the
unwanted

PAUL BREER

Table of Contents

1. The Incident 1

2. A Trip to Oaxaca 9

3. The Funeral 17

4. Two Years Earlier 27

5. Alma 41

6. Northward Journey 50

7. Nogales 54

8. Friends & Coyotes 59

9. The Desert 65

10. Macuahuitl Unleashed 74

11. Ambush 78

12. Out of the Desert 82

13. Phoenix 87

14. The Job 90

15. The Sheriff's Office 95

16. Marisol 100

17. The Sheriff's Boy 107

18. Picking up the Scent 113

19. The Library 117

20. Anna's Family 123

21. An Unexpected Ally 135

22. Trouble on the Highway 140

23. Paula 158

24. Murder on the Rails 165

25. The Train of Death 176

26. When Predator Becomes Prey 192

27. A Talk with Javier 199

28. The Tunnel 205

29. An Orange Jacket 210

30. First Meeting..219

31. Surveillance 229

32. Bristlecone Drive 234

33. After the Funeral 238

34. The Trial 243

35. The Raid 259

1

The Incident

Earl Culpepper stands before his dresser mirror, tucking in a black and white checkered shirt he has bought for the occasion. Even when allowed to hang loosely from his belt, the shirt does little to hide a gut that protrudes conspicuously from his six-foot two frame. He looks again and sighs. There was a time not too long ago when he viewed that gut as a symbol of his authority in the community. After all, he is more than just another man; he is the Sheriff of Mariposa County, hardly someone to be trifled with. Back in Alabama where he grew up, any man who achieved something noteworthy in life had a prominent gut. In that world of dainty ladies and stout-hearted men, some degree of belly overhang was a requirement in the upper ranks of business, the professions and law enforcement.

Earl had only to look to his father, Billy Joe, also a sheriff, for an authority figure who projected power through the enormity of his paunch. The same could be said for his granddaddy who, while never a sheriff, rose to the rank of lieutenant in the Montrose police force before dying of syphilis contracted from a black woman who confessed to an affair after the funeral. People said his gut was so big he had to have his shirts made from discarded parachutes.

Earl stands there now, his broad shoulders hunched, his gray-blue eyes staring out from a pale white face, his jowls sagging, his mouth curled in a downward arc. It is obvious that these are the looks of a man who is more than just tired. Something deeper is going on, something to do with how he sees his place in the broad scheme of things. His eyes, once clear and bright, have taken on a faint mistiness; his jaw is slack now, no longer thrust forward in readiness for battle. You might surmise that his inner gyroscope, once his most reliable guide, has been knocked askew, set to wobbling, no longer able to tell him what path to take next.

He squints at the image in the mirror, then runs his hand across his stomach. The sensation is familiar but something has changed. Where once he took pride in his estimable girth, he now has doubts, can even feel a hint of shame. He reaches for the badge on the dresser…suddenly remembers where he is going today and puts it back…careful to place it in the upper right-hand corner about three inches from the edge. In a final bow to convention, he slides his Western bolo tie under his collar and pulls it tight. As he turns to leave, he catches a glimpse of his wife in the mirror; her face is taut, her lips quivering.

"Are you coming back?", Emma whispers.

He says nothing. Grabbing his suitcase from the bed, he brushes past her into the living room. She follows, unwilling to let go. She knows it's too late but says it anyway. "Eric needs your help." With the mention of his son's name, Earl's eyes draw smaller, his lips curl into an unconcealed sneer. Without another word, he yanks open the front door and heads down the walk to where a cab is waiting.

Once in the taxi he slumps back in his seat, relieved to be alone. His thoughts turn to the events that lie immediately ahead. With eyes closed he summons the image of his young friend Santé whose funeral is tomorrow in Oaxaca, Mexico. He gropes for that once familiar face, a handsome face, cocoa-skinned with the high cheekbones, straight black hair and deep brown eyes of his Indian ancestors.

Instead, it is Emma's face that returns.

"What did I ever see in her?" he asks silently, not even wanting an answer. Unbidden images of her youth loom before him, blotting out the pasty, bloodless face he passed just a few minutes ago. "Her features are pretty much the same," he reflects, "the girlish figure, the natural auburn curls, the tantalizing C-cup breasts. But she's changed; Jesus has she changed.

What the heck is it? Why can't I stand being around her anymore? Sure, she's no longer a girl, but 40 is hardly old these days. And I haven't felt turned on for God knows how long. It can't be her looks; it's gotta be the way she acts toward me. And that's been a long time in comin'. It seems like as soon as Eric was born she lost interest in me as a man; all her playfulness and sexiness vanished overnight. Or at least it seemed that way to me. From that day on, she poured all her love and affection into the baby…*her* baby she kept callin' him. I remember how she drove me wild in those days, goin' out of her way to cuddle the kid just when I was getting hard. And that's been goin' on for years now. In 18 years nothin' has really changed. Sure, he's too old now to be suckin' on her tits, but that doesn't keep her from treatin' him like a little boy.

He sighs again as they approach the airport. "Jesus Christ…now she wants me to protect him from the police. I know goddamn well the kid is guilty. What am I supposed to do…forget that I'm the Sheriff? Does she really think I'm gonna hide the evidence…risk my job just so he don't have to go to jail?

He pauses to refresh his memory. "The Mexican boy's death was all over the news the next morning…his white pickup found at the bottom of the canyon…apparently forced over the cliff by another vehicle. According to Phoenix police, streaks of black paint on the boy's left front fender indicate that the offending vehicle was black…most likely a pickup of the same size as the victim's. No other information was given.

"At first I didn't pay all that much attention until I heard the kid's name… Asanté Aguilera, the Mexican boy I had been watching play soccer every Saturday. Seein' how much I had come to like the kid, the news was joltin' enough…but it wasn't 'til later that things got a lot worse. I was comin' home from work, enterin' our driveway, ready to put the car in the garage. When I pulled up to the right of Eric's truck, I couldn't help seein' the fresh paint job on his right front fender. At first I was concentratin' on the fact that the paint didn't quite match the original. I remember thinkin' how hard it is to get a perfect match with a vehicle as old as this one. It wasn't until I knelt down and ran my fingers over the paint that the truth hit me. That's when I saw a few flecks of white paint lodged in one of the dents that ran the length of the fender. I remember yelling, 'Oh my God…what the hell is he up to? Was he up on Bristlecone Drive the other night? Is he the one who forced Santé over the cliff?'"

Earl sighs as the details come back. "When I got inside and pinned him against his bedroom wall, he finally admitted that he had been there. 'It was an accident,' he screamed. 'I was comin' down the hill ready to pass this white pickup when an 18-wheeler suddenly come around the corner headin' right up the hill toward me. The only way I could avoid getting crushed was to move to the right. I honked several times, figurin' the pickup would hit his brakes and let me pass but he just kept goin'. Dad, I didn't have any choice…believe me.'"

The cabbie looks back, checking to see if his passenger is O.K. For Earl, still deep in his thoughts, his son's explanation doesn't ring true. In his 22 years as a law enforcement officer he has developed an uncanny ability to read faces. His colleagues are convinced that their boss is better at ferreting out liars than a formal polygraph test. "I want to believe him," he mutters. "I tried like hell to believe him, but the story doesn't make any sense. Eric's a good driver; why would he try passin' in that kind of situation? And why didn't he hit his own brakes the second he saw the 18-wheeler comin' toward him? Didn't he have time to slip back behind the white pickup?"

He looks through the car window at the passing traffic…then shakes his head as more of the story unfolds. It's early morning; he's sitting at the breakfast table across from his son. Without even looking at the eggs on his plate, he begins: "So what were you doin' up there on Bristlecone Drive that night? You makin' out with a new girlfriend? If so, is she goin' to back you up?"

"No." Eric replies softly. "It was a beautiful night and I just wanted to… (*starts coughing*)…"

"Earl…give the boy a chance," Emma says. "Let him eat his breakfast."

"He can eat his breakfast when I'm finished with him," Earl shouts. "Now Eric, what the hell were you doin' up there at that time of day?…(*pounds the table*)…I want the truth.'"

"I told you…it was a beautiful night and…."

"Cut the bullshit. You knew goddamn well that Santé would be there. That's the road he always takes when he leaves his girlfriend's house…yes?"

Emma *(dropping her fork)*: "And how do you know that?"

Earl turns quickly to his wife. "One of the detectives over at the Phoenix office interviewed Santé's girlfriend, Anna, and she told him about the boy's movements."

"The newspaper said his name was Asanté," Emma interjects. Why do you keep calling him Santé?"

"Because that's his nickname."

Emma folds her napkin and sets it down. "I don't see why you're so concerned about this Mexican boy when you've got a son of your own."

"I haven't had a son of my own since you stole him from me 18 years ago."

"Well, Eric has tried to be close to you. But you can't blame him when he sees his father going off every Saturday to watch some other boy play soccer. And then take him out to lunch."

"How the hell do you know what I do on Saturday?"

Emma suddenly reddens.

"Have you been following me?" he barks. When no answer is forthcoming, he stares at her, then breaks into a wry grin. The image of his wife's playing detective is too much. "You don't even have your own car," he says, "so how could you…." He stops…then shifts his gaze to Eric. He waits until his thoughts fall into place. Once he is certain, he strikes quickly, "So it was you who followed me, you who observed me at the soccer field. You watched when I sought out Santé after the game, stopped to chat with him and took him to a restaurant. You saw all that, didn't you?"

Eric looks down at his oatmeal, saying nothing.

With his prey hopelessly trapped, Earl moves in for the kill. "That means you *did* know about Santé…(*pause*)…So why were you following me?"

When Eric says nothing, Emma answers for him. "He thought you were having an affair. It was out of loyalty to me."

"And when he discovered that I was not having an affair but befriending a Mexican boy, what happened?"

"Well, imagine how you would feel if your father went to some other boy's soccer games every Saturday…but never to yours?"

"Eric plays soccer? When did that happen? As far as I know, the only game Eric ever played was tiddlywinks."

"You're being cruel. Eric doesn't deserve to be treated like this."

"So how should he be treated? I don't know for sure, but his role in Santé's death is beginning to look awful fishy."

Emma lifts her fork, holds it for a second, then puts it back down. "But Earl, nobody knows that Eric was on Bristlecone Drive that night. Nobody saw him. Right now the police don't suspect him of anything. As far as the world is concerned, Eric doesn't even know this Mexican boy."

"But you and I know what happened. We know there *was* a relationship. Eric knew about my friendship with Santé and probably had some negative feelings about it. Now…just how negative were those feelings? And how far was he willing to go to express them?"

As the cab makes its way through traffic, Earl tilts his head back and closes his eyes. His brain is aching from the thoughts swirling inside. "There can't be any question about it," he murmurs. "If he did it, that's murder…first degree." He pauses to breathe. "Jesus H. Christ…my own kid…a prime suspect for murder. And now Emma wants me to get him off the hook. Does she think I'm goin' to give up everything for a kid I can't stand being around? She's gotta be crazy. Would I do it if my job weren't at stake? I don't know. For almost 20 years I've watched her baby him…take his side in any argument, excuse him whenever he done somethin' wrong. She's the one who raised him; she's the one who made him the weakling he is today. And to think I used to love him…even adored him when he was a little kid. That's not so strange, is it? He was our only child, the only one left to carry on the Culpepper tradition. Another sheriff, I thought when I first saw him at the hospital, maybe even a prosecutor or judge. But now he's on the other side of the law. Yes, I know nothin' has been settled, but that's the way it looks to me right now. He could be headed for prison… for a long time I would guess…25 years, maybe even life."

He sits up in the cab to see where they are. Much as he craves peace, he can't stop replaying the events of yesterday morning. When his eyes close, Eric's face appears once more, gaunt from lack of sleep. "That's when I told 'im he has to turn himself in. And if he doesn't, I'm goin' to drag 'im to the station when I get back from Mexico and make 'im admit that he was up on Bristlecone Drive that night. Of course, he'll offer his own explanation and they might be inclined to believe 'im…especially if I don't mention that I saw 'im coverin' up the white paint on his fender. He could even admit he was there that night but claim the collision was an accident. And then if I do say somethin' about the paint job, he could respond that it wasn't meant to cover up anything…he was just fixin' the damage to his fender."

The thoughts keep coming. "From what I learned at the breakfast table I'm pretty sure that Santé's death was no accident. But how's the prosecution goin' to prove it without my help? How are they goin' to establish a motive for first degree murder without evidence of a relationship between the two boys? Even if I testify about those Saturday trips to watch Santé play soccer and the lunches we shared afterwards, Eric can deny that he ever followed me. Maybe I'm gonna have to testify about my feelings for the Mexican boy and how this made my own kid jealous. But I don't want to fly off the handle…a kid's future is at stake here. Does Eric deserve to spend the rest of his life in prison because his father rejected him for another boy? How the hell do you answer a question like that?…*(pause)*…I don't know. I'm just glad to get away from it all for a few days while I attend this funeral in Oaxaca. Maybe when I get back things will be clearer. Goddamn it…I hope so."

As they enter the airport, the cabbie breaks the long silence. What airline?"

Earl sits up. "Mexicana."

"Got it. What city you goin' to?"

"Oaxaca."

"Vacation?"

"No… a funeral…a friend's funeral."

"Oh. Sorry."

2

A Trip to Oaxaca

As the Sheriff stretches out his 6'2" frame, he is reminded how glad he is he got an aisle seat. As the plane prepares for takeoff, he checks his jacket pocket for Santé's family's address, the one he got from the Immigration and Naturalization Service...the same people who sent the boy's body to Oaxaca along with a bill for $1,700 which they do not expect to be paid.

According to his ticket, he should arrive in Oaxaca around 2:30 P.M. which will give him the afternoon and evening to look around before the funeral on Friday morning. He looks out the window; there's not a cloud in the sky. The pilot announces that they may reach their destination a few minutes early.

As predicted, the plane lands in Oaxaca at 2:25, leaving plenty of time to seek out Santé's family...in particular to find out where the cemetery is and when the funeral is to be held. He hails a cab just outside the airport, checks his notes again and instructs the cabbie to take him to Panoramica del Fortin Calle.

"Que nombre?" the driver asks.

Drawing on some high-school Spanish, Earl responds "Tres, cinco, seis (356)." Once he arrives, he finds himself at the bottom of a steep set of stone-slab stairs...at least 50 in all...leading to a house up on top. Alongside the stairs, there are several small buildings, some with a door and windows but none with a separate street number. He looks confused. As he starts up the stairs, he is suddenly approached by a young man.

"Maybe I help you?" he offers in English.

"I'm looking for the Aguilera residence," the Sheriff says, "Santé Aguilera's family." The boy points to the top of the steps. "But what about these other houses," Earl asks. "I don't see any numbers on them."

"Some relatives…some no relatives. You want me take you to top? I can show you Santé's house."

"Yes, thank you. I'm sorry I don't speak much Spanish. Your English is pretty good. By the way, what's your name?"

"Marco." Earl reaches out his hand; "I'm Earl."

As they make their way up the stairs, Marco jumps ahead while Earl toils behind, hoisting his 230 lbs. step by step. Half way up, Earl spots a shed over on the left. The door is open but it's too dark to see inside. He pauses, partly to catch his breath, partly out of curiosity. "Goats or sheep?" he calls to his guide. The boy comes back down a few steps, clearly bewildered by Earl's question. "No goats or sheep, Senor…people house."

Earl stares into the shed. "People live there? he asks, unable to disguise his incredulity.

"Si, come look."

Earl peers inside the unlit building. At best, it is 8 by 8 feet square with a dirt floor and no bed, table or chairs. "You say people live here?"

"Si Senor, a woman and her four children. She is Santé's prima…how you say?" He struggles for the English equivalent but can't find it. Stooping to the ground, he picks up a twig and makes a dot. "Here is Santé" Next he makes two holes above that of the first…forming a triangle. "Santé's Mama and Papa." Earl nods. Marco then makes another hole to the left of Mama. "Sister de Mama." Below the sister, he makes a final dot…Santé's prima."

Earl smiles. "Oh, O.K.…cousin…got it."

"Si, this is cousin's casa."

After checking again to see if anyone is home, the boy pulls the door all the way open and beckons Earl closer. "Come…she not here."

Earl stoops to enter. When he stands to look around, he suddenly grows quiet. As the boy looks on, Earl struggles for something to say. 'Oh my God' finally tumbles from his lips. The "house" is dark, windowless, illuminated only by patches of sunlight peering through cracks in the rotting, slabwood walls. The entire building consists of a single room no bigger than the office Earl has in his home. He shifts his gaze from one wall to the other. The rear of the shed consists of soil and rock dug out of the hill on which the shed sets. Overhead is a piece of corrugated iron perforated here and there with ominous holes. A single unshaded bulb hangs precariously from the roof. He looks again, shaking his head. "I don't see any beds or table or chairs. Where's all the furniture? Where do they sleep? Where do they eat?"

Marco smiles, seemingly amused by this gringo's ignorance. (*Pointing*) "See cardboard along wall. They sleep on cardboard."

"You mean no bed, no mattress?"

"Same way for most people here…Santé's family too."

"But where do they eat…how do they even prepare meals here?"

Marco steps outside and motions for Earl to follow. There, on the ground just outside the door, is a small cast-iron grate. Under it sit the ashes from a recent wood fire.

Earl can't help scowling. "You mean they have to come out here three times a day and cook their meals on that thing? And then sit on the ground while they eat?"

Marco squints, then answers just loud enough to be heard, "They no eat three times every day."

Sensing his guide's discomfort, Earl softens his tone. "I see. What do they have for breakfast, Marco?"

"Tortillas…when they can buy or make own."

"You mean tortillas filled with beans and rice…or maybe chicken?"

"No…just salt on tortillas. Salt is cheap."

Earl sighs as images of his own breakfast of bacon, scrambled eggs, English muffins, jam and coffee swirl through his head. Taking a last look inside the shed, he says, "I don't see any refrigerator. How do they keep anything cold? It gets pretty warm around here."

Marco reaches for the door, "No refrigerator…she buy milk in small carton. Everything else eat warm."

"Even meat?" Earl asks.

"Meat not go bad for two days, Senor. Lots of chilis make good taste."

Marco pushes the door shut…or at least as shut as he can make it. "You want to see Santé's house?

"Yes, but I don't want to intrude."

"Intrude?"

"You know…get in the way"

"They not home…all at church I think."

As they continue up the stairs, Earl grapples with what he has just seen. "On a typical farm in Alabama," he muses, "you'd have a shed like that out back for a goat or two. I still can't believe this is home for a woman and four children. With five people in there, it's gotta be impossible to move around. Christ, in my own house I can walk from the kitchen to a large living room; along the way I pass three bedrooms, a dining room and a little office. I also have a two-car garage with a work bench in the corner. And then there's an attic where I can dump stuff I don't want but am not ready to give away. This woman has none of that…nothing but a single room with an uneven dirt floor, a single bulb overhead and not a scrap of furniture."

When he catches up with Marco, Earl stops, breathing heavily. "She's divorced?" he asks.

"No, husband is in prison. Hit another man in eye…now can no see. Husband must stay in prison three years."

"So this woman, Santé's cousin, has to support her four children alone?"

"Si…she work in laundry…leave children with mother or aunt."

"Does she get to see her husband very often?"

(*Smiling*) "In Mexico wife allowed to spend three days with husband in jail. She go every few months…come back pregnant. She now ready for fifth child."

"Oh my God. How will she ever feed them all? Is there even room for another child in there?"

"She find a way."

"Don't they believe in contraception?"

Marco shakes his head, "No. Never. Very wrong to do."

The top of the hill is another 25 steps. By the time they reach the house Earl is exhausted. He sits down on the edge of the deck which runs the full length of the house. The house itself is twice the length and width of the cousin's place below.

"Nobody home here also…but door closed," says Marco. "Not right to go in…but we look through window." Earl gets up and comes over to the window Marco is referring to. "This is Santé's house…where he grew up."

"You were his friend?" says Earl.

"I like him but me friend of Santé's brother Raul." Together they peer into the house. Again, it is a single room with no furniture other than two children's chairs. The floor is brick rather than dirt. Over in the far corner there is a yellow, soiled mattress…no bed, just the mattress. "That's where Santé's mama and papa sleep. Other eight children all sleep on cardboard…like prima."

"Eight children…all in this one room?"

"Si…everybody sleep in same place at night…baby next to Mama and Papa, then bigger children…all the way to corner where Vicente the oldest sleeps. When Santé was here, he sleep there (*pointing*), next to Raul. Now more room since Santé and Raul both gone."

"How does the father support such a big family?" Earl asks.

"In other year, he have farm in Tecultepec…maybe two acres…for maize, cebolla, calabaza, tomate. Give them food for family…sell rest in market. Then NAFTA change everything. Everybody buy cheap corn from Canada and U.S. The Aguileras must sell farm and move here to Oaxaca. Now Mama and older daughter make clothes for children and sell in zocalo. Children no go to school after nine or ten grades…books and uniform cost too much…beside family need them to work."

"And what does the father do?"

"He the hefe, the boss…he tell others how to do."

Earl coughs. "He tells his wife and daughter how to make children's clothes?"

(*Smiling*) "He help carry clothes to market."

"Why doesn't he get a real job?"

"He have accident five years ago; knee still hurt where hit by car. He walk funny. And no more front teeth since ox kick him in mouth when he put yoke on. Now he embarrassed to look for job."

Earl is about to ask about cooking for such a large family when he spots the familiar cast-iron grate on the ground just beyond the deck. Instead, he asks, "I don't see a bathroom; is it outback somewhere?"

Marco giggles. "Everybody pee on ground near house; for other things they go over there (*pointing*). Earl shields his eyes and looks where Marco is pointing; what he sees is an outhouse built of slab wood, 30 feet away down the hill. As he continues staring, an unpleasant memory from years ago rises before him. It is 2003; he is in a hotel in northern Mexico, confined to bed with a severe case of diarrhea, a problem contracted from drinking unpurified water. While his wife and son explore the town, he remains tucked under the covers, sweating and feverish. Every few hours he feels himself about to explode and rushes for the safety of the toilet. Half the time he doesn't make it, soiling bed sheets, underwear, and floor in the process. He shudders at the memory.

A call from Marco draws him back to the present. He shifts his gaze outward to what he can see from the deck. "At least there was a toilet next to the bedroom," he mutters. "How in the world do you survive a case of diarrhea when the toilet is outdoors, 30 feet away down an unlit path? And it could be raining as you race to relieve yourself."

Marco senses Earl's discomfort and offers, "People here not fussy like in your country. (*Laughing*) Whole world a bathroom." Earl grins and starts back down the steps. Half way down, Marco taps him on the shoulder from behind, saying, "I have question for you Senor Earl. People here think Santé die because la migra chase him…make him drive over cliff. What you think?"

Earls' stomach tightens at the question. In a flash he pictures the events on Bristlecone Drive. He sees Eric coming up alongside Santé's truck, then watches as his son steers hard to the right, pressing against Santé's left fender. "Now what?" he asks himself. "Was there any honking? There must have been. Did they look at each other? What was the expression on Eric's face? Did he watch as Santé slid over the edge? Did he go back to look?"

The question brings Earl to his knees. Marco rushes to catch him as he stumbles. "Sorry…bad question, Senor Earl."

"It's O.K. Marco…I'm sorry…I still haven't digested the whole thing." He stands up and rubs his eyes. "About the Immigration Service, I'm sure they get caught up in their work sometimes, but I don't think they were chasing Santé at the time. It must have been something else."

Once they reach bottom Earl stops to thank his companion. "Just one other question," he says. "What time is the funeral tomorrow morning… and where is the cemetery?"

"I don't know about time…maybe ten in morning. Come back here and wait until you hear music. Then follow people to cemetery." Earl reaches into his pocket and pulls out a $100 peso note…worth about $8.00 U.S. When he pushes it toward Marco, the boy pulls back. "Thank you, no," he says, grinning. "If you friend of Santé's, you friend of mine."

"But I want you to have it; you've gone out of your way to help me." As Marco turns to leave, still shaking his head, Earl gets an idea. Pressing the money into the boy's hand, he says, "Is there a store nearby where you can buy me a Coca-Cola. After all those stairs, I'm too winded to go myself." When Marco hesitates, Earl adds, "I'll be right here when you get back. O.K.?" Marco nods, then hurries off down the street. By the time he returns with the drink and change Earl is five blocks away, heading for the zocalo.

"I had no idea," he whispers to himself as he makes his way to the center of town. "How could a 16-year-old boy have come so far…from a one-room shack without beds, tables or chairs…armed with nothing more than a 10th grade education…and wind up in an apartment in Phoenix with his own pickup truck, a steady job, and realistic hopes for a college degree in engineering? As far as I can see, he had no support, no money, no passport, no friends in Arizona, and no knowledge of the English language…nothin' but guts, nerve, and a refusal to waste the rest of his life in a Oaxaca slum."

He passes a billboard featuring a picture of a professional soccer player drinking Coca Cola. As he looks, an image of Santé scoring his team's only goal just days ago brings a smile to his face. The smile disappears when he remembers there will be no more Saturdays together…no more games… no more lunches. As he turns the corner on Hidalgo Calle, Santé's face suddenly gives way to an image of his wife. He stops at the curb as her last words echo in his head. "Are you coming back?" she whispers. Stepping off the curb, he shakes his head. "I don't know. I doubt it."

3
The Funeral

Just like Marco said: all he'd have to do is listen for the music. Although he still can't see any mourners, he can make out the trumpets, the drums, and a few trombones…even a clarinet or two. At the end of the street, a policeman is blowing his whistle as cars and trucks yield to the passing assemblage. Finally he sees them…perhaps 40 in all, counting the band…men dressed in dark, wrinkled suits, women wrapped in black rebozos, children hand in hand or holding onto their parents. In the middle of the cortege is the casket, assembled from wood and held aloft by six young men, presumably relatives or friends of the deceased. The music is both loud and out of tune as the group passes by, although no one seems to be disturbed by the dissonance.

As the last of the mourners passes the intersection, Earl steps into the street and joins them. His six-foot two frame towers over the men on either side, no one of which can be over 5 feet three or four. As Santé had explained at lunch one day, contemporary Mexican Indians are descended from the Aztecs, Mixtecs and Zapotecs of pre-Spanish times and tend to be both shorter and darker than the Mestizos who are of mixed European and Indian heritage. Like the boy they are carrying, these diminutive men trace their roots and genes to an ancient civilization that once rivaled the Roman Empire in its splendor. Today, they are the poorest of Mexicans, hobbled by a culture that glorifies tradition and stability over the acquisition of wealth. All that is forgotten on this sunny morning as they say goodbye to one of their own, a boy of 16 who ventured to the north in search of a better life and who was devoured by the world he hoped to conquer.

They are now a half a dozen blocks from the Aguilera home and approaching the edge of town. The streets here are no longer paved and the sidewalks non-existent. Long rows of maguey plants, used for making mezcal, can be seen in the nearby fields. But it is the dry season and not much else is growing. What the farmers do at this time of the year is a mystery.

Up ahead is an intersection; the dirt road they are on continues out through the fields while a short road paved with worn-out cobblestones turns left and into the cemetery. The band is still blaring its off-key dirge as the cortege enters through the graveyard gate. Two young girls are standing on either side, holding purple and pink bougainvilleas. From his position in the rear Earl can see that the cemetery is divided into family lots, each with its tilting wooden crosses and vases of flowers stained with the passage of time. A few yards ahead, where the path turns right, a small group of people has already assembled around a freshly dug grave. It is here that the band comes to a full stop and plays its final hymn to the departed. The rest of the mourners take positions around the casket which has been placed on the ground in front of the priest. As the white-robed padre reads from the gospels in Spanish, Earl turns his attention to the short, squat Indian woman standing closest to the grave. It must be Santé's mother. After eight births, her body looks assaulted, crushed…her once pretty face draped in dark brown wrinkles, her back bent from carrying one infant after another, three of which are now buried just a few feet behind her.

As her son's body is lowered into the grave, the mother's knees buckle. A young woman with pale face and black, wavy hair reaches forward to grab her. To Earl's surprise, the old lady regains her balance and resumes standing. All is silent. With her right hand she picks up some dirt and sprinkles it onto the casket. There is no wailing, no outburst of despair, just the power of a face tilted downward, drawing grief into itself as it whispers its last goodbye. The father watches from behind her, his lips drawn tight against his toothless upper gums. His narrowed eyes defy anyone to ask him what feelings lie buried within.

Earl's own eyes turn to the young, American woman next to the mother. "Could this be Santé's girlfriend from Phoenix?" He waits until the others begin to leave and approaches her with hand extended. "You're not Anna by any chance, are you?" he offers, forcing a smile. "Yes," she replies, taking his hand in her own, "and you must be the Sheriff Santé told me about, the one who came to his soccer games and took him out to lunch. I thought it might be you when I saw the band come in. (*Smiling*) You make all these Zapotec people look like midgets."

"Is that what they are? I remember Santé talking about his Indian ancestry several times. He seemed pretty proud of it."

"Yes he was…(*pause*)…Look it, Sheriff, I'd love to talk, but I've got to give something to Santé's mother first…O.K."?

"Certainly…but I wish you'd call me Earl. 'Sheriff' sounds a bit stiff, don't you think."

(*Smiling*) "I do…Earl."

With that, she turns and approaches the mother, handing her an envelope. In Spanish she explains: "This is Santé's last mail; it was in his box, so I picked it up because I thought you would like to see it." The mother takes the envelope, focusing her attention first on her son's name, then on the return address. Slowly, she opens it, then hands it back to Anna. She can't read it.

Anna speaks slowly. "It's from Arizona State University. It says, 'We are happy to inform you that you have been accepted for admission to the freshman class of 2013. If you wish to….'" Then she stops, her words drowned in a sea of tears as the significance of the letter hits her. After two years of studying English and passing the required language exam, Santé's dream of going to college in the U.S. had finally come true. She hands the letter back to the mother and summarizes in Spanish. "Santé has been accepted at the university." The mother smiles and slips the letter into her dress pocket. When she turns to her husband, he says nothing. While he is fully aware by now what the letter says, his scowl makes it plain that he has other matters on his mind…money for instance. Without the remittances Santé has been sending every month, he is worried that the family can no longer survive. Hobbled by both a bad knee and no upper teeth, he wrestles in silence with a growing sense of unworthiness. To those around him, the drooping of his mouth hints at the doubts gnawing within. After all, in this land where machismo trumps all, what is a man who cannot provide for his family?

Although standing several feet away, Earl is privy to most of what is said between Anna and the mother. When Anna turns to leave, he comes up beside her. "Want some company on the way back?" he asks shyly. "If you'd rather be alone I can understand." She answers by taking his hand as they head out the gate. Out on the road he gives her hand a squeeze and asks, "How close were the two of you? I know he thought you were pretty special."

She waves to a girl who is passing on a bicycle. Turning back to the Sheriff, she says, "Well, I'd say pretty close. We were talking about marriage… not right now but after I finished law school and he finished engineering school. That's what makes the letter from A.S.U. so hard to swallow. I don't know if he told you, but he had to take the English language exam three times before passing. They're pretty strict about that…you have to score 85 or better to get in. But once you make it, you can qualify for scholarships and grants just like kids who were born in the U.S. Santé would have been ecstatic if he had been here to open that letter today. Unlike most Mexican men, he was pretty open with his feelings. That's one thing I really liked about him."

Earl slows his pace. "I noticed that too. We have several Mexican-born men in our office back in Phoenix; if you ask them about anything personal, you rarely get a straight answer. So I've learned to stop asking. But Santé was something else. He talked a lot about his family, about you…but especially about his desire to become an engineer. I was flattered that he trusted me enough to tell me all those things."

"Santé was like a son to you?"

Earl coughs. "Well yes, I guess you could say that."

"I think it's wonderful that a sheriff can become friends with a poor boy from Mexico. That makes you pretty special."

"Well, to be honest, I wasn't always this way. I used to be pretty rough on the illegals…it's not something I'm proud of."

"Is that what you called them…illegals?"

"Yes…or aliens."

"As if they were from outer space?"

"Sounds stupid I know. Santé helped me change all that."

Anna turns to look at him. *(Softly)* "I take it you don't have a son of your own."

When Earl stumbles, Anna reaches to grab him by the arm. "Are you O.K., Sheriff?" she asks. Without speaking, he struggles to his feet, then smiles and points an accusing finger at a stone in the road. Outwardly she returns his smile but begins wondering.

She stops to pet a dog so thin she can count its ribs. "Don't they ever feed you?" she whispers. From across the street two school girls point at the dog and giggle. Now it is only another step or two to the intersection where the cobblestone path from the cemetery meets the dirt road into town. As they turn right onto the dirt road, they are suddenly confronted with a herd of steers coming down the road straight at them. At the rear of the herd a farmer is waving his stick frantically and pointing to the right, a signal to the pedestrians to get out of the way. There are no sidewalks to step up on…nothing but a telephone pole that sticks out from the stone wall on the right-hand side of the road. It is to that space between pole and wall that the Sheriff and Anna race now.

When Earl realizes there's not enough room in that space for both of them, he moves to the side of the pole, allowing Anna to squeeze in behind him. The front row of animals, perhaps seven or eight across, is only a few yards away now and heading directly for them. Unless the steers move to the other side, which is unlikely, their horns, sharp as daggers and pointed forward like reverse handlebars, will almost touch the pole as they pass. Adding to the hazard is a massive gray ox, a giant of a beast standing a foot or more above the rest of the herd. Unlike the steers which are content to look straight ahead, the ox stares balefully at Earl, seemingly troubled by the movement around the telephone pole. Without turning its massive head, it rolls its nearest eye and snorts. Fortunately, its horns slant backward and pose little threat to Earl's balloon size paunch. Nevertheless the sheriff begins to tremble. From her position behind him, Anna senses his anxiety and whispers in his ear, "I just wish Santé was here; he'd know what to do."

Her comment, innocent enough in its motivation, stirs something deep in Earl's psyche. It threatens the core of his self-image for a young girl to wish that someone else was there to protect her. For a split second, he ponders her question. What indeed would Santé do? In response, a picture of the boy appears, his broad shoulders, muscular arms and determined jaw as vivid now as they were on the soccer field back in Phoenix. With Anna's words ringing in his ears, he tries to think and feel like Santé. Gradually his arm muscles swell; his eyes flare. In his mind's eye he grabs the beast by its horns and twists it to the ground, forcing it to yield to his newfound might. While the act is sheer fantasy, his victory whoop is real enough to send the whole herd bolting. Although she can't see her protector's face, Anna can feel the change and pats him on the shoulder. Just a few feet from the pole, the ox stares blankly, then turns away and resumes its place in the herd.

As they step out into the road again, Anna turns to Earl, asking, "What went on back there? I think you scared them all away, especially that ox that was heading right for us."

"I don't know. I'm not even sure it was me."

"Hmm. What exactly do you mean by that?"

Earl stops to ponder the question. "This is all confusing to me, Anna. I may need a little time to figure it out." As they continue on down the road, Anna chooses to respect his privacy and says nothing more. For Earl, however, the questions refuse to go away. Silently he reviews what happened. "Yes, I did feel strong back there…strong enough to take on that mammoth creature and wrestle him to the ground; I could probably have broken his neck if necessary. But let's face it; it was only a fantasy…and part of me was aware of that. What's crazy is that it worked; just thinking I was Santé changed the way I felt…and the way I probably looked to that ox. Sure, I drove that beast away and scared the shit out of the whole herd, but what does it mean? What's all this saying about me, Earl Culpepper? Can I be proud of what *I* did? What would I have done if Santé didn't exist; what if I had just been myself, Earl Culpepper, a middle-aged guy with a paunch who's tryin' to protect the friend of a friend?"

As he continues walking, the question settles deep into his psyche where certain issues, some of them potentially troubling, have lain dormant for years. This experience with the ox, trivial as it is, threatens to expose those issues to more honest scrutiny. He stops, wipes his brow…then waves Anna on ahead. Of this he is aware: something is on the verge of crumbling inside; certain barriers, erected years ago, are in danger of coming down. For someone who has always lived in a world where outward conformity is demanded and introspection discouraged, this is new and perilous territory. Yet the events of the past few days…the death of his friend, the possible imprisonment of his son, the potential breakup with his wife… have turned everything upside down. At this moment, standing in the middle of a road in southern Mexico, fresh from a funeral and startled by his encounter with an ox, he is ready to open up.

He starts with a question: "Why did I feel so weak when we first saw the herd coming toward us…but so strong a few minutes later? Everything seemed to change when Anna leaned against me and asked what Santé would do in this situation. I can hear her words right now. They made me ashamed of being afraid. They made me want to act like Santé…to become Santé …instead of just being myself. The desire to please her was so strong that I somehow changed myself into Santé…at least it seemed that way. And it worked; the fear disappeared and I felt all this new power wellin' up inside me. That ox could see it for sure."

He pauses to kick a small stone to the side of the road. "It worked, yes, but what does it say about Earl Culpepper? Is it sayin' that I have to become somebody else in order to feel strong?" He shakes his head in disgust. "That's hard to believe. I've always felt strong; just ask the people I work with. They'll tell you."

Anna turns to wave, then continues on by herself.

"For Christ's sake, I'm the Sheriff, right? I love being the Sheriff. People respect you; sometimes they fear you. It's a powerful position to be in. I'm careful not to abuse that position, but it does make me feel strong." He drops his head. "But that's not the way I felt a few minutes ago when that ox was comin' at me. How come? What's the difference? What happened to the confidence I usually feel in tight situations?"

By now Anna has stopped by the side of the road to wait for him. As he approaches, she smiles and asks, "Well, have you figured it all out…you know, what happened back there with the ox?"

The sweetness of her voice dispels the last of his resistance. "Well, I'm workin' on it, Anna, but I still don't get it. I'm usually very confident but back there I was…if you'll excuse the expression…shittin' in my pants… until you asked what Santé would do if he was there. Then, all of a sudden I felt all this strength…Santé's strength really…I could actually see his face…in my mind of course…but it was enough to scare the ox back into the herd."

"Yes, I thought you were wonderful."

"But it wasn't really me. That's the point I don't get. I was actin' and feelin' like I was Santé, not Earl Culpepper, Sheriff of Mariposa County."

Anna turns to look directly at him. "But perhaps that *is* the point, Earl. Down here, you're no longer the Sheriff. You're just a friend who came to attend Santé's funeral." She pauses to check his reaction before continuing. "Look at yourself; you're not wearing a uniform; you don't have a badge on your shirt; you're not carrying a pistol. You're dressed like any another man, a gringo for sure…but not some representative of the law, not somebody people have to be afraid of."

The simplicity of her words sends Earl reeling. "What are you saying… that it's got something to do with the way I'm dressed?" He grimaces, then turns away.

(*Softly*) "All I meant was that maybe without your uniform you're a different person." As his face reddens, she adds, "Tell me if I'm speaking out of turn. I hate it when other people do that to me."

Earl lets out a deep breath. "No, please…I'm new to this sort of thing. It still doesn't make any sense to me."

Anna steps closer. "I guess the thing to ask yourself is who you really are…you know, without the uniform and pistol. But that's a big question; I know." She pauses. "It's hard for anyone to be honest with their answer. I certainly have trouble. For example, when I was with Santé, I acted in a way that pleased him. I became sweet and submissive like a good Mexican wife. But I'm really not that way. When I'm with other people, I tend to be pretty outspoken."

Earl shuffles his feet, kicking up a little dust. "You know, maybe the uniform makes more of a difference than I thought. I never stopped to think about it. It does make me feel powerful…probably a lot more powerful than if I was wearin' somethin' else. When I have the badge on my chest and a pistol on my hip, I can see the way other people look at me. I can see the awe, even the fear, in their eyes. So, you're right. It does affect the way I feel. It makes me a different person…bigger, stronger, more intimidating."

(*Smiling*) "I think it would make anybody feel that way …especially if they see you driving a cruiser, with overhead lights blinking and the word SHERIFF painted on the side of the car."

"But it's not just the uniform or the pistol or the cruiser. It's what being a sheriff means to me. Remember, both my father and grandfather were sheriffs before me. It's in the Culpepper blood." He stops to wipe the sweat from his forehead. "More than anything else, it's what makes me me. (*Grinning*) I remember the day I was sworn in as Sheriff of Mariposa County. My chest was ready to explode. What struck me was the fact that several thousand people had voted for me. And those votes carried a message: 'We're givin' you a badge, a pistol and a cruiser. We're trustin' you to protect us. And boy, was I determined not to let them down."

"That's bound to make you feel powerful."

"Yes…but like you said, down here it's different. I'm no longer the sheriff. I'm not anybody special. For the first time in years, I feel naked…no uniform, no title, no authority. It feels like something has been taken away from me…my life's blood or whatever you call it. Suddenly, after years of being somebody, I'm just a regular Joe. It's goddamn frightening…or at least it was when that ox come toward us. Without my uniform and pistol, I had no way to defend myself…until you mentioned Santé's name."

"So you were no longer Sheriff Culpepper, but you could still identify with Santé…and that gave you the strength you needed."

"Yes. Sounds crazy, doesn't it? But why? Just because I couldn't be a bigshot in uniform? Why did I have to become someone else? Why couldn't I just be myself?"

Anna nods. "Interesting question…(*pause*)…Any answers?"

Earl looks away, then resumes walking. There are still two miles to go before they can hail a taxi. No longer interested in talking, he is already picturing himself back in the hotel tub, whiskey in hand, soaking away the day's troubles. Softly enough so that Anna cannot hear, he mutters, "There'll be time to think about all this when I get home."

4

Two Years Earlier

Santé wakes up and looks around. Papa is still asleep in the corner. Vicente, his older brother who recently returned from the United States is next to him on his left. There is more room now that his sister Alma has gotten married and gone to live with her husband. Quietly he throws off his blanket and leans the cardboard carton he has been sleeping on against the wall. Mama is the only other person awake… making tortillas outside next to the fire. When he approaches her, she looks away.

Memories of last night quickly fill his head. The sky was darkening when Papa called him outside and made his chilling announcement. His words come back now, as cold and unyielding as the starless night. "It's time for you to go north and begin sendin' us money. With Vicente back home and not working and Alma gone to live with Felipé, we're not bringin' in enough money to pay the rent and buy food for everybody." Santé pauses by the fire, letting the words settle before summoning an image to go with them. Papa is much more intimidating than his diminutive size would suggest; he is only 5'1", barely 100 pounds, dark-skinned and balding but has the enviable ability to put down bigger and younger men with his eyes alone. Those eyes, hard and penetrating, speak of a life wrested from adversity through willpower, of a battle with despair won by denying himself the things everyone else had. His own father died when Papa was only twelve years old. As a result, he never got sent to school…never learned to read or write…and is even today more fluent with Zapoteca than Spanish. Thanks to the ox which kicked him in the mouth, he has no upper teeth, slurs his words and has to chop his food into tiny pieces before eating. But in all these years, no one has ever heard him complain.

His final words return to haunt Santé now. "Your family needs you to go." That's all that was said but his reasons were clear. Santé was well aware, for one thing, that his older brother, Vicente, had recently been sent home from a hospital in Texas. Apparently he had tried to cross into the States without enough money and became prey to drug dealers who lured him into serving as their mule. Newly flush with cash, an apartment and car, he began experimenting with the drugs he was delivering and quickly became addicted. After being detoxed in Houston, he was returned to Oaxaca for further treatment. Although he is now back with his family, he is still shaky, unable to concentrate and not emotionally strong enough to handle a job. From Papa's perspective, he represents another mouth to feed without paying his way.

But it's Alma too. Her departure means one less mouth to feed but also one less person capable of cooking and making children's clothes for sale in the zocolo. At 18, she is already an accomplished seamstress; so this is a big loss. Mama must now do the bulk of both cooking and sewing which means less time to make clothes. Although Alma has only been gone for a few weeks, the drop in income is already noticeable.

All this makes sense to Santé as he stands by the morning fire. It does not, however, lessen the bitterness he feels at what he is being asked to do. With his eyes half-closed, he replays more of the scene from last night. His own voice comes back, thin and frantic. "But Papa, I want to graduate…maybe go to Mexico City for classes in engineering. I'm considered one of the top students in the class here; just ask Senorita Bautista. She's convinced that if I finish school here, I can get a scholarship to college and get a good job afterwards. She knows that things are tight in our family but she was willin' to pay for my uniform and books next year…out of her own pocket. Papa…that's how much she likes me."

Santé moves closer to the fire as the scene continues unfolding. Father raises his voice, "Jis' because a man got some schoolin' don't mean he can support a family. Look at your Uncle Javier…he finished secondary school and he's jis' as bad off as we are."

Santé bites his lip in desperation. "But I can help the family if I stay here. I'm already making almost 100 pesos a week workin' on people's radios and TVs. It can only get better as more neighbors get sets of their own." He is referring to a little business that started as a hobby…tinkering with the family radio.…getting it to work again after Papa smashed it in a fit of anger. Once he learned how to do it, he offered to fix neighbors' radios for free…then did it for things in trade…finally charged real money. People say he has the gift for figuring out what makes machines tick…and how to fix them when they stop ticking.

Papa is unyielding. "Nobody in this here family has ever gone beyond 10th grade. No reason why you should go just because some teacher likes you. Who knows what she's up to anyhow. Your first owe is to your family. We give you food and shelter for 16 years; now it's for you to pay us back."

The scene nears its end as Santé drops his head, sobbing. "When do I have to go?" Papa scowls. "As soon as you can git yir things together. In a few days maybe."

Santé looks up, astonished. "You sayin' I can't even finish school this year?" Before Papa can reply, Mama, who has just come out onto the deck, takes up her son's case. "It won't make that much difference if we let him stay two more months, will it?" With further pleading on her part, Papa relents. It is agreed that Santé can stay until school ends in June. But then he must go.

As Santé wrestles in his sleep that night, images of his father's face pass back and forth before him. Sometimes the eyes are enormous, seeming to pop from his head. At other times his lips are twisted into a violent sneer, a sneer made more hideous by the fangs it reveals. Most frightening are those times when his father's head swells, then moves toward him, expanding to fill the whole room before shrinking again. No words are ever spoken; the images say it all.

The next day Santé goes to visit his Uncle Javier in Colonia Pistore, a barrio as impoverished as the neighborhood where Santé lives. Javier is as fat as Papa is thin and not even five feet tall. It's easy to see from his broad chest and long arms why people call him "Bear." Unlike his furry namesakes, however, he laughs easily, even when he is the butt of a joke. Ever since his wife died of cancer five years ago, he has lived alone and has built his life around his sister's family, Santé being his favorite nephew.

He earns his living as a carpenter…helping to build or remodel houses for affluent clients. He also builds wooden toys for children and birdhouses just for fun. He was one of the first to give Santé a radio to fix…and later encouraged him to start a little appliance business. Through conversations with his sister, Theresa, he is aware that Santé's parents have been thinking about sending Santé north. The moment he opens the door and sees his nephew's face, he is aware that a decision has been made.

"Come in…I've been expecting you." Santé enters the house without a word, his lips tight and shoulders drooping. "Bad news?" Javier asks. The question goes unanswered as Santé heads for the pillowed cane chair in the corner. Javier takes the tattered leather one opposite. It is clear from their behavior that the ritual of lemon tea is to be bypassed in favor of the business at hand. As soon as Santé is seated, Javier gets right to the point. "I take it you have to go…(*pause*)…So, when do you have to leave?"

Santé turns to look out the window, then drops his head. "As soon as school is over…in June."

Javier squints. "So soon? I was hopin' you could stay until you graduated… that's what…two years from now."

"Yeah…me too. Papa wanted me to go right now, but Mama told him they should let me finish this year. So, I've got two more months."

(*Smiling*) "Assuming you don't get kicked out of school out before then."

Santé bristles. "Those fights weren't my fault. What would you do if somebody called you a 'dumb Injun'?" He shakes his head. "Bunch of Mestizo assholes who think they can push us around because they're bigger than us. I ain't scared of 'em."

(*Smiling*) "Yeah, but Santé, you didn't have to break that kid's nose and hit the other one so hard you knocked him unconscious."

Santé pauses, his lips twisting into a poorly concealed smirk. "They don't say those things no more now…so I guess they're scared of me."

"Well, you're right about their attitude. Most Mestizos consider all of us Zapotecs inferior…Mixtecs and Aztecs too. What a bunch of crap…as if having a little European blood makes you better than anyone else." He pauses to lean back in the chair. "You'll see something like that up north where the whites treat the Indians like trash. The difference is that in the U.S. there aren't many Indians left whereas here in Mexico there are still millions of us hangin' around."

Santé continues staring at the floor. "I guess they look down at us because we're smaller and darker."

"And poorer. We don't own any land and we don't have much education. And because of that we're stuck with the poorest paying jobs."

(*Looking up*) "I don't get it. I thought at one time the Zapotecs ruled this whole area around Oaxaca…you know, from their city up on Monte Alban. The books we read in school said that our people were great fighters. Not scared of anything. Weren't they the last people to hold out against the Aztecs?"

Javier warms to the subject. "Sure…they defeated the Aztecs in several key battles with the help of the Mixtecs, their neighbors. Sent 'em runnin' back to Tenochtilan with their tails between their legs. But the great city our ancestors created up on Monte Alban broke down around 900 A.D.… everybody up and left. Nobody knows for sure why…maybe disease or lack of food and water, or probably the strain of constant warfare. Good land was scarce in the Oaxaca valley and every village chief was fighting to get a bigger chunk of it. The Zapotec people got the lion's share for a while but in the end, the Aztec Triple Alliance proved too strong for everybody else. We've been an oppressed people ever since."

Santé squirms in his seat. "But why couldn't we defend Monte Alban against the Aztecs…even with their allies? Were there too many of them… or maybe they had better weapons?"

"We did defend it for a while. As I said, nobody knows for sure why we finally gave up and left. But I don't think it was a matter of weapons. Both sides had all kinds of things they could use. One of the best, shared by Aztecs, Mixtecs and Zapotecs alike, was the macuahuitl."

"The what?"

"The macuahuitl." He pauses, then rises from his chair, smiling. "This was supposed to be a surprise, but since we're talkin' about it, I might as well give it to you right now. I made it for your 16th birthday…which is two weeks from today, right?"

"Yes."

"Let me go get it."

Javier returns a few minutes later and hands the weapon to Santé. "It's not an original *(laughing);* they're all in museums. You can see several at the Cultural Museum in town…you know, down by the Cathedral. This one I made myself…so its only a replica…but a pretty accurate one I think."

The weapon he is talking about is somewhat longer and narrower than the wooden bat the English use in cricket. Unlike any cricket bat, however, it has sharp flakes of obsidian stone, each five or six inches in length, sticking out from its right and left hand edges. From top to bottom, excluding the handle, it has six or eight such flakes wedged into each side of the weapon. Because of all the inserts, it could be swung in either direction…like a double-edged sword.

Santé grips the handle. "So this is what our people used when they defended Monte Alban."

"Well, so did the Aztecs…and the Mixtecs for that matter. All the armies back then used it. They had other weapons of course…like the javelin, sling, and dart thrower…but the macuahuitl was the most popular… probably because it was the most deadly."

Santé tries swinging the weapon back and forth. "I think I've heard of it before but I ain't never seen one…or even a picture of one. *(Running his fingers along one of the blades).* Wow! It's really sharp. You could take somebody's head off with this."

Javier nods. "It's light enough so you can swing it rapidly in either direction. And that's what made it perfect for hand-to-hand combat. A single blow to the arm or neck was usually enough to finish off your enemy…*(pause)*… Just don't take it to school, O.K.?"

(*Grinning*) "I promise…but I better take it with me when I go north. Who knows what I could run into up there?"

Javier leans forward in his chair. "That brings us to the question of how you're going to get there. What are your plans?"

Santé opens his back pack and stuffs the macuahuitl in as far as it will go, then sits back down."I haven't had time to think about it…(*pause*)…You were there once…how do you think I should go?"

"Well, that was a long time ago Santé. Lots of things have changed since then, but this much I know. The worst way to go is by train…you know, the way kids without any money do it. They go down to Chiapas where the freight trains come in from Guatemala and hop on one of the cars for a cheap ride north. Hoppin' on a movin' train is dangerous enough, but once they're sittin' on top, things get a lot worse. First they get robbed by bandits who take what little possessions they have, sometimes even their clothes. Then they get picked up by the Judiciales who either beat them or demand bribes. Some of the slower kids never even make it on board; they slip and fall tryin' to climb up the side of a car as the train is roundin' a corner. I've seen pictures of kids your age and younger with legs cut off just below the knees. It's horrible."

"So, what's a better way…hitchhike?"

"I'd go by bus if I was you. It's the safest way to go. It'll cost you a little, but I can probably help you out there."

"You mean a bus from Oaxaca…to…where?"

"When I went…and this was 10 years ago…I took one bus from here to Monterrey…and then a second one up to Nuevo Laredo which is right on the Rio Bravo or what the gringos call the Rio Grande. From a spot outside town, it's only 50 yards across the river to the U.S. After that it's a day's ride to Houston and the big city."

"So how'd you get across the river?"

"In the old days, you hired a coyote who would paddle you over on a raft…a flimsy thing made from inflated tires. But those days are gone

forever. Now…and you can read this in the papers…the Border Patrol…
you know, the migra…are on the other side just waiting for people to try it."

"You sayin' you can't get through that way no more?"

"Maybe a few make it…by swimming over in the middle of the night…
but I wouldn't try it even if you knew how to swim…"

"…which I don't."

"Nogales…northwest of Laredo…next to Arizona…is probably a better
bet these days although from what I've heard they've got 17-foot fences
guardin' the town. With all those fences, it's just about impossible to sneak
across one of the main roads."

"But people still make it, don't they? I got friends who did it this year…at
least that's what I heard."

"O.K.…but where did they cross?"

"I don't know. I just heard they made it."

Javier smiles as he sits up in the chair. "Well, like I said, I haven't been
there for 10 years and things have changed. But I've kept in touch with
people who've made it to the other side. They tell me that all the cities
along the U.S.-Mexico border are now blocked off with giant fences. That
means that the only place left to cross is the desert that lies between towns.
In the Sonoran desert, for example, the border is nothin' but a string of
barbed wire you can step over. You can still cross that way, but you take
your life in your hands. Hundreds of migrants, healthy enough when they
start out, die every year from heat exhaustion. They don't take enough
water and their bodies burn up in the desert sun. In the summer, desert
temperatures can get up to 120 degrees; your only hope is to travel at night
when it's cool and rest during the day. Trouble is, there's hardly any shade
to hide under when the sun's up. And there are rattlers all over the place
at night …(*pause*)…How would you like to be poking along, guided only
by moonlight, and step right on top of one of them?"

"Jeez. Ain't there some other way?"

(*Grinning*) "Well, yeah. You could apply for a passport and visa…then hop on a plane from Oaxaca to Phoenix. Of course, you might have to wait a few years to qualify…and the documents plus the plane will cost you over ten million pesos. To make things worse, the visa they give you is only good for six months…then you have to leave or they boot you out."

"Sounds like they don't want us to come."

Javier nods. "It depends who you're talking about. The business people want us to come and do their dirty work…you know, the kind of stuff no self-respecting gringo wants to do, things like picking fruit, mowing lawns, cleaning houses, and slaughtering cows. We're welcome in those places… as long as we stay out of trouble. The rest of the gringos don't want us to come at all. They see us as 'aliens'…unwanted invaders who take jobs away from white folks and clutter up schools with our kids."

"If we're not welcome, why do we try so hard to get there? I mean, why stick your neck out to get to a place where people hate you?"

"It's obvious; just ask around. For most people, it's a chance to make more money than you can possibly make here. In Oaxaca you break your back shuckin' corn or pickin' grapefruit and you're lucky to make 200 pesos a day; in the U.S. you can make three or four times that much doing the same thing. And that's money you can send back to your family…money for rent and food."

"Yeah, I want to help my family…but I gotta think of myself too. If I'm gonna get anywhere, I need to put away some money. I just want a chance to go to college and learn how to be an engineer. Maybe I can do that up north…(*pause*)…Is that being selfish?"

Javier shakes his head. "Why can't you do both…send some of your pay back here and save the rest for college? You just have to live cheap…rent a trailer with several other guys, don't go to restaurants, don't waste your money on girls. Besides, I've heard they have scholarships up there. It might be hard to get one without legal papers…but who knows?"

"But I won't even have a high school diploma when I get there. What college is gonna to take me without a degree?"

"My friend Paco…remember him?…he told me he took a test up in North Carolina. Well, he had to take it several times before he passed…but they let him count it as a secondary school degree. Then he applied to college."

"Did he get in?"

(*Laughing*) "No…but he's still tryin'."

Santé shrugs his shoulder. "Maybe I'll never be an engineer but I should be able to get some kinda job."

"Hey, with all you've learned about repairing radios and TVs, you shouldn't have any trouble at all…especially in a big city like Phoenix. Everybody's got a TV up there…and they all have radios in their cars. That means lots of work for people like you, my friend."

Hearing the word 'friend' lifts Santé's sagging spirits. He manages a slight grin.

Javier is good at reading thoughts. "Remember, you can always call me if you get into trouble or need money. When you get there, buy a telephone card. Paco uses a card to call me now and then; he says it's much cheaper than long distance…(*pause*)…Hey, but first things first; you've got to get across the border. That means finding a coyote who knows the way."

Santé straightens up. "And how do I find a coyote?"

"Just go the bus station in Nogales. From what Paco tells me, there will be lots of guys like you waiting to cross. Hang out there for a few hours and a coyote will find you. The price these days he said is somewhere around $1,500…that's U.S. dollars or about $18,000 Mexican. But don't pay more than half up front…some of these guys are thieves and will take off as soon as you pay them. Look for a coyote from Oaxaca if you can; they're less likely to screw you since news of their treachery would get back here and ruin the family's reputation."

"Where am I supposed to get 18,000 pesos? Couldn't I just buy a map, get directions from someone who's crossed before, and take off by myself. I like to hike and I'm in pretty good shape."

"Well, where are you going to find someone who has made it recently? You need to get fresh directions since the migra are always changing what they do. They even have helicopters now…that means you can be seen from the air and in the desert there aren't a lot of big trees you can hide under. Paco also said they've placed sensors in the ground along routes that migrants usually take. So you need a coyote to tell you where those sensors are… and how to avoid being seen by a helicopter…(*pause*)…I admire your guts my friend, but I don't think you or anyone else can make it without the help of someone who knows all the tricks."

"But the money?"

"Do what most of them do…go to Nogales and get a job. Save your money and use it to pay the coyote."

"But it could take months to save enough money, couldn't it?"

Javier squints. "Maybe. With your repair skills, my guess is that you could do it faster than most guys. But you will still need to work for a while before attempting to cross…(*pause*)…And you should time your trip so you don't cross in the middle of the summer when the desert is hottest. For example, go up there right after you finish school here in June, work for a couple of months, then make your attempt in early fall."

(*Forcing a smile*) "You say 'attempt.' You don't think I'm gonna make it right away?"

"I don't know. With a little luck, maybe you will. But the majority of people who try don't make it on their first attempt…or even their second. They get caught by the Border Patrol and sent back. Paco tells me that some of the men he met in Nogales were getting ready for their sixth or seventh go at it."

"What happens when they get caught? You say they get sent back, but is that all?"

"The coyotes are put in jail if they're caught, but the people who pay the coyotes are usually just reported. Their names and addresses are written down; then they're put on a bus and sent back to some city south of the border. Some give up at that point, but most just get a ride back to Nogales and try again. If they're caught enough times, they're punished somehow…probably a few months in jail. That's a chance most are willing to take. After all, if you've come all the way from southern Mexico or even Guatemala or Honduras, you're not going to give up easily, not when returning home means sleeping on a dirt floor and watching your kids go hungry every day."

Santé rises and paces the floor. "Do you think it's worth it? You were there once…but you came back. Why didn't you stay? Didn't you like it?"

"I was willing to stay, but my wife, Cochita, missed her family and wanted to return. We fought about it for a few months and then I gave in. Most people who go north…and that goes for men as well as women…expect to come back to their villages in Mexico. Cochita thought that way. Before heading north, migrants often promise their families they'll only stay until they make enough money for a second floor on the house…or until they can buy a used car…or until they can pay for somebody's operation. But then they get used to the big paychecks; some may meet a guy or gal they like…and within a year or two they decide to stay, despite prior commitments here in Mexico. They may still return each year for a local fiesta, but their home is now in the U.S."

Santé nods his agreement. "Yeah, Alma's friend Gloria had something like that happen to her. Right after she had a baby, her husband went off to L.A. with a few of his buddies…just for the citrus season he said…but after a few months he stopped sendin' her money. A year later a friend told Gloria that her husband was livin' with another woman who was pregnant with his child. Gloria hasn't heard from him since…*(pause)*…How can a guy do somethin' like that?"

"Men can do pretty much anything they want here in Mexico. If you look around, you'll see lots of women, usually with a couple of kids, living alone because their husbands never returned from a trip north. The lucky ones are those who still get money each month. Those who are abandoned have to provide for their kids by themselves…by taking in laundry or selling home-made pastries from their front yard. I don't see how they make it. Take the woman who lives down at the end of the street, Alicia.

Her husband left for the States three years ago and has stopped sending money. He's even stopped writing to her or calling. Her only hope now is to find another man…someone with a job…and then pray that he doesn't want to go north."

Santé hangs his head. "I guess the only reason I wouldn't come back is if I graduated from a university and got a job as an engineer. But even then, I'd want to help the family with money…and come back at fiesta to see everybody."

(*Nodding*) "That's what you say now, Santé. And that's good to hear, but we'll see how things turn out…(*pause*)…But look, let's concentrate on how you're going to get there. Here's the advice Paco gives his friends who are heading for Phoenix and planning to cross the desert. First, take plenty of water and good shoes."

"How much is plenty?"

"I don't know? You better ask people in Nogales…but don't scrimp just because it's heavy. Put at least one jug in your backpack and carry another. And take a cap with a visor to shield your eyes from the sun. It's going to be hotter there than the hottest day you've ever known in Oaxaca."

"How will I know where the trail starts?"

"Your coyote will show you. The entry point into the desert won't be in Nogales itself; more likely several miles to the west. Paco says there are some trails there, but you can get lost easily, especially since you'll be traveling at night. Carry a map of the area just in case."

"O.K. Let's say I get across the desert without stepping on any snakes or getting caught by the migra, how do I get to Phoenix?"

"Your coyote will make arrangements for you to be picked up in a van on the other side of the desert; that's included in the payment. If you get that far, you'll be in the United States…so before you go, buy a pocket dictionary. That way you'll be able to read signs and other English words. Phoenix is best place to head for but don't try to hitchhike if the van never comes; you'll just have to take a bus. Paco says there are migra everywhere looking for crossers. So, once you're across the border, try to blend in as much as you can. Take a clean shirt and a pair of pants in your backpack. Dirty clothes are a dead giveaway that you're crossing illegally."

The meeting ends with a bear hug from Javier and a quiet 'gracias' from Santé. As the boy heads down the hill, Javier suddenly remembers a book he wanted to tell Santé about called The Devil's Highway. It's about 14 Mexican migrants who died while attempting to cross the desert outside Nogales, the very area Santé will be heading for. "Yes, the book is frightening," he murmurs, "but it also has useful things to say about migra hiding places, favorite coyote tricks, and how the sun can affect your brain…information that could save a person's life." As he picks the book up, he nods approvingly, "I'll give him my copy next time he comes over."

5

Alma

Out on the deck, the Aguileras have just finished their evening meal of tortillas, frijoles and white Oaxaquena cheese. The fire on the ground is still burning when Santé brings out Uncle Javier's gift to show his brother Raul. They sit down at the edge of the deck, away from everybody else. With no more than a few words of explanation, Santé hands the weapon to Raul who immediately runs his fingers across the obsidian blades. "Ow, that's really sharp," the boy yells, then watches as blood appears on his fingertips.

Santé laughs, ""I warned you, jerk." He takes back the macuahuitl and jumps off the deck. "Imagine me up on Monte Alban," he shouts, his body coiled, his eyes afire. "Down there (*pointing to the steps*) are the Aztecs comin' toward us." He raises the weapon for a strike…then swings wildly, slicing through the evening air.

There is a loud 'thud' as the macuahuitl cuts into a young grapefruit tree just beyond the deck. "What the hell are you doin," cries the father who has just come out of the house. "Gimme that goddamn thing before you do somethin' crazy." He goes over to inspect the tree. (*Shaking his head*) "I planted this tree five years ago…it coulda given us some fruit in a few more." He runs his finger along the cut in the bark. "Thanks to you, it ain't gonna make it now. Maybe you can send us money for a new one when you get up north."

Santé gets back up on the deck and slowly hands the macuahuitl to his father, handle first. No words are exchanged. The ensuing silence is broken a moment later when Raul shouts, "Lookit, somebody's comin' up the steps…(*pauses*)…and it's no Aztec. It's Alma."

As Alma approaches the deck, smiles of welcome turn quickly to looks of horror. Her cheek is bruised like a piece of fallen fruit, her left eye half-closed. Sobbing, she wipes the blood from her chin, lurches forward and falls into her father's arms. "My God, child, what happened to you?" he cries, still hanging onto the weapon with one hand. She stares into his eyes, unable to find words for her pain. When neither speaks, Santé approaches, takes her by the arm and whispers what she cannot bring herself to say, "Felipé?" She nods, covering her face with her hands, but says nothing. Even here, surrounded by her own family, she is determined not to speak ill of the man she has married.

"You musta done somethin' wrong Alma," Papa says, "but he shouldn't hit you so hard."

Alma looks up, begging with her eyes.

"But you can't stay here," the father says, dropping his arm and backing away. "What are people gonna say? You gotta go back to your husband… (*pauses*)…That's your home now."

Alma cringes but still says nothing. Santé shakes his head in disbelief, then runs to his father's side, tears the macuahuitl from his hand and races down the steps. It is nearly three miles to the village where Alma lives but he knows the way, having visited there often. Once he reaches the bottom of the hill, he sets off at a gallop, gripping the macuahuitl firmly in his right hand.

By the time Santé has reached the street below, Theresa has joined the others on the deck. Like so many other mothers, her hands are red from kneading tortilla dough, her eyes still watering from the fire. One look at her daughter's face is enough to tell her what happened. She winces. Memories from her own past surface quickly…images of a husband's clenched fist, the sound of a blow to her cheek, a mother-in-law's sneer as she stands watching…and a misshapen face for months to come. Slowly she leads Alma into the house and sits her down on the mattress. As she dabs at the cut to her cheek, she asks, "How did it happen, honey? What dya do to bring him on like that?"

Alma opens her mouth to speak but is forced to stop as blood from inside her cheek fills her throat. Still sobbing, she traces her gum with her finger, sighing when it becomes clear that she has lost two lower teeth. The mother watches anxiously. Whispering, she repeats her question, "What dya you do to make him so angry."

Slowly the sobbing subsides. She opens her mouth. "You know I usually go shopping with Estella…and…" She grabs her mother's arm as the trembling returns.

"Take yir time Alma; he can't hurt you now."

(*Crying*) "But Papa says I gotta go back."

"We'll see. Your father's worried 'cuz the neighbors gonna talk. And I know it. Once a girl gets married, she's s'posed to live with her man's family. Our people always done it that way; everybody's goin' to get riled up if you don't go back. You can come visit us, but you belong to your man now."

"She's gotta stay even if her man beats her?"

(*Biting her lip*) "Yes. He can do that if she disobeys…(*pause*)…But what happened?"

Alma takes a deep breath. "Well, I hadda go shoppin' yesterday mornin'… so like always, I went to Estella's house since we do our shoppin' together. Her mother-in-law come to the door and said she was sick in bed and couldn't come out. I got scared; I knew we needed corn for the tortillas and sugar for the tea…but I couldn't go…"

Mama leans forward. "I know…you couldn't go inta town alone; people would say you was bein' unfaithful to your husband."

"I knew that…but what was I s'posed to do? We was all outta corn and Felipé, he gets real ornery if I don't have fresh tortillas on the table when he gits home from workin'."

Mama nods. "Of course, a man works har' in the fields all day and is tard' and hungry when he gits home. Your father was like that when we had our farm out in Tecultepec."

"I knew I was takin' a chance, but I figured since I was wearin' a long dress and had my rebozo pulled up over my head, nobody was goin' to think I was tryin' to attract a man."

"Oh dear God, that's where you was wrong child. It don't matter what you is wearing. A woman who walks into town by herself is tellin' everybody she's available. That's the way people here think. You shoulda known that."

(*Starting to cry again*) "I did know it Mama, so I took the back road… until I come to the center of town. Then I waited until no one culd see me before I went inta the store."

"Was there anybody in the store when you got there?"

"Besides Senor Alfonso? Just one…that old witch Graciela…you know, the one with brown teeth and a cane."

"Oh yes…the one who tells folk's futures. You think she's the one who tole Felipé's mama you walked inta town alone?""

"She couldn'ta. I was only gone for an hour. And we don't have a phone at home."

"So how did Felipé find out? Somebody musta told 'im."

Alma sighs. "Everything was jus' normal at first. Felipé ate his dinner and went back out to Carlos's Place for a beer. Nobody said nothin' about my trip into town. It wasn't 'til this mornin' that his mother, Reyna, come back from talkin' to her friend, you know, the woman in the house next to Estella's. Well, the minute she got home she rushed inta Felipé's room and shut the door. He was in there relaxin'. I got scared and stood outside so I can hear what they're sayin'. That's when I heard her tellin' 'im Estella was sick yesterday and I went inta town all by myself."

The mother begins to tremble. "Did he come out and ask you why you done such a thing?"

"No. He jus' opened the door and grab me by the throat. When I see him make a fist, I tried to pull away. Next thing I knew I was on the floor rubbin' my cheek and spittin' blood. I think maybe I fainted for a bit.

When I made like I was goin' to get up, he kicked me back down and called me a whore. Then he left."

"And Felipé's mother?"

"When I sat up, the first thing I saw was Reyna's face. She was smiling."

"She didn't do somethin' to help you?"

"She went and got a wash cloth and handed it to me. While I tried to stop the bleeding, she stood there watching but never offered to help. She kept shaking her head and smiling. The only thing she said was, 'I hope you learned a lesson.'"

"That's all?"

"Well no. She finally got down on her knees and picked up two teeth that I had spit out. They were covered with blood. When she asked me if I wanted them, I said no. So she got up and threw them in the trash."

"And then you left. Where was she when you got outta there?"

"She was right there at the door, hanging onta my arm. She's tiny but very strong. We fought for a minute until I pulled free and headed down the street. The last thing I heard her say was, "You better come back here tonight or Felipé will give it to ya again."

Theresa takes her hand. "So you walked all the way here…still spittin' blood. Did anyone stop to ask what was wrong?"

"No. I kept myself covered up…(*pause*)…So, can I stay here Mama?"

"I'll talk to your father about it. When he hears what you jus tole me, he might change his mind…(*pause*)…My worry now is Santé. He's got such a temper. You remember the trouble he got inta at school? Two times they sent him home for fightin'."

"I remember. But he might think twice this time. Felipé is four years older…and bigger. And he has a temper of his own (*rubbing her cheek*)."

(*Smiling*) "I can see that."

Rising from the mattress, Alma heads for the door. "I love Santé for wanting to get back at Felipé, but I don't want him to get hurt…*(pause)*… By the way, what's that thing he was waving around out on the deck?"

Mama shakes her head. "Somethin' your Uncle Javier give 'im for his birthday. He made it outta wood and some kinda stone. I think it's s'posed to be a weapon like our ancestors used up on Monte Alban."

Alma's eyes open wide. "So, why did he take it with him? He doesn't mean to use it, does he?"

Mother smiles. "He's probly tryin' to scare Felipé. Nothin' more than that."

* * * * * * * * * * * * * * * * * *

After running non-stop for an hour, Santé is relieved to see the road turn to dirt and gravel. Here, at the outskirts of the city, there are fewer eyes to stare as he races by. Another 15 minutes and he will be in Tecultepec; from the center of the village it's only a few minutes to Felipé's house. By now his lungs should be burning, his legs aching, his hand limp from clutching the macuahuitl. Under ordinary circumstances he would be totally exhausted, but these circumstances are anything but ordinary. Given the urgency of his mission, pain is a luxury he can no longer afford. With each step toward Felipé, the image of Alma's battered face becomes clearer. He speaks to her in fantasy now, demanding to know what happened. She takes his hand and through her tears tells how she was knocked to the floor with a sudden blow to the face. He sees the terror in her eyes, the blood on her lips. As he visualizes the scene, his head begins to throb; his heart is racing. There is a fire burning in his gut, driving aside all reason.

As he races toward his target, he has plenty of time to think about what he's going to do, but no such thoughts arise. There is no room in his psyche for anything but fury. No questions of intent, purpose or strategy can survive the fire that is consuming him; no fear of the consequences can compete with the image of Alma's battered face. He is at the mercy of his rage. What will happen will happen.

He picks up his pace; the two towers of Santa Cruz de Tecultepec lie straight ahead. Turning west along Avendida Zaragoza, he tightens his grip on the macuahuitl. Dusk is descending on the village. A boy on a bicycle comes up on Santé's left, challenging the runner to a race…then veers away when Santé refuses to play. Further on, an old man waves from his yard but drops his hand quickly when there is no response. Houses are passed unseen; horns go unheard. When a dog in the road awakens from its sleep, growling at the intruder, Santé refuses to deviate from his path. Nothing exists now but the sound of feet on dirt…and a sister's face. One more block and he will be there.

As he turns the corner and heads down Montero Calle, he slows to a trot, then stops to look around. Alma and Felipé's house, a one story, two-room house made of cinder blocks, is just ahead on the right. No one can be seen from the road. His heart is pounding, his lungs on fire but there is no stopping now. Slowly he approaches the front door, knocks firmly and waits. As expected, it is Felipé's mother, Reyna, who comes to the door.

Before opening, she rehearses her little speech. "We knew you'd be back," she sneers silently. "Now, get inside and prepare your husband's dinner. Be grateful that he's letting you return." Confident in her words, she sets her jaw and opens the door.

She gasps at what she sees. The figure towering over her is not the contrite daughter-in-law she expected. It is Santé. A quick glance at the macuahuitl in his hand triggers screams of "Felipé, Felipé!" Her cries fill the house, reaching the bedroom where her son is resting. In desperation she tries to push the door shut, but Santé is too strong. He forces his way in, then presses the tip of his weapon against her shriveled chest, knocking her to the floor.

Once inside, he scans the room for Felipé. Seeing no one, he heads for the bedroom, macuahuitl held high in readiness. Before he gets there, the door opens and Felipé, eyes flaring and knife in hand, throws himself at the intruder. Santé braces himself for the attack. Felipé, who is tall for an Indian and muscular from his work in the fields, raises his hand and brings his knife down on Santé's neck. It never gets there. Midway to its victim, the knife falls from his grasp as the macuahuitl, swung in an upward arc toward the bigger man, glances off Felipé's shoulder and buries itself in the side of his head. Blood gushes from his temple as he falls to the floor, gasping.

Reyna watches in horror as a pool of blood forms on the floor. When Santé turns and heads for the door, she rushes to her son's side, pressing her apron to his temple. "That boy is a monster," she mutters. "I'll go get the police." Felipé rolls over on his back and takes his mother's hand. With eyes still half-closed and teeth clenched in pain, he whispers, "No…don't say nothin'. It's jus' between him and me. I'll make him pay." He pauses to wipe blood from his cheek, adding, "Alma musta tole him about this morning. She's gonna pay too."

Outside the house, Santé pauses to examine his macuahuitl. One of the obsidian blades is covered with blood. He looks around, then rips a leaf from an overhead plum tree. Once the blade is clean, he drops the blood-soaked leaf on the path. Breathing more slowly now, he smiles contentedly, then sets out for the long walk home. It will be dark when he gets there.

Everyone is still up when he arrives an hour later. Anxious to hear what happened, they add wood to the fire and draw close. Santé breathes deeply then looks from one to the other, fixing his gaze finally on Alma who sits shivering under a frayed blanket. He starts slowly, deciding to include some details while leaving out others. As he approaches his encounter with Felipé's mother, he recognizes the folly of any pretence and begins relating exactly what happened. His account of the fight with Felipé, told blow by blow, elicits a variety of responses…whoops of joy from Raul, a scowl from Papa, and a nod of the head from Alma. He finishes with a simple statement, "She can't go back there now; it ain't safe."

No one speaks…but all eyes are on Papa. Mama reaches out to take Alma's hand then looks over at her husband. He hesitates for just a moment then nods his head.

"The police may be here in the morning," Mama says, breaking the silence.

"I don't know," Alma whispers from under her blanket. "I'm not sure. Calling the police would make Felipé feel weak. Besides, he'd have to tell them why he beat me."

Santé nods enthusiastically. "And that would say he's not macho enough to control you. I don't think he could stand havin' folks laugh at 'im."

Mama looks at Santé. "So, what you're saying is…."

"…that he's better off not telling anybody. Just keepin' it to hisself."

"Yes…but won't he try to get back at you somehow?"

"Sure…but I'll be in the U.S…remember?"

6

Northward Journey

Santé takes a seat in the bus, sets his backpack next to him, waves goodbye once more to his family and allows himself the luxury of a deep breath. The bus, a 1990's relic whose only extravagance is a tiny toilet in the rear, backs slowly out of the terminal. Santé pulls the nearest window open as the driver weaves delicately past an assortment of indiscriminately parked buses and trucks. In his haste to complete the obstacle course, the driver makes no attempt to avoid the ubiquitous puddles left from the rains which have been falling steadily here since early June.

This will be Santé's first trip outside Oaxaca. His ticket, purchased mainly with funds from Uncle Javier, will take him first to Mexico City and from there to Guadalajara and on up the West coast to Mazatlan, Culiacan, Hermosillo, and Nogales. The trip will take at least three days and nights, all of it to be spent on one bus or another. From the map he has studied, the route will run through territory alternately flat and hilly, treeless in places, with occasional views of the Pacific Ocean and temperatures in the high 80's and 90's. For two months he has been looking ahead to this day, sometimes with dread of the unknown, sometimes with the anticipation of discovery. Right now it is neither; El Norte is a long way off and there is much to be seen out the window.

As he gazes at the passing scenery, he pays special attention to the houses along the road, unconsciously comparing them to his own. Some have curtains in the window; others have bicycles and toys in the front yard. He begins to see his own circumstances in a broader light. Where exactly do we fall on a scale from rich to poor? His thoughts turn to his family. Alma is back home now…with no intention of returning to Felipé. Since the police have not shown up, it is safe to assume that the fight never got reported, just as Santé figured. Nor has Felipé made any hostile gesture, either to confront Santé or to get his wife back. When Raul saw him in the zocolo last week, his hair seemed much longer than usual, apparently a move to cover up the scar above his left ear.

He can relax now; so far things have turned out alright. As the bus lumbers through the forest toward Mexico City, he feels an itch in his nose and reaches into his jacket pocket for a tissue. As expected, the tissue is there, but it is not alone. Hidden below is a small cylindrical package wrapped in plastic. "What's this?" he exclaims quietly as he withdraws the package and pulls off the plastic. Inside there are twenty 10-peso coins, each worth about 80 cents in the U.S. or a total of 16 dollars. There can be no question who put them there. "But my God," he whispers, "where did she get the money?" As his mother's face rises before him, he battles first with tears then with an overwhelming urge to hold and kiss her. Turning his head toward Oaxaca, he whispers a prayer of gratitude, then closes his eyes as the bus heads northward into the enveloping night.

In Guadalajara he changes buses again. This time there are more passengers and Santé is lucky to get a seat…lucky in one sense but not so lucky in another. While the man sitting next to him appears to be sleeping and thus poses no threat, the odor emanating from his body suggests that he has been drinking heavily and is now nursing a hangover. He also reeks of nicotine. To Santé's dismay, the combination of the two smells is strong enough to bring on nausea and thus jeopardize his breakfast. In self defense, he reaches across the man's body and pulls the window open. Relieved at the difference it makes, he sits back in his seat and looks around. His actions have not gone unnoticed. A man and woman standing in the aisle, both in their 50's, flash smiles of appreciation. A girl of 14 or 15, standing next to them, perhaps their granddaughter, nods shyly. Santé nods back and closes his eyes.

The next stop is Matzalan which is right next to the ocean. A few passengers get off but many more get on, filling the bus to capacity. Many of the newcomers, now standing in the aisle, are wearing the standard gear for border crossing…caps with visors, backpacks, and sneakers. Some carry plastic bags filled with fruit and tortillas. Most are men in their 20's and 30's…probably on their way to Nogales, just like Santé .

No more than two minutes after the bus has left the station, a man of about 35, sporting tattooed upper arms and a faded t-shirt with the logo 'Take No Prisoners' on the front, makes his way brusquely through the crowd, not stopping until he reaches Santé's seat. He looks first at Santé, then at the man slumped next to him. Certain that he has found the man he is looking for, he reaches across Santé's lap and grabs the sleeping man by the arm. "Hey Miguel, wake up…it's Artemio." Miguel wakes up, looks around, shakes his head, then smiles at his friend. Still groggy, he rubs his eyes. "So, whatcha doin' here," he asks. Artemio laughs. "Hey, amigo, that's a long story." He then turns to Santé and says, "How about gettin' outta that seat and lettin' me and ma friend talk?" When Santé fails to answer, he jabs him in the shoulder. "I said we wanta talk. So git."

Santé clutches the backpack in his lap, with the handle of the macuahuitl sticking out. Still not sure what to make of the request, he turns to look at Artemio. As their eyes meet, each gauges the other's size, probable strength and emotional state. Artemio is around 5'7" and weighs close to 160 pounds. His protruding jaw and curled lip suggest an impatience with anything less than total submission. He reads Santé's eyes carefully, looking for any sign of fear. Instead of a twitch or blink, Santé responds with a glare and a tightening of his fist.

It is Miguel who strikes first. Breaking out of his stupor, he turns to face Santé and gives him a shove toward the aisle. As Santé falls forward, Artemio grabs him by the shoulders, pulls him into the aisle and takes his place on the seat. The passengers nearest the men immediately back away. It takes a few seconds for Santé to regain his balance and locate his fallen backpack. He kicks it to the side, then turns to face Artemio. Still sitting, Artemio flashes a smile of contempt, then whispers something to Miguel. With his head turned, he doesn't see Santé raise his arm. The sound of bone on bone can be heard throughout the bus as Santé smashes his fist into Artemio's right cheek. Amidst shrieks of pain, blood spurts from his mouth, spattering Miguel's shirt. Before his victim can recover, Santé's hands are around his throat, dragging him out of the seat and into the aisle. As Artemio lies coughing at his feet, Santé turns to Miguel and with a jab of his thumb, orders him out of his seat. Miguel hesitates for a moment, stares at his bloodied shirt, then does what he is told. Muttering to himself, he drags his semi-conscious friend to the rear of the bus and pulls out a dirty handkerchief.

With both men gone, Santé turns toward the front of the bus to look for the man and woman with the young girl. They are still in the aisle, their eyes riveted to the scene before them. With his hand, Santé motions them to come and take the two vacant seats. Slowly they inch forward, the man in the lead. Carefully he studies Santé's face, using what he finds to decide whether it's safe to sit down. Sensing his concern, Santé smiles, then offers his hand. From behind her husband, the woman, more experienced in gauging personality than her mate, pokes a finger into his back. He turns to acknowledge her judgment. Together they nod their appreciation to Santé and move into the empty seats. The girl remains standing. Later Santé finds a seat to stretch out on and passes the night curled up on his backpack.

7

Nogales

Early the next morning, Santé is awakened by the sound of passengers heading for the bus door. He sits up and looks out the window. The morning sun is shining directly on the façade of the Nogales Hotel as the driver announces their arrival in Nogales, Mexico. Just yards to the north he can make out some of the new office buildings in the sister city of Nogales, Arizona…buildings that loom airily above the 17-foot fence separating the two cities. Exhausted after three days and nights on the bus, he stumbles to the door and follows the others into the terminal. The first thing to greet him is the aroma of freshly made tortillas filled with rice and beans. Reaching into his jacket pocket, he rubs the coins put there by his mother, then withdraws enough for breakfast.

The terminal is filled with passengers from his own bus as well as many from other buses. Almost all have either a backpack or a bag of some sort strapped to their shoulders. Some are carrying gallon jugs of water. The ubiquitous baseball caps and sneakers suggest that most if not all are here to cross into the United States. He moves close enough to listen. The constant hum of conversation centers around the desert…how hot will it be…how dangerous are the snakes…how do you avoid the migra?

Santé is surprised that so many seem about to cross in June when the temperatures are still climbing. It is already hot here in the terminal as evidenced by the fans running full blast. Perhaps they're eager to make it before the temperatures get even higher …or before they extend the barrier fences out into the desert. Who is to say? To the 16 year-old kid who has never been outside his home state, it seems obvious that the best thing to do is work first, make some money and then try crossing in the fall. This is the advice his Uncle Javier gave him and thus far there seems no reason to question it. Reassured that he has made the wise choice, Santé buys a cheese and bean burrito, then wanders outside the terminal and into town.

Nogales is in the Mexican state of Sonora. From what he has read, Santé figures it's about half the size of Oaxaca. According to a book Senorita Bautista lent him, Nogales is poised above an old mountain pass which divides the town from its sister city Nogales, Arizona. Many of the main streets follow the path of former arroyos, running steeply downhill to the border where they deposit huge amounts of water during the rainy summer season. For Santé this is all very different from Oaxaca which is situated in a gentle valley surrounded by mountains on either side.

As he walks around town, Santé is more interested in what he can see at a distance than what is right there in front of him. Nogales, Mexico is interesting…more cosmopolitan and commercial than Oaxaca…but just across the way is the United States…the world every peasant in Mexico dreams about…the Eldorado of the North with its promises of food, cars, college, a career and money to support a family. Where he is standing, he is high enough on the hill to see over the 17-foot fence marking the international border. On the American side a cluster of office buildings gleams in the morning sun; further from the center there are several shopping malls, each with its own mammoth parking lot. Private residences, most of them with deck, lawn, garden and attached garage, dot the surrounding hillside. It is suburbia at its best.

On the Mexican side of the fence, houses give way to shanties. Late model Explorers and Tauruses yield to rusted out vans and pickups. There's a church on almost every block here, vivid testimony to the role of faith in assuaging the stress of everyday life. Pedestrians are dressed differently too. More skirts and dresses on the American side; more jeans and blouses on the Mexican side. Down in the area next to the border where people tend to congregate, Santé notices another difference: lots of smokers among the locals but hardly any among the American tourists shopping there. He walks down the hill toward the border. At the pedestrian crossover that links the two cities, he stops and stares through the opening into the other Nogales. "Why can't I just walk through?" he murmurs. "Why do I have to risk my neck hiking through the desert when I could cross here in 10 seconds?"

Further on down the street he passes a store featuring bedroom furniture and is reminded that he needs a place to sleep tonight. Turning, he hurries back up the hill to the terminal where there are people who should be able to advise him. From what he has already heard, most of the crossers gathered there plan to spend the night in the park…with nothing more than a thin blanket to shield them from the cold. This is apparently illegal but so many do it the police have given up trying to stop it. When Santé approaches a boy his own age and asks what he plans to do, he is told that if you want to save money, the best alternative is a flop house at the East end of town…no beds or mattresses…only one bathroom for the whole house and it rarely works; you sleep on the floor or on a piece of cardboard if you can find it. While it doesn't sound like much, the boy adds, it only costs 50 pesos a night. To Santé who has slept on a piece of cardboard his whole life, it doesn't sound all that bad…at least until his informant adds that the place reeks of pot and alcohol…and that drug dealers pass through there every day looking for new delivery boys. Memories of what happened to his brother Vicente come quickly to mind; he crossed successfully but was penniless by the time he got to L.A. Desperate for work, he became a mule, bought a car, began experimenting with cocaine, became addicted, was hospitalized, then sent home to Oaxaca. Now, instead of working hard and sending money home which was the original plan, he lies around all day, physically unfit for work, a dead weight on his family. Santé thanks his informant for the information, asks for directions to the park and takes off. "Git yirself a blanky," the other boy cries out.

"There's a sweater in my backpack," Santé answers. "That should do it."

The "park" is nothing more than a field with a couple of paths running through it. Maybe once it was a real park but with so many migrants camping here, trampling down the grass and littering the place with beer cans and Styrofoam containers, it has all the appeal of a garbage dump. No one complains, however, unless it is the prostitutes who parade through here night after night hawking their wares. "We know you is away from home and horny as hell," they cry. "You too cheap to enjoy a woman's body?" Men pretend not to hear; they huddle under their blankets and dream of the cars they will buy in El Norte.

In the morning Santé rises and heads for the terminal where he purchases three plain tortillas, adds a little salt to each and sits down at a table. With his last gulp, he rises, goes to the telephone booth in the corner and picks up a tattered copy of the Yellow Pages. Turning quickly to 'Appliance Repair', he copies down the names and addresses of the two companies listed. Fortified with his three-peso breakfast, he returns to the counter, shows the clerk the names and asks for directions.

First on the list is a company on Montoya Avenida, several blocks to the southeast. Santé arrives at the office shortly after they've opened. He introduces himself and explains his position. "I'm looking for a job as a repairman. I've fixed a lot of radios and TV's back in Oaxaca…so I don't need no trainin'."

The office manager looks him over carefully. "Your family jis' move here… or you lookin' to cross over?"

Santé studies the man's face. "How honest should I be? The guy seems interested, but how long does he expect me to stay?" He decides to tell the truth. "I need to make enough to pay a coyote…then I'm headin' for Phoenix…(*pause*)…but I'm a real hard worker…I can even work durin' lunch hour if I have to."

The man smiles, then shakes his head. "Sorry kid. I'd like to take ya on but it's not worth it for me to teach you the ropes and then have you up and leave after a couple of months. If I was you, I'd try Gomez TV Repair over on Jaurez Calle. They're bigger than we are and might take you jis' for the summer…(*pause*)…but it might be good to play down this Phoenix business. And be sure to tell 'em what ya tole me…that you don't need no trainin'. That should help."

On his way over to Gomez TV Repair, Santé rehearses his little speech. When he gets there, he omits any mention of his plan to cross over. Conscious that he is lying, but aware he has little choice, he tells the manager his family has just moved to Nogales from Oaxaca where they had trouble feeding themselves and that he needs to make money to help support them. The combination of his apparent sincerity and good looks convinces the manager to give him a job. "We're short somebody workin' on car radios," he says. "Have you worked on cars before?" Already uncomfortable with his previous lie, Santé confesses that he hasn't but adds that he is a quick learner. "We'll see," says the boss. "C'mon on in tomorra and we'll give it a go. We open at 8:00…there's some paper work to fill out; jis' don't be late."

8

Friends & Coyotes

Santé's new job works out fine; he has no trouble learning how to fix car radios and CD players. In the next two months he spends as little as possible and is able to save most of his money. He does buy a blanket and piece of plastic for rainy nights in the park; other than that, nothing except food. Every morning he goes to the bus terminal to clean up. It helps that the slight fuzz on his upper lip doesn't need shaving yet. Typically, he leaves the terminal with five frijoles-filled tortillas, eats two on the way to work, and saves the other three for lunch.

While at the terminal, he receives several offers from coyotes. The going rate is now US $1,800; that includes a van to Phoenix once they get over. While hanging out at the terminal, he also meets a boy named Luis from El Salvador. Luis has a sister in L.A. who has paid for his bus trip all the way to Nogales. He plans to live with her until he can get his own place. Right now he has a job cleaning tables and floors at the Café del Sol and is making 35 pesos (US $3.00) an hour, less than half what Santé is earning at the repair shop.

The two manage to meet for a few minutes every day. When Luis asks about the strange bat sticking out of his backpack, Santé tells him what happened with Felipé. His curiosity aroused, Luis asks to see the weapon, then runs his fingers along blade just like Santé did at first. "You could really take somebody down with this motherfucker. You gonna use it if la migra catch you?"

Santé laughs. "No...I really don't have any plans to use it; it was a gift from my uncle; just takin' it with me as a reminder of home....and my ancestors."

As they lie next to each other in the park, Luis responds with his own story of what happened in San Salvador when his sister, Amalia, and her two kids visited from LA. "We was driving along in this rental car when Amalia's cell phone rings. It's a strange voice sayin' he knows who she is and that she's visitin' her parents and brother. He talks real creepy. She wants to know who he is, but he don't answer. Then the guy says she's gotta give him US $2,000 by the next day or he'll kill both the children. She goes whacko, drives back to our parent's house, calls Jorge her husband in L.A. and tells him to send the money right away.

Santé raises his eyebrows. "Why didn't she go to the police?"

"Hey, she knows the police won't do nothin'…maybe they in on whole thing…maybe the guy who calls is policeman too. You can't trust the police in San Salvador…bunch of crooks."

"So, did your sister pay?"

"Yeah, she got money from the bank and went to the spot where he says to leave money in paper bag. I go with her thinkin' maybe I can do somethin' to stop the guy, but he's big and carries a knife. So we pay and Amalia takes plane home to L.A. next day."

"It's not so scary in Oaxaca, Santé replies. "Some fightin', sure, but nothin' like what you said. It's mainly unions wantin' more money from the government. Food is more of a problem…lotsa beggars on the sidewalks near the zocolo…lotsa kids searchin' in dumpsters for somethin' to eat."

"But you got mucho drug problems in Mexico, yes? Cartels fight each other?"

"Not that far south. It's more of a problem up here near the border. And it's not jis' drugs anymore. I hear one guy say drug cartels are startin' to take over the coyote business…yeah…right here in Nogales. Pretty soon if you wanta be a coyote, you gonna hafta join a cartel."

Luis nods enthusiastically. "Yeah, and that means they gonna try to 'liminate guys who try to be coyote on their own."

"Right…and they're gonna try to keep other cartels from movin' in here. We could end up in a crossfire…(*pause*)…"

"So whatcha gonna do?

Sante pauses. "I'm waitin' until I find somebody from Oaxaca…somebody whose family I know."

"But what if you wait and ain't nobody from Oaxaca comes along?"

Santé pulls out the macuahuitl. "I'll go anyway…but I might have to use this."

By the end of August Santé has enough money saved to pay a coyote… plus something for food and a room in Phoenix while he looks for a job. But Luis proves to be right; no one from Oaxaca comes along. Santé settles for someone from Veracruz, the state nearest to Oaxaca. The boy he chooses is only 19, but according to others at the bus station, he's already experienced, having successfully guided several groups through the desert. He dresses just like any other migrant: sneakers, baseball cap, dirty pants, backpack…just in case the group gets picked up by the migra. If caught, most migrants will get off easy; first they will be sent to a holding center, then, as soon as there are enough to fill a bus, they'll get shipped back to Mexico. Coyotes, on the other hand, are usually fingerprinted and sent to jail for three months. The leader of Santé's group goes by the name of El Chacal (*The Jackal*), a name given to him by the pollos (*chickens*) he has taken across previously. While not entirely flattering, he accepts it as a sign that others see him as especially clever, a description that fits his self-image. Some would say that it also fits his looks: thin frame, braided black hair falling to his shoulders, eyes narrowed to a slit, and a mouth that turns up at the corners in a smirk. After some hesitation, he accepts Santé's offer of half the $1,800 now, the other half to be paid when they reach Phoenix.

On the first of September the group meets at the bus station for breakfast and final instructions. There are nine in the group including El Chacal. All are short with dark skin suggesting an Indian heritage. There are no introductions, just a short speech by the leader in which he cautions against taking too much time to cross the desert. "There's gonna be migra everywhere…jis' waitin' to grab us…so we hafta keep goin'. If you walk too slow, yir goin' to git lef' behind. And if you fall behind, yir on yir own. Don't count on me for no help…*(pause)*…We gonna take a van to Quitobaquito, then go into the desert for a mile. That's where the border is. Don't worry, it's jis' a string of barb wire…we can step right over it. Then we gotta wait 'til dark before beginnin' our little hike. We'll spend the days hidin' out anywhere we can find some shade."

At first, silence…then a graying man in his fifties speaks up: "You say 'little hike'….but just how little is it? I got a wife here with a heart problem; she's not prepared for a lot of fast walking."

Santé turns to look at the man, convinced he's seen him before. Before El Chacal can continue, it hits him. "On the bus…yeah, he was the guy I gave my seat to…him and his wife. Nice people…thanked me twice."

El Chacal stares at his questioner. "Like I said, you gotta keep goin'… *(smiling)*…but don't worry, I got some medicine here that will keep you slow pokes movin' along. A hundred percent guaranteed."

No one asks about the 'medicine.' Each one in the group has his own hunch about what he means. It could be a traditional herb of some sort or maybe an illegal drug like cocaine. The latter is especially worrisome to Santé given what happened to his brother. He decides to keep a close eye on El Chacal when he begins dispensing his 'medicine.'

A second question comes from a 20-year-old man with a Guatemalan accent. "So how long is it gonna take to get across…you know…how many nights we gotta hike?"

"Depends," El Chacal answers. "If we don't hit no trouble with la migra, two nights at most. If they's waitin' for us…you know…ambush us, we gotta scatter. Then it's every man for hisself. Git the hell outta there, rapido. When the migra leave, double back and head for Quitobaquito. You can git a ride there back to Nogales."

"If we don't make it across, do we get our money back?" The question comes from a lean, squinting man in his late 20's, a man Santé later learns is the Guatemalan's brother. "Seems like we should."

"Fuck no," El Chacal responds with a sneer. "If we git ambushed, that ain't my fault; it's jis' bad luck and I get to keep what you already give me. If I go the wrong way and git us lost, that's different. Then you git yir money back. But I ain't gonna do anything stupid. I never do."

Santé ponders the last statement. "If Chacal takes the wrong turn and gets us all lost, when is he gonna pay us back? Don't make any sense. If we're lost, we're probably gonna run outta water and die from the heat. No, he's jis' talkin'. We ain't gonna git our money back no matter what." He shakes his head. "It took me the whole summer to save that $900 and I don't wanna have to do it all over again. No, I gotta make it on this first try. If he gets us lost, I'll jis' go my own way." For reassurance he reaches into his pocket and pulls out the map he bought. "It's all right there," he mutters, "the trail into the desert from Quitobaquito, the valley on one side of the Growler mountains, the town of Ajo on the other side, and the route from Ajo into Phoenix. I can do it alone if I hafta."

Just as the group is preparing to leave, Luis enters the bus station and heads immediately for Santé. They exchange brief hugs. "Hey, you comin' with us?" Santé asks. "I thought you said that you didn't have enough…."

"No, I jis' wanted to say goodbye. You tole me you was leavin' this mornin'….so I come over to wish you luck…(*pause*)…Maybe I can meetcha in Phoenix…as soon as I save up the $1,800. Probly 'nother coupla months."

"It'll be cooler then," Santé replies, "so hikin' through the desert should be easy. But look, when you get to Phoenix, check the yellow pages for the TV repair shops. If things go O.K., I should be workin' in one of them. It would be fun to get together on the other side."

"Yeah, maybe we could git some leather boots and one of them cowboy hats, then find some girls and take 'em to a bar."

Santé smiles. "Let's rent a car…then we could take 'em anywhere we want."

Luis claps his hands. "Why rent…let's buy us one…maybe one of them old Chevies…you know, the kind with the fins and shiny hubcaps. We go cruisin' the streets with one of them jobs and the chicas, they gonna jump right in."

(*Laughing*) "Let's get over there first. Remember, look for me in one of the repair shops. I'll be waitin' for you."

At the door they say their final goodbyes. As Luis heads down the street to the restaurant, Santé climbs into the van and takes a seat behind the couple he met earlier on the bus. "I'm Santé," he says, extending his hand first to the man and then to his wife. "We were on the bus together…comin' up from Hermosillo."

"Oh yes," says the man. "I'm Alessandro; this is my wife Guadalupe; we're from Tlacalula in Tabasco. I remember….you gave us your seat. Those guys were really mean to you but you stood up for yourself. I'm glad you're comin' with us. (*turning to the seat across the aisle*) Have you met our granddaughter? Come here Maya…say hello to Santé."

Maya is about 14 or 15…too skinny to be attractive but blessed with large brown eyes and a cute, turned up nose. Her 'hello' is shy enough to suggest an interest in the boy she is being introduced to. Santé acknowledges her with a nod and leans back in his seat.

The driver closes the door and revs up the engine. All talking stops as the bus moves out onto the road. There is a slight chill in the air, the sign perhaps of an early fall. The sun is already high in the sky, not to be denied its daily climb to glory. Let the desert cringe it seems to say. I am the master here.

9

The Desert

The bus rolls on to the village of Quitobaquito where it leaves the highway and heads into the desert, stopping when the makeshift road ends about a mile later. At the road's end there is a trail leading into the hills, the beginning of the infamous Camino del Diablo (*The Devil's Highway*). Just outside the bus, the migrants gather to survey their new surroundings. Nothing is moving; no birds, no animals; it is eerily silent. Alongside the trail there are a few creosote bushes, several saguaros and some large sandy-colored rocks. Nearby there is evidence of previous migrants: plastic jugs, candy wrappers, tampons, toilet paper, and feces blackened by the sun. El Chacal leads everyone to the shade of a mesquite grove. "We'll rest here…wait until dusk before movin' on. Take it easy on the water. You'll need plenty tomorra."

"No medicine yet," Santé whispers to Alessandro, a twinkle in his eyes.

"Later tonight," the other replies, making a place for himself besides Santé among the rocks. "He'll probably bring it out when we start walking. But I'm not taking any. I don't know what kind of drug he's talking about but whatever it is, my wife's heart is too weak for that kind of thing…(*pause*)… Are you going to?"

"Nope," comes the brief response. "I don't need anything special to get me movin'." Sliding deeper into the shade, Santé opens his backpack and pulls out a beef torta he bought the night before. The lettuce is already wilted and the tomatoes limp but he pretends not to notice. Before closing the pack he makes sure that the other three sandwiches are still there. He takes two brief swigs of water from his plastic jug and lies down on his back. There is nothing to do now but wait.

By 6:00 the sun has spent its glory and is getting ready to slip behind the mountains to the west. El Chacal calls the group together and gives another little talk. "The boundary is jis' up there (*pointing*)," he says. "It's only some barb wire but once we cross it, we're in the U.S.…and that means la migra. You guys that got flashlights gotta keep 'em turned off. They'll be copters overhead all night long lookin' for crossers like us so we gotta stay hid. We got about 10 hours of dark we can use for walkin'…and then we gotta lay low when the sun comes up. So you gotta keep movin'…anybody who falls behind is gonna git left behind…(*pause*)…You hear that?"

By the time he says 'You hear that?' his eyes are fixed on Alessandro and his wife. He stands stiffly, his chin thrust forward as if readying himself for a protest. None comes. Without a further word he turns abruptly and starts up the path, not bothering to check if everyone is following. The Guatemalan brothers quickly fall in behind, followed by Antonio, a husky 20-year-old from Chiapas and Jesus his younger cousin. Alessandro, Guadalupe and Maya come next; Santé brings up the rear. Using fallen branches, some fashion walking sticks for poking the ground in front of them…a useful tool when you can't see where you're going. Others are content to rely on instinct.

El Chacal sets a blistering pace…walking steadily for a full hour without rest. The only light shining is that of a moon rising in the east. As the column feels its way up the trail, some tapping their walking sticks, others trusting to the protection of their sneakers, everyone is focused on the threat of rattlesnakes sleeping in the dirt. What they are unaware of, at least in the beginning, is the presence of overhead mesquite branches. On more than one occasion a sudden bump to the head is followed by a loud cry…and a quick warning from El Chacal: "Shut up you asshole…you want the migra to hear us.?"

When El Chacal finally stops, he waits for everyone to catch up, then reaches into his backpack for a bottle of pills. "Some of ya are gittin' tired already; I can see that. I'll tell ya this: if we slow down, we're gonna get caught…the migra are everywhere in the desert. The more time we spend here the better their chances of catchin' us. Two nights a walkin' is all we got…and we already behind…(*pause*)…If ya wanta git to Phoenix, ya gotta go faster. If ya like goin' slow, that's O.K. too…jis' be ready to get picked up and shipped back to Chiapas or Guatemala or wherever the fuck you come from…(*pause*)…Now, all of ya can use some help. These here pills are guaranteed ta pick ya right up."

With that brief introduction, he takes several pills from the bottle and hands a few to the Guatemalan brothers, then to Antonio and his cousin Jesus. Alessandro holds up his hand, palm forward, a clear 'no thanks.' El Chacal skips past Guadalupe and Maya, then turns to Santé who simply shakes his head. Not bothering to conceal his disgust, El Chacal puts the bottle back in his pack and shouts, "O.K.…get yir asses movin'. We gotta make it to the mountains 'fore dawn. Without a further word he heads up the trail, never once looking back.

As the path steepens, Alessandro's family falls further and further behind. By 1:00 A.M., they are over 100 yards behind everyone else…except Santé who has chosen, for reasons not entirely clear to himself, to bring up the rear. It is obvious from her labored breathing that Guadalupe's strength is giving out. Even with her husband holding one arm and Maya hanging onto the other, she can barely move. Yielding to the inevitable, the three of them sit down to rest. Santé stops with them but remains standing.

Up ahead their absence does not go unnoticed. The older of the Guatemalan brothers, Enrico, is the first to confront El Chacal. "We gotta wait for the ole guy and his wife," he says. "The woman, she can't go so fast."

El Chacal stops just long enough to scowl, then spit next to Enrico's foot. "They stupid not to take my medicine. Now they gotta pay. Like I tole 'em, ya fall behind, ya git lef' behind. There ain't no other way to do it."

"Yeah, but if ya leave 'em there, you gotta give 'em their money back…yes? They pay $900 for you to get 'em to Phoenix; now they not goin' to make it. You gotta stop and give 'em their money back."

El Chacal says nothing. Instead he reaches into his pocket and pulls out a folded knife. With a snap, the blade pops out, a foot from Enrico's chest. "Look, you dumb injun. You come with me, you go by my rules. If you don't like it, you can join those assholes back there. They should never try to cross desert; they too old. Now they gonna get robbed by bandits, caught by la migra, or burned alive by the sun. Take yir pick; or come with me and keep yir mouth shut."

Further back on the trail, Santé sits down next to Alessandro. By now the moon is at its zenith, throwing soft shadows on both sides of the path. Santé whispers: "You think if we rest for a while she can keep goin'?"

"She's a tough old bird," the older man answers. "With a little rest she should be ready to walk some more. It's the heart…gets beating too fast… makes it hard for her to breathe. If we stop here, take something to eat, and get some sleep, she'll be ready to go tomorrow night…(*pause*)…but you go on now. Maybe we can catch up with you later…have a beer together in Phoenix (*laughing*)."

Santé forces a smile. "Do you have a map?" When Alessandro shakes his head, Santé responds quickly, "Well, how you gonna know which trail to take in the dark? If you get lost you gonna run outta water before you make it to Ajo. You betta take mine. I remember it real good."

Alessandro takes the map and nods a 'thank you.' With Santé's help, he goes over the route they plan on taking. First north along the desert floor, then east up over the Growler Mountains, down the other side into the town of Ajo and then west into Phoenix on the highway. Once he is assured he knows his way, he turns to Guadalupe and smiles. "We're O.K. now, thanks to Senor Santé.

Santé, the 16-year-old, chuckles, adding, "You sure you don't mean Don Santé?"

Guadalupe is close enough to hear their conversation but remains dubious. She nudges her husband. "But what about bandits?" she asks, not attempting to conceal her anxiety. "They know we have money to pay coyote in Phoenix. They know we all go on same trail…so how we hide from them? Tell me that."

Not for the first time in their 30 years of marriage, Alessandro is at a loss for words. His failure to answer intensifies her frustration. With voice rising she blurts out, "I think we go back now. We know this trail. If la migra catch us, that's O.K.…better than bandits."

"But we have nothing to go back to," the husband replies softly. Remember, we sold our furniture, gave our clothes away, and let your cousin and her three kids move into our house. Where are we going to live?"

Guadalupe is unmoved. "We still have the $900 hidden in my jacket… and a little extra. We can rent an apartment until my cousin finds another place. She will understand. It's not our plan, but is better than gettin' robbed or even killed…yes?"

Alessandro drops his head in defeat.…then turns to Santé. "What do you think we should do?"

Santé hesitates to get involved, especially with people much older and presumably wiser than himself. What changes his mind is the image of the three of them being attacked on their way back to Quitobaquito…with no means of defending themselves. "It's probly no safer goin' back than goin' forward," he offers. "We've been lucky so far, but maybe the bandits are too afraid to attack a large group. With only three of ya, it would be easy pickins."

Alessandro sits up. "You sayin' we should go on?"

"That sounds best to me," Santé replies.

Guadalupe bites her lip. "If we go on, you stayin' with us?"

"If you want me to, yes."

She relaxes enough to lower her voice. "You good boy…(*pause*)…I notice somethin' stickin' outta your bag…with a wooden handle. What is it?"

Santé opens his backpack and pulls out the macuahuitl. As he hands it to Guadalupe, he adds, "Careful, the edges are very sharp. My uncle made it for me…said everybody used it in the old days. Nowadays bandits carry knives when they rob people…and they know crossers don't have nothin' for protectin' themselves. So, when they see this thing, maybe they get shook up in a hurry." To underscore his point, he takes the weapon from Guadalupe, stands, and slashes at an imaginary assailant. His audience is startled into silence. "So," he asks, holding the weapon aloft, "which would you rather have…this or a knife?"

Alessandro murmurs his approval. Guadalupe says nothing but is clearly impressed. Maya smiles shyly and looks away. Santé can see it in their faces: the decision to keep going has been made.

They spend the rest of the night bunched together next to the trail, leaving the decision of where to seek shade until morning. Gradually the talk shifts from bandits to more personal matters. Alessandro confides that he is a school teacher from a small village outside Mexico City, the first in his family to graduate from college. They have one son, Adrian, who is married and has a daughter, Maya (*pointing to the girl*). Adrian took a job as carpenter's apprentice but there wasn't enough work, so he and his wife Paolla left for the U.S. when they were both in their 20's. They left Maya with us, promising to come back in a year or two. That was seven years ago. They've been sending money back ever since, but have changed their minds about returning to Mexico. They're now living in Phoenix; that's where we're heading.

"But why did you leave your village?"

"Farmers there are no longer able to make a living on their campos. Ever since they passed NAFTA, the price of corn has plunged. Most campesinos have moved to Mexico City or the U.S; there's hardly any young people left in the village. The school was finally shut down for lack of students; now I teach Maya at home. There are only a couple of stores left, no doctors or dentists; the roads are in terrible shape…huge pot holes…some so bad that trucks can't bring food into center of town. They've set up a temporary mercado out on the highway. If you want to buy food, you have to walk or take a bicycle out to the highway and buy food there…then bring it back to your house.

"So, without students, how do you make enough money?"

"I tried commuting to Mexico City for a part-time teaching job but couldn't make enough to support us, even with help from Adrian in Phoenix. So, we finally decided it was time to move."

Santé responds with details of his life in Oaxaca, focusing on his father's decision to pull him out of school and send him north to make money for the family.

Guadalupe, who has been quiet but listening carefully, turns to Santé. "You really like school? I never like it. I was glad when I stop at end of 8th grade. Maybe you smarter than me (*giggle*)."

Santé shifts uncomfortably. "I had good teachers. Senorita Bautista was the best. She wanted me to go to college…even offered to help pay for it… (*pause*)…That's what I really want…to get more education and become an engineer."

"But your father had to think of the family," Alessandro adds, his frown lost in the shadows. "Education is no good if you're starving. Look at me. I don't know what I'm going to do in Phoenix…maybe clean bathrooms or mow lawns…nothing that my college degree has prepared me for, but I'll do it just so we get enough to eat. Your father was putting the family first…like a father should."

Santé stops breathing, his face suddenly taut. He struggles for the right words. "My father never went to school…so he never appreciates what education does for you. He can't read books…can only write his name. Everybody says he is ignorant man."

"You shouldn't talk about your father like that," Guadalupe responds sharply. "He's only tryin' to help his family. You should be happy that he worry so much about his wife and children."

Santé says nothing, then gets up and walks down the trail.

Maya taps her mother on the arm. "I think you make him mad. Maybe he's goin' to leave us now."

"Well, maybe he will. Maybe jis' talk when he say he stay with us."

"No, I think he's serious…but you hurt his feelings. He wants to stay in school, but his father say no…you must go to U.S. and get a job so you can send us money."

"Of course," mother replies, "The man never went to school hisself. How's he s'posed to know what it's like. Besides, he has to take care of a whole family, not just Santé…(*pauses, then smiles*)…You gettin' to like this boy?"

Maya's face reddens. "He's nice, that's all."

When Santé returns, he sits down at a slight distance from the family. Maya opens her mouth to speak but stops when her father touches her arm. Nothing is said. Instead she lies down, her heart throbbing, forced to watch as the moon inches its solitary way across the midnight sky.

At daybreak, the group begins looking for shelter from the sun. When Santé spots a rock overhang facing west, they all crawl underneath and spread out their belongings. By noon when the sun is directly overhead they will have to find an overhang facing east. In the meantime there is little to do but sit still and take occasional sips of water. What little conversation there is centers around the heat…and how much further it is to Ajo. Santé and Alessandro pore over the map, trying to locate the trail that leads up over the mountain. "Trouble is," Santé says, moving his finger to the base of the mountain, "even if we find the main trail, there gonna be migra waiting for us. My uncle's friend says they hide behind rocks and then jump out at ya with their big lights turned on. Then they grab ya and take ya away in trucks."

"Then how do we get over the mountain?" Alessandro asks.

"I think we hafta look for an animal trail…you know, the kinda path deer use when they're movin' around. If it's far enough from the main trail, the migra won't see us climbin'…so we can slip over the mountain without gettin' caught. Harder for bandits to find us there too."

"But how are we goin' to find such a trail…then follow it in the pitch dark?"

"You got a flashlight?"

"It's in Guadalupe's pack."

"O.K. I got one…so that makes two. We jis' go real slow and keep the lights down. Won't be no 'copters to spot us at night, but it's important we stick together so nobody get lost."

With a plan in place, they settle back under the overhang and wait for noon. Their next destination has already been agreed upon…an east-facing overhang about 20 yards back down the trail. When the sun's tentacles approach their doorstep, threatening to bake everyone alive, they gather their belongings and hurry to the new overhang. An empty plastic jug in the rear tells of a previous occupancy. Huddled once again in the shade, they breathe in the cooler air and spin fantasies about the person who sought shelter there before. Santé lies back on the rock, his head on his backpack. Gradually his thoughts shift to the night ahead and the trail they must find. At any point along the way, he muses, the migra may be hiding, ready to pounce in the dark. But what can they really do, he adds, except send them back to Mexico where they can try again. That's not that bad; no, the real danger is bandits…bandits with knives…fellow Latinos desperate enough to rob their own people…men who will do anything for a buck. Unconsciously, he reaches for his backpack and pulls out the macuahuitl. Reassured, he closes his eyes and falls asleep.

10

Macuahuitl Unleashed

By 6:00 P.M. the group is headed deeper into the desert, aiming for the path that will eventually lead them over the mountain and down into the town of Ajo. Using a walking stick fashioned from a mesquite branch, Santé leads the way, constantly poking the ground to warn any rattle snakes that might be sleeping just ahead. Alessandro brings up the rear. The group's snail-like pace is set by Guadalupe who must stop every five minutes to catch her breath. Each time they stop, Maya sits down and takes her hand.

Around 1:00 A.M. they come to the spot where the valley trail they've been following intersects with the trail leading up over the mountain. Santé puts his finger to his lips, "A friend tole me this is where the migra hang out; they're probly further up the trail waitin' to jump on us when we git near the top…(*pause*)…Let's keep goin' 'til we find a deer path we can follow… (*turning to Alessandro*)…Be sure ta keep yir light down."

About a hundred yards further, Santé stops and points his flashlight at a well-worn deer trail leading up the mountain side. "Here it is," he whispers. "It's gonna be hard to foller with all these bushes in our face…but the migra won't be able see us from the main trail. We jis' gotta be quiet."

The pace is even slower now, not because of Guadalupe's heart but because the path leads uphill. The vegetation is also much thicker with branches pressing in from both sides of the trail. And underfoot, sharp rocks lurk in the dark, waiting to trip the unwary.

Two hours into the climb, Alessandro signals that his wife needs a rest and pee stop. A large, sandy clearing next to the trail makes a convenient place for the group to spread out. Santé, Alessandro and Maya sit down to snack on tortillas and sip water while Guadalupe takes the flashlight and goes behind some creosote bushes to do her thing. When she returns, she hands the light to Maya who heads for the same spot. When all three family members have relieved themselves, Santé puts on his backpack and shines his flashlight into a grove of mesquite trees on the other side of the clearing. On his way there he steps carefully, anxious to avoid twigs on the ground that might make a crackling sound. At this time of night the moon is sinking to the west but still luminous enough to throw tree shadows across the clearing. He stops to listen for the sound of distant voices. Hearing nothing, he moves into the grove, turns his back and unzips his fly.

Before he can actually pee, the night's silence is broken with a scream from Guadalupe. Santé whirls around in time to see the back of a man racing toward Alessandro. A second man is standing over Maya. A few feet away, Guadalupe is on her back, struggling to get up. Bandits! Two of them. He turns off his light and reaches for the macuahuitl.

Gripping his weapon tightly, he slips into the clearing, then races for the man standing over Maya. She is on her back, her bony thighs already exposed, her cries for help frantic. The man has dropped his pants and is preparing to kneel. From behind, Santé raises the macuahuitl in readiness. Just as he is about to strike, he hears a loud "No!" from Alessandro on his left. Then "Shut up, you fucker!" followed by an agonizing "Aaargh" from the old man. Suddenly all is quiet. The would-be rapist turns his head toward the voice. Santé's arm is cocked in mid-air, his eyes fixed on the man in front of him, the macuahuitl frozen midway through its lethal arc.

The silence is suddenly pierced by a second scream as Guadalupe stumbles toward her prostrate husband. As if ordered by some unseen force, the macuahuitl resumes its interrupted flight, slices through the air and buries itself in the assailant's neck. Blood spurts from his severed artery, spraying both Maya's skirt and Santé's chest. As the man rolls over, clutching his neck, a cry from Maya alerts Santé to someone approaching from behind. He turns, macuahuitl held high, as the second bandit lunges toward him, his face contorted with fury, his knife still dripping with Alessandro's blood.

In his haste for revenge the intruder fails to see the strange weapon in his adversary's hand. Now it is too late to turn back. Battle cries rend the night air as knife and macuahuitl both seek flesh, one aiming to disembowel, the other to behead.

With so little light to see by, neither happens. The macuahuitl glances off the bandit's upper arm, knocking his knife to the ground. For a split second the two stare at each other in shock, their breathing hoarse and labored. With the assailant's face just inches away, the odor of tobacco and mescal is inescapable. Without a word the bandit picks up his knife and flees into the brush. Santé chases for a few yards before giving up and coming back to the clearing. He flashes his light on the ground. New blood indicates that the intruder was wounded, perhaps badly. But too badly to return? Silently Santé vows vigilance.

At the edge of the clearing Guadalupe sobs while holding her dead husband. The rest of the night passes in prayer and tears. Despite entreaties from her granddaughter, she vows to remain here with Alessandro's body until she too is dead. With morning comes new light and a new perspective; Maya and Santé have little trouble convincing her to bury her husband here and continue on to Phoenix. As silently as possible, the three scrape out a shallow grave, slide Alessandro's body in and cover it with as many rocks as they can find. On top of the rocks they erect a cross made from branches cut from nearby mesquite trees. Once the work is completed, they sit down to map out a new strategy. It is agreed that it is too dangerous to stay in the clearing any longer. As they prepare to go looking for a new hiding place, Maya turns to take one last look at her grandfather's grave. Grasping Guadalupe's hand, she whispers, "It's a beautiful little shrine. God will look after him."

Fewer than fifty yards away they find another clearing surrounded by rock ledges that will offer protection against the morning sun. Guadalupe and Maya put down their packs and crawl beneath the largest of the overhangs while Santé picks out a nearby mesquite tree. Within an hour, all three are asleep, oblivious to the presence of last night's intruder who has returned seeking revenge for his brother's death. Santé, mindful of the previous night's attack, has the macuahuitl lying next to him as he sleeps. The intruder waits until he is convinced that no one is awake, then edges closer. Confident that he is alone, he inches his way to the place where Santé is sleeping, knife drawn. He stands and looks down at his victim, then smiles.

Suddenly, there's a scream to Santé's right. It's Maya. A second later, the would-be assailant topples over backwards with the girl clinging to his neck. In a single motion, Santé bursts from his sleep and grabs his macuahuitl. He turns in time to see the intruder getting to his feet, clutching his knife. In the early morning light there can be no doubt: it is the same bandit that tried to kill him last night…the rapist's partner. Santé's muscles tighten as adrenalin floods his body. In a flash, every bullying suffered at school, every injustice and put down endured on the streets of Oaxaca explodes into consciousness, triggering a fury that demands expression. The intruder sputters an epithet, then lunges forward. From behind, Maya, back on her feet, tries to grab his arm but falls to the ground. With macuahuitl raised, Santé leaps aside to avoid the intruder's thrust, then, as the man stumbles, swings swiftly to catch him under the chin. The assassin falls to the ground, spitting blood, his hand on his throat. Still writhing, he looks up at Santé…gurgles a curse…then rolls over dead.

Maya struggles to her feet, then collapses into Santé's outstretched arms. With her head on his shoulder, she gasps, "I think he was the other man's brother…you know…the man who was going to hurt me."

"Yes, I know. He can't hurt you now."

Guadalupe runs to join them, embracing her granddaughter before covering Santé with kisses. "What would happen if you no stay with us?" she asks, not waiting for an answer. Santé nods, then walks to a nearby tree where he picks several leaves. When he sits down to clean the blood off his macuahuitl, Maya and Guadalupe join him, anxious to hear his plans for the coming night. He is too innocent to see it but there is a new look in their eyes. Any doubts they had of his ability to protect them are gone, vanquished with two strokes of his magical weapon. He is only sixteen but he is now their leader, their savior…their young Moses sent to guide them through the desert to a promised land of milk and honey. Silently they cross themselves and give thanks.

11

Ambush

It is Santé's plan to avoid the main trail as they make their way up the mountain…then, assuming they haven't been detected, to head down into Ajo where their erstwhile coyote said there would be a van to pick them up. He is aware that since the other group is moving much faster, the van will probably have come and gone by the time he gets there… and that alternative transportation will be needed. There is reason to be optimistic, he explains, since the pick-up spot is on Indian land and some of the people who live there make extra money by arranging transportation for migrants into Phoenix. Buoyed by its prospects, the tiny troupe heads up the mountain, eager to find a shady place to spend the rest of the day.

Toward evening Santé calls Guadalupe and Maya together for some last minute details. "We're gettin' low on water," he says. "No more drinkin' 'til we get to the top…(*pause*)…and no talkin'. La migra will be listenin' for anything that sounds like people. We'll stick to this animal trail 'til it runs out… and then…"

"And then what?" Maya asks.

"I dunno. "Maybe we'll have to bushwhack the rest of the way. We'll see."

Soon after they set out, the trail narrows, then forks into two smaller paths, one leading to the left, the other to the right. Santé studies the situation briefly, then chooses the path on the right. It will prove to be a fateful decision. The right-hand trail, unbeknownst to the three travelers, intersects with the main trail where the migra have set up their surveillance operation. Just a few yards above the intersection two Border Patrol officers, both armed, sit in a truck with headlights turned off, waiting, listening.

Jose Garcia, the officer in charge, nudges his assistant, Jorge. When out in the field they use their native language. "D'ya hear that?" he whispers in Spanish. "Somebody's comin'. Get ready to turn the lights on. I'll get down in the bushes."

Santé realizes his mistake the minute he steps out onto the main trail. Before he can reverse course, the lights flash, blinding all three hikers. As they shield their eyes from the light, Jose steps out from the bushes and shouts in Spanish, "You're under arrest. Sit down with your hands on your head. Move and you'll git shot."

The three crossers sit and put their hands on their heads.

Jorge gets out of the jeep and comes over to where the migrants are sitting. He examines each of the three carefully, looking into their faces, then their clothing. Satisfied they are crossers, he moves behind to see what they are carrying. Could they be mules working for one of the drug cartels? He stops behind Santé, then without warning reaches down and pulls the macuahuitl out of his backpack. "What the hell is this?" he asks, holding it up for his partner to see.

José comes to where Santé is sitting and takes the macuahuitl from Jorge's hands. He carefully runs his fingers along the obsidian blades. "Jesus Christ…this is sharp. You could take somebody's head off with it. What the hell are you doin' with this in your pack?"

When Santé refuses to answer, Maya turns to face José. "He saved our lives with it when bandits tried to hurt us. There was two brothers and…" She is about to elaborate when a stern look from Guadalupe stops her in mid-sentence.

José comes to where Maya is sitting. Looking down at her, he asks, "So, what happened?"

Maya drops her head.

"C'mon, I need to know," he continues. "Did anybody get hurt?"

Guadalupe turns to Maya and then to José. "They killed my husband… that's what they did. We buried him a few miles back. And they woulda raped my granddaughter here if Santé hadn't helped us."

"So how'd he help you?"

Silence.

Santé shifts uneasily. "I had to kill him…the one who was gettin' ready to rape the girl."

"How? You mean with this thing (*holding up the macuahuitl*)?"

Santé nods.

"Jesus Christ…a goddamn murder right here on our shift."

Jorge comes over to Maya. "You say there was another brother. What happened to him?"

"He's the one who killed my grandfather. And he tried to kill Santé but Santé hit him with his macua…I forgit what to call it…and he run off. But he come back in the night and tried to stab Santé but I jumped on him from behind and pulled him down."

"Then what?"

Silence.

José moves over in front of Santé and looks down. "So ya killed him too?"

Santé squirms.

"What the fuck…two murders in one night."

With that he walks over to the truck and tosses the macuahuitl into the front seat. "We gonna need this here weapon for evidence."

José turns next to Guadalupe. "So where'd all this happen?"

"Back there (*pointing*)," she whispers. "Near the bottom of the hill."

José turns to Jorge. "That's on the U.S. side, right?. So it's in our jurisdiction."

"Yeah, so we gotta take 'em in."

"José takes a deep breath. O.K. folks, you're in serious trouble. Jorge… tie'em up…all three…and git their backpacks. We're takin' 'em back to headquarters."

Suddenly, as Jorge bends to tie their wrists, Santé springs to his feet and races to the truck. He pulls the door open and grabs his macuahuitl. Before either of the officers can respond, he dives into the brush and disappears into the dark.

Two shots ring out as Jorge fires his revolver into the brush. He waits for a sound indicating a lucky hit. With the dying of the blast, all that can be heard is the distant snap of breaking branches as Santé heads up the mountain. Accepting temporary defeat, Jorge goes to the truck and picks up the phone. "We're bringin' in two crossers…two women; there's a third…a kid who escaped into the brush…he's probably headed for Ajo… armed with somethin' like a machete…watch it…he's dangerous…already used it to kill two bandits."

12

Out of the Desert

Santé crouches in the bushes, listening for a sign that he's being followed. No one comes. The next sound he hears is that of the Border Patrol truck starting up. It's only 20 yards away. The truck appears to be turning around and heading back to Ajo, presumably with Guadalupe and Maya in tow. Santé shifts his position until he can see the tail lights of the truck as it heads toward the mountain top. He fixes the position of the road in his mind, then sits down to rest. Images of the family he has just left come quickly. In his mind's eye, he sees Maya on her back with the bandit standing over her. As he strains to see the details of her face, he feels an unfamiliar softness, a desire to hold her, to protect her. Then a sound explodes in his head…his macuahuitl crashing into the assailant's neck, followed by a scream from Maya. The memory returns. He turns to face a stranger with a knife, the brother seeking vengeance. A clash of weapons, obsidian against steel, Zapotec versus Aztec…a battle unfinished until the next day when Maya again alerts him and the macuahuitl takes its second victim.

As the memory of the second bandit looms before him, he grips the weapon at his side, his body still heaving with rage. Despite the setting…an attack in the middle of the desert…what he feels is strangely familiar, not unlike what he felt when he saw his sister stumbling onto the deck in Oaxaca, her face swollen and bloody. And the incidents at school…the ones that got him expelled…the same thing again…a wrath beyond reason, a hunger to destroy, a craving to bring the oppressor to his knees.

He stretches out on the ground. Gradually the bloody scene recedes, allowing another to rise in its place. It is Maya again…lying on her back, sobbing, preparing for the thrust that will bring her childhood to an end.

In his imagination he kneels and places his hand on her forehead. There are no words; it is all too new for a boy who has never even had a girlfriend. He looks down at her, his eyes fixed on her lips, his heart racing. He caresses her cheeks and bends closer. She smiles and opens her arms. "Can it be?" he asks. "Do you really want me?"

A sudden rustling among the leaves wakens him from his trance; thoughts of the present return. Both Maya and her grandmother will probably be sent back to their home in Tabasco, unlikely to try again now that Alessandro is gone. Perhaps years from now Maya will make another attempt. He may even see her in Phoenix. After all, stranger things have happened.

In the dark, without flashlight now, Santé takes a few steps up the narrow deer trail, his face bleeding from the overhanging branches, his knees aching from tripping on sharp rocks. The slope is steep, the air getting cooler and thinner. At this elevation breathing comes hard for anyone accustomed to life in the valley. Exhausted and thirsty, he reaches for his water jug only to be reminded that in his haste to escape, he left it behind. No water, no food, no backpack, nothing left but the macuahuitl. Nervously, he reaches into his shirt pocket for the map. Breathing a sigh of relief, he withdraws it and spreads it on the ground. There is just enough moonlight to make out the general topography of the area. The distance between contour lines tells him that he has reached a flat area near the top of the mountain. That means that making his way down the other side should be a lot easier. He checks to see where the road is on the map, then folds the paper and returns it to his pocket. By now his strategy is clear: get back on the main road and spend the rest of the night walking as fast as he can. If the Border Patrol truck returns, duck into the bushes and wait. With any luck it should be possible to reach Ajo by daybreak; from there he can thumb a ride into Phoenix. Buoyed by his plan, he leaves the deer trail and fights his way through the brush to the main road. As he steps out onto the road, it suddenly occurs to him that in their haste to get the two captives back to headquarters, the BP officers may have left his backpack behind…or at least his jug of water. Instead of heading up the mountain, he turns back toward the spot where his group was apprehended. Luck is on his side. There, beside the road, is his backpack. He opens it quickly and is relieved to see his jug, now half full of water. Just below it at the bottom of the pack is the set of street clothes he will need when he reaches Ajo. Overjoyed by his discovery, he turns around and heads up the mountain, a soft whistle on his lips.

The night is cool, perfect for fast walking. Stopping only occasionally to sip some water, he makes even better time than he thought. When he reaches the top, he pauses for a just a minute or two before continuing. On the way down the mountain he breaks into a jog. Toward daybreak he comes to a point just west of town where the mountain road he is on intersects with a blacktop highway. Several cars pass. On the other side of the highway he sees a sign but is too far away to read what it says. Checking first to make sure he cannot be seen, he crosses quickly and reads: "Do Not Pick Up Hitchhikers." Under the words is the insignia of the Border Patrol. He reaches into his backpack and pulls out the pocket dictionary he bought back in Nogales. More cars pass as he looks up each word. The words make sense…but why the Border Patrol insignia? Then it hits him. The BP doesn't want drivers to pick up hitchhikers because they might be migrants crossing illegally.

Sensing danger, he crosses back to the other side of the highway and slips into the brush. Better not to take any chances now that he has come so far. Orienting himself to his map once again, he sets out to the north, sure of very little other than he doesn't want to be seen on the highway, even in the clean clothes that he brought with him.

As the sun rises, it brings with it the thirst all crossers dread. Santé pulls the jug from his backpack, checks its meager contents then drains it. When he has consumed the last drop, he tosses it into the bushes, acutely aware that his time is running out. His only hope now is to find someone who is willing to drive him to Phoenix…for a price. He still has plenty of money…the second half of the $1,800 promised to the coyote plus $300 for extras like food and lodging once he gets to the big city. What makes finding someone difficult is the necessity of avoiding the migra while he looks. That means leaving the highway behind and hiking through an arid landscape. But this present terrain is less dangerous than the desert; there are people living here. Looking around, he spots a house in the distance and decides to head for it, taking his chances the owner won't turn him in.

After hiking several hundred yards, he comes to a sign indicating that he is about to enter the O'odham Reservation, a territory set aside for the Indian tribe of that name. There are no walls here, no barbed wire…just a sign to mark where the reservation begins. According to his map the area is huge, running north from the Mexican border and east toward Tucson. The house he can see in the distance is well within the boundaries of the reservation, meaning that it's in Indian territory.

By the time he reaches the house, Santé can barely stand up. He is greeted at the door by an old Indian with tobacco-colored skin and hair tied back in a pony tail. "You a crosser?" the man asks from inside the house. Santé nods, no longer willing to play games. Through the screen door they negotiate a deal in which the Indian agrees to take him to Phoenix in the morning for $200. He then invites Santé in, offers him water, frijoles and beans. Santé drinks slowly until his appetite returns, then falls into bed. He sleeps fitfully on his side with a hand across his chest grasping the macuahuitl. Several hours into the afternoon he is awakened by the sound of the bedroom door opening. He continues to lie still, his hand tightening on the macuahuitl. When he feels a hand sliding into his back pocket, he opens his eyes…just far enough to see a man's shadow on the nearest wall. He is totally awake now. When the intruder's hand goes deeper into his pocket, groping for a wallet, Santé whirls around…bringing the flat side of the weapon down on the man's back. The man screams and slumps to floor, his pony tail sticking up like a handle. Santé jumps out of bed, grabs his backpack and runs from the house. Allowing no more than an occasional look over his shoulder, he runs until he can no longer see the house behind him. A half a mile from the house, he pulls up next to a tree and sits down to catch his breath. According to the map, he is still in the middle of O'odham country but there are actual streets further to the north; that means more houses and cars…and a possible trip to Phoenix. Despite his troubles at the previous house, he is buoyed by the prospect of reaching the big city soon. After all, he is already in El Norte and has over $1,000 still sewn into his pants. If all goes well, in another day or two he should have a place to live and be out looking for a job. He just has to stay on his toes.

To avoid the afternoon sun, he moves from tree to tree, taking advantage of whatever shade is available. But since there is no trail here and he is without a compass, he must rely on the position of the sun to guide him. Every few minutes he turns around to make sure the sun is over his left shoulder. The going is slow and uneven. By evening he is once again exhausted and low on water despite having filled his jug at the house where he was attacked. He decides to rest until morning when he will have more energy. Sitting down under a large mesquite tree, he puts on a second shirt, the clean one reserved for Phoenix, and folds his arms against the coming cold. Before closing his eyes, he takes a last look at his surroundings. The moon is coming up in the east, climbing slowly, pale yellow and half full. It is the only light in the sky. On earth, all is dark and still.

13

Phoenix

It is around mid-morning when he sights a house on the crest of a distant hill. With energy renewed, he picks up his pace until he is close enough to see several men milling around a van. He creeps closer, made more wary now by his run-in with the pony-tailed Indian. From behind a tree, he makes out their faces, then stifles a gasp when he recognizes El Chacal. None of the other men are familiar….suggesting that Santé's original group of polleros is already in Phoenix and the coyote has returned to take a new batch in. Santé takes a deep breath and walks out into the open. He is seen as he slips through a barbed wire fence just beyond the house.

El Chacal waves him closer. "So, it's you again. Where the fuck you been?"

Santé stops a few yards away. "Maybe I ask you the same question."

El Chacal laughs. "We waited for ya…but we couldn't wait forever. There's migra all over the desert now. Maybe you didn't notice."

Santé flashes his own grin. "I noticed. They noticed me too but I got away…(*pause*)…Right now I need a ride to Phoenix. You got room for one more?"

El Chacal hesitates. "I think so…but there's a little matter of money we got to settle first."

As the other men come closer to listen, Santé offers a well-rehearsed answer, "I'll give ya $200."

El Chacal forces a laugh. "Sure you can spare it, injun? Let's negotiate when we git to Phoenix. Go ahead…git in the van…we gotta get goin'."

A total of 13 men pour into a van designed to hold seven passengers. Once they are on the road, the conversation remains muted, reflecting the anxiety felt by the crossers as they enter the final phase of their journey. All are aware that to be caught and sent back now, after all they have endured, not to mention the money they have spent, would be a disaster.

No more than 10 minutes into the trip, El Chacal pulls the van off the road and tells everyone to get out. "There's a checkpoint a mile ahead… you gotta get out now and walk around it through those woods (*pointing to the trees bordering the nearby field*). The path is easy to find…we done it hundreds of times already. The van'll be waitin' for ya about a mile beyond the checkpoint. You can see me from the woods…(*pause*)…Any questions?"

A short, squat man in his mid-twenties steps forward, his voice soft and trembling. "How do we know you won't just take off and leave us here?"

"Because you still owe me $900, asshole. You think I'm stupid?"

A murmur of approval ripples through the group.

The hike through the forest proves uneventful. Through openings in the trees the crossers can see the checkpoint below where cars and trucks are being stopped and inspected. "El Chacal sure knows what he's doin'," one man says, giving voice to a thought shared by all. "Yeah, but we're payin' 'im good money for it," answers the man behind him. After a two mile walk, they spot the van down on the highway and make their way across the field. As they approach the road, El Chacal beams a self-congratulatory smile and orders them to get in.

Two hours later the van pulls into one of the poor barrios of South Phoenix and parks outside a house used to put up crossers while they look for jobs. El Chacal waits until everybody's up on the porch before speaking. "OK. You can stay here for three days, then ya gotta get out. That's included in what ya already paid me. Now you all owe me another $900. So let's see it."

He pulls a small sack from his back pocket and slowly makes the rounds… collecting $900 from each crosser. When he comes to Santé, he opens the sack and smiles. "O.K. injun, your turn…I want 900 big ones. Santé looks into his face and hands him four $50 bills. El Chacal, who is considerably taller, squints. "Hey, where's the other $700?"

Santé bristles, his heart racing. "I ain't payin' for somethin' I never got. The $200 is jis' for the van."

"You signed up for $1,800….half up front and the other half when we get to Phoenix. In case you can't read road signs, we is in Phoenix, so ya owe me another $700."

Santé shakes his head vigorously. "You never did nothin' for me or the family I was with. You went on ahead without us…so we had to find our way with a map. I'm the only one that got this far. The old man got kilt by a bandit and the migras picked up the woman and the girl. You wasn't there to help us through any of it. So we don't owe you nothin'. The only thing you done for the $900 we give you back in Nogales was to show us where the trail starts."

El Chacal lets out a snort, then smiles. Still grinning, he reaches into his pocket and pulls out his knife, then snaps it open close to Santé's chest. Santé backs away, not as El Chacal assumes, to avoid begin cut, but to give him room to swing. Not stopping to breathe, he reaches over his shoulder into his pack, grabs the handle of his macuahuitl and in a single motion brings it down on his adversary's hand. Thanks to the jackal's animal quickness, the blade lands short of its mark, knocking the knife to the floor.

"You dumb fuck. You almost got my hand," El Chacal yells as he stoops to pick up the knife. Santé, now driven by the same instinct to rebel that has gotten him into trouble before, grips his weapon and waits for an opening. It's not long in coming. As El Chacal rises, knife at the ready, his mouth open and frothing with epithets, the macuahuitl falls on his upper arm, burying itself in his flesh. The scream can be heard throughout the building as he falls, clutching his left arm. Santé tears the money sack from his other hand. Taking out a wad of bills, he counts out $3,600…$900 for himself and $2,700 for the family that got left behind…then tosses the sack aside. Rising, he mumbles, "I know what town the family come from…somehow I'll get 'em their share." With that, he stuffs the money into his pocket and dashes out of the building.

14

The Job

Santé walks quickly, constantly turning around to see if he is being followed. Assured that no one is coming, he sits down on a street bench and counts his money. He has close to $5,000, about $2,000 of it his own, enough to get some new clothes, some food and a place to stay while he looks for a job. For months he has thought about these first days in Phoenix…whom to avoid (the police), what to wear (clean clothes), where to look for a job (the yellow pages) and how to behave (imitate other people). Now it is time to act.

After buying two new shirts, a pair of pants and some street shoes, he picks up a copy of the local newspaper and begins searching for a room or apartment. There are many being advertised. After stopping three different people for information, he finds himself at the door of a multi-apartment building in a run-down part of town. When the landlady (Senora Mendez) sees his roll of cash, she immediately warms up, going so far as to introduce her 16-year-old daughter, Mirasol. "You can eat breakfast and dinner here too if you want," she adds. In a city much larger than any he has ever seen and filled with people who look different and speak a foreign language, it is a relief to find someone who is not only physically similar but who talks the same way. He inspects the apartment (a small room with closet plus full bath) and hands her enough money to cover room and board for the next two months. Once all has been decided, he changes into his new clothes and lies down to rest, the macuahuitl at his side. His sleep is fitful and punctuated with dreams of knives and blood. An hour later he is up and ready to hit the streets.

His first stop is a public phone booth where he finds a copy of the yellow pages. Turning quickly to the section on television and radio repair, he writes down the name and address of several companies with big ads. Once armed with concrete targets, he returns to his apartment and shows Senora Mendez his list of addresses. Anxious to please, she invites him into her kitchen and pulls out a city map. Mirasol, standing demurely in the corner and clearly fidgeting, is asked to join them. Together they find all three of the companies on Santé's list, circling each in pencil. One of the three appears to be no more than four or five blocks away and can be reached in ten minutes while the other two are out in the east end of town and will require taking the San Felipé bus. He decides to start with the one closest to home. When Mirasol offers to show him the way, he responds with an awkward 'No thanks' and heads out the door.

It is clear when he arrives at Maricopa TV & Radio Repair that his lack of English is going to be a problem. The man who greets him knows just enough Spanish to understand that Santé is looking for a job. Once he is clear about the boy's interest, his first impulse is to say no and send him on his way. He hesitates to do so only because his wife who is fluent in Spanish chooses that moment to enter the shop from the apartment out back. Seeing Santé, she offers to translate. "Hello, I am Senora Edmunds. What can we do to help you?"

Santé, who has been away from home for months, is immediately drawn to her bronze skin, warm smile and full breasts. "My name is Asanté Aquilera," he says hoarsely, "but people call me Santé. I fix lots of radios back home and want a job in Phoenix."

Senora Edmunds steps closer, her eyes not wavering from the visitor's handsome face. "Santé…nice name. So where is home for you, Santé?"

"Oaxaca."

"Oaxaca, Mexico?"

"Yes."

"Do you intend to live here in the States?"

"Yes. I want to."

Turning to her husband, she says in English, "Could we use some more help?"

"Not really," he answers. "Maybe if business picks up we could…but not now."

Senora Edmunds turns back to Santé and gazes again into his face. Far from prying eyes, thoughts of what it would be like to have a son like this begin stirring deep inside. Now in her early forties, she has come to accept that she will never have children. It is an ache that will never go away. She has tried to assuage the pain by surrounding herself with pets…a dog, two cats and a canary…but to no avail. After years of trying, the hole is still there.

She looks again at the dark-skinned, muscular boy in front of her. "Do you fix TV's or just radios?" she asks, once again in Spanish. Her voice is smooth and gentle, masking the longing she secretly feels.

"Most of the time, just radios…but two times I fix old TV's for our neighbors. They work for a little while…then they buy new ones."

 She turns back to her husband. In English, "Couldn't we take Santé on as an apprentice…let our men teach him about television?"

"Paula, we can't afford it," he answers quickly. "You should know…you make out the paychecks."

Listening carefully to their interaction, Santé picks up the word 'pay' which he has learned from conversations at the bus station back in Nogales. He turns to the owner, "How much you pay now?" (*pointing to men at work inside the shop*). Mr. Edmunds looks at his wife for a translation. She covers her mouth to conceal a smile, "He's asking how much we pay our employees…how much an hour I think he means."

"Well, go ahead and tell him."

She turns back to Santé, her eyes fixed directly on his. "O.K. Santé, for our experienced people, we pay $25 an hour; for beginners we pay $18. Some of our workers started with us as beginners but they are all old-timers now."

Santé's heart leaps at the news. Without thinking, he blurts out, "I will work for nothing…one month….after that, if you like me, you give me half of beginner's pay…$9 an hour."

"That's a generous offer, Santé," the woman says, still smiling. Turning to her husband, she translates what he has said, adding several nods to indicate her approval of the arrangement. "But we still don't know what he can do," Mr. Edmunds answers. "He says he's fixed lots of radios in Oaxaca but that could be just talk."

Senora Edmunds shifts uneasily. "Well, we could give him a chance to show us. How about setting him up with a radio that needs fixin'? We can see right away what he does with it."

The husband shrugs. "Why not? What can we lose?"

With eyes sparkling, she turns to Santé. "Before taking you on, we would like to see what you can do. If we give you one of the radios waiting for repair, would you be willing to work on it?"

"Oh yes," the boy replies. "I can fix it very fast."

"Good. There's a work station in back that no one is using. Come…take a look."

An hour later Senora Edmunds comes back to the station where Santé is working. "So, how's it going, Santé?, she asks, looking over his shoulder.

"Almost done, Senora. It wasn't very hard. I just need a new TR-63 transistor, the small kind."

"Nice. You do work fast…(*pause*)…Whenever you need a replacement, just go to the spare parts department in back and tell Jerry what you need. We'll probably have it…if not, we can order it…(*pause*)…Don't worry; he speaks Spanish."

Still standing behind him, she watches as he removes a burned-out transistor. His hands move gracefully across wires, capacitors and battery…almost as if he were caressing them. "Like a pianist," she murmurs, shaking her head in silent admiration. When he goes on working, seemingly unaware of her continued presence, her eyes shift to his neck and the small area between hair and shirt. She reaches to touch him. Just inches from his skin, she pulls her hand back and presses it to her breast, sighing secretly with the pain of pleasure foregone.

Thirty minutes later Santé is in the office, holding the radio in his hand. Mr. Edmunds looks up and smiles, "How'd you make out? Any trouble?" His wife, standing nearby, translates.

"No Sir. Very easy. Want to see if it works?"

"Yeah. Go ahead. There's a plug over there (*pointing to the wall*)."

When the radio immediately blares out a pop tune, Santé breaks into a broad smile. Senora Edmunds, who has been waiting impatiently, cries out, "You did it. Well done Santé." Turning to her husband, she adds, "I guess it's a deal then...is he hired?"

"Well yes...but on the terms we agreed to before...one month as a volunteer...than we'll see about paying him."

 Senora Edmunds turns to Santé. "Do you have enough money to get by for a month? I suppose we could always..."

(*Interrupting*) "Oh yes...I got lotsa money (*slapping his pocket*). Thank you. I will work very hard...you'll see."

Mr. Edmunds stands to shake hands. "Our hours are 8:00 to 4:00. Don't be late. There's a morning break at 10:00 and lunch break at 12:00. Bring something to eat; you won't have time to buy it elsewhere." Senora Edmunds translates.

As Santé heads for the door, she reaches out to shake his hand. In a whisper, she asks, "Do you have a place to stay, Santé? If not, we..."

(*Interrupting*) "Yes. I rented a room this morning...on Juarez Avenue...nice lady and her daughter. I am very happy...so glad to be in Phoenix now." With that, he opens the door and dashes out onto the sidewalk. "At last, at last," he shouts, "I am in land of milk and honey. Thank you, Dios. I will work hard....and send money to family...make everybody happy. El Norte...I love you."

15

The Sheriff's Office

Earl Culpepper, Sheriff of Maricopa County, sits back in his revolving chair and puts his feet up on the table. The other officers in the room, the lieutenants and sergeants who have been with him for years, take this as a sign that it's time to relax, to shoot the breeze… air out any complaints. It's something they do every day just before going out into the field. Since it's their only chance to share ideas and feelings, they consider it their favorite time of the day. Today, as is often the case, a member of the Border Patrol has dropped in to share information on migrant activity.

As usual, Earl says nothing, waiting for someone else to start the discussion. He doesn't have long to wait.

Tom Flaherty, the visitor from Border Patrol, is the first to speak. "Last night we was zeroin' in on this group of illegals out near Post 2…could see with our night visions that they were on their last legs. None of them carried jugs of water which meant they had finished all they brought. We're all ready to swoop down on 'em and what happens…they spot a water tank… you know the kind put there by those gonzos from 'No More Deaths'…big green tanks set right next to the path along with empty plastic jugs for fillin'…all nice and easy…like, c'mon over…we're happy to see ya. And then they…"

Fred Ogilvie, a newly-minted sergeant from Mississippi, breaks in, "I don't know why they're allowed to do that. Here we are bustin' our asses to keep the bastards out…usin' all the latest technology and spendin' millions of dollars…and these assholes undermine the whole thing by puttin' out the welcome mat. It should be a crime to set out water tanks like that. It's just helpin' 'em break the law."

(*Flaherty, continuing*): "Yeah. Like I was sayin', these people we were watchin' spotted the tank, grabbed some jugs, filled 'em with water and scattered. We never did find 'em after that." He shakes his head. "Thanks to the do-gooders, those crossers probably made it into the U.S. last night and are already beggin' for handouts. You know what that means…more mouths to feed, more kids fillin' our schools, more aliens drivin' around without a license. It's a goddamn shame."

Jim Jaccoby who worked for the Immigration and Naturalization Service before moving to the Sheriff's Office, uncrosses his legs and leans forward, "We jis can't seem to win. No matter what we do, they keep comin' like locusts. Out in the desert we cover the trails with alarm sensors and they jis' walk around 'em. In Nogales we build 17-foot walls and they climb over 'em. We dig tunnels to catch the rains and what do they do…they use 'em as walkways into the U.S. They're like cockroaches…you just can't keep 'em out."

From Ted Polk standing in the doorway, "Hey…some of 'em even live in those tunnels down in Nogales…mainly kids I hear…you know, the ones who come over with their parents and got separated. They sit there in the dark waitin' for crossers to come through and then mug 'em for money or jewelry…whatever they can get. Can you believe that? Their own fuckin' people and they hit 'em up for every last centavo. Goddamn animals."

Earl sits up straight in his chair. "It's the drugs that bother me the most. You see this more and more now…the big Mexican cartels are movin' into the migrant business…puttin' their own coyotes in the field…offerin' a free trip to crossers in return for luggin' a bundle of marijuana. It's scary. Accordin' to stats from the front office, about a third of the people we catch these days are totin' some kind of drug."

Walt Baker, tall and lean but still a sergeant after working with Earl for 15 years, slides down from his desk and turns to face Jaccoby. "I tell ya, Jim… there *is* a way to keep 'em from comin'…but you gotta get tough. To my way of thinkin', this politican from Kansas got it right…put helicopters in the air and when you see somebody tryin' to cross, shoot 'em. When folks read about that in Mexico, they'll think twice about tryin' to come up here."

Earl forces a smile. "Well, that's goin' a bit far, Walt. I don't think we have to get that tough. After all, we do have this new law in Arizona. If we catch somebody speedin' or goin' through a stop light, we now have the right to ask for documentation of legal status. No need to do that for white folks but for Latino types it should net us a lotta aliens."

Baker, getting back up on his desk, responds with, "Yeah, Chief, but the Supreme Court might knock down that law because only the feds are supposed to have jurisdiction over immigration."

Earl nods. "Perhaps. But we gotta do somethin'. The situation is gettin' outta hand. You know how big the Latino population is now in Arizona… it's over a third and getting bigger all the time. They say that ten or fifteen years from now Latinos will outnumber us. Yeah, believe it or not we're gonna be the minority here…we, the very folks who settled the Southwest…built roads and houses, irrigated the desert, made the land livable. We're gonna be the minority because the aliens are breedin' faster than we are."

"That means they'll be able to outvote us," adds Flaherty.

Earl nods again, then pounds the table with his fist. "They're already takin' away jobs from white folks…they're so hungry when they get here, they'll work for close to nothin'."

Walt flashes a smile. "And they live like termites…ten to a trailer…parents and children in the same bedroom….sometimes in the same bed for Christ's sake."

Jim, the undeclared intellectual of the group, nods approvingly. "They're changin' our culture. We're already a two-language society…pretty soon Spanish will be the primary one. I can see it now…everything in Spanish…road signs, bank accounts, books that kids read in school, even TV programs. Jesus, if this keeps up, we're gonna need English subtitles to understand the evening news."

Earl smiles. "Jim mentions the change in culture that's goin' on. I see it in religion too. Just think, the whole Southwest used to be mainly Protestant…Baptists, Methodists and Evangelicals. Now more and more

Catholics are pouring in…bringin' their Latino brand of Papism with them. That means they take their orders from Rome…so, if the Pope says contraception is a sin, you're gonna get a lot more babies. And those babies are gonna grow up and vote the Hispanic way. It's a cycle that's hard to stop once it gets underway."

Jaccoby throws his hands up, "So, what can we do, Chief?"

Earl pauses before replying. "I think we gotta be patient until anti-immigrant sentiment gets stronger…and then we can get tougher…you know, let the Border Patrol use their guns out there in the desert. Right now, people want us to be gentle and tolerant. If we catch somebody, we're supposed to put 'em on a bus and send 'em back to Mexico. That's stupid. We all know they'll just try harder next time. Until we impose some kind of punishment for crossin' illegally, they'll keep on tryin'. Lookit…if they've come all the way from some village deep in Mexico or even Central America, they're not gonna give up tryin' to cross jis' cause we caught 'em once. To make 'em stay at home, we need stiffer penalties…like jail time."

Walt lets out a whoop. "Or helicopters and guns."

Earl forces a smile. "Maybe Walt, but the public is gonna have to get a lot angrier before that can happen."

Flaherty, rising to leave, lets out an audible sigh. "For all of us over at BP, the sooner that happens, the better. (*looking around*) Hey guys, great discussion. See ya all next week."

Alone again, Earl turns back to his desk, mulling over the ideas he just heard. Although nothing particularly new was brought out, the sheer intensity of the meeting has him thinking. "How's all this gonna affect me and my family? What's it gonna be like for the three of us if we have to live in a world dominated more and more by Hispanics? Is it time to get outta here…maybe move back to Alabama where there are fewer Latinos… or somewhere up north where they haven't infiltrated yet? I don't wanna move, but Jesus…things are changin' so fast now, I dunno. I'll probably be out of a job in ten years…outnumbered, outvoted. Then, what the hell am I gonna do?"

He turns to look out the window. Gradually despair gives way to anger as he pictures a horde of illegals pouring across the border, spreading out into the city like locusts, consuming people's homes, their streets, their jobs, their schools…leaving nothing behind…like a field of corn devoured and leveled…everything edible turned to dust. Gritting his teeth, he rises and pounds his fist on the desk. Not stopping to tell his secretary where he's going, he slams the office door and jumps into his cruiser. For a full minute he sits there, tight-lipped, revving the motor until the secretary appears at the window, clearly alarmed. When she wraps on the pane, he pretends not to hear, then bursts out of the parking lot, lights flashing, siren wailing.

16

Marisol

At dinner that night mother and daughter want to know all about Santé's job. He enjoys being the center of attention; it's similar to Oaxaca where the women asked questions and the men talked about themselves. Then too, being able to talk Spanish after hearing nothing but English all day is a relief.

As soon as dinner is finished, Senora Mendez leaves the kitchen table to go watch a favorite TV program, leaving Mirasol and Santé alone for first time. She picks up where mother left off…asking questions about Santé's family back home and his trip across the desert.

On subsequent nights the ritual is repeated. When Mirasol speaks warmly of their new boarder, Senora Mendez begins entertaining the possibility of marriage. To be on the safe side, she warns her daughter about the dangers of promiscuity, going so far as to quote scripture on the immorality of sex outside of marriage. "Be careful what you wear," she cautions. "Cover yourself at all times. Remember what happened on your date earlier this year." She was referring to a high school dance which Marisol attended with a boy from the class ahead of her. The date ended in disaster. While in the front seat of his father's car, the boy began pawing at her bra and pulling on her dress. She escaped only by clawing his cheek with her nails and jumping out of the car. She arrived home early to find her mother waiting in her nightgown. The girl's tears were enough to convey what happened; the gruesome details were added the next morning. That was her first and last date of the year.

Mirasol is not the prettiest of girls…and she knows it. When she looks in the mirror, what she sees is not encouraging. There is a plainness to her face that cannot be masked with lipstick, eye shadow or rouge. For one thing, her eyes are too far apart, leaving a dull, almost bovine emptiness above her nose. Her thick, unplucked eyebrows only add to the inelegant image. Below her nose things get no better. Her lips are naturally red and swollen and droop at the corners, giving her a perpetual look of being both wanton and depressed. On the inside she is neither, but finds it difficult to counter the impression conveyed by her face. All in all it is an awkward anatomy. The parts are there but don't seem to go together…rather like a living room where the chairs are too far apart for easy conversation, the coffee table askew, and the couch buried under a plethora of over-stuffed pillows.

Her figure, however, is something else. As Santé is quick to notice, her breasts are more than ample and ride particularly high on her chest, giving the impression simultaneously of a girl conscious of her youthful charms and a grown woman capable of providing succor. At 5'4" and 110 pounds, her frame is slight, which accentuates her breasts all the more. Her legs are long and athletic without being muscular. Conscious of her assets, she chooses her wardrobe carefully…eschewing long, loose dresses in favor of tight-fitting blouses and short skirts. At least this is what she would prefer to wear. According to her mother, however, it is clothes of that sort which got her into trouble at school where she was seen by the older boys as coming on sexually. Having learned from that experience, she now leaves her more seductive apparel in the closest, reserving the low-neck blouses and skimpy skirts for a time when she meets the right kind of person.

While Santé is aware of Marisol's charms, he is too caught up in his own life to pay more than cursory attention. This does not keep her from staring. What she sees when she looks across the table is a boy, now almost a man, with intense brown eyes, a straight Roman nose, full cheeks, and jet black hair falling uncombed to one side. To Marisol it is the hair that defines his character. Unlike other boys from Mexico who comb their hair forward, pulling it up at the very front to form a bird-like crest, Santé seems content to push his hair back with his hand, letting it fall naturally wherever it wants to. The effect is a kind of manliness, neither smug nor complacent but compelling in its indifference to what others might think. She finds it mesmerizing. When he talks, he often looks down at the table, unaware that she is scrutinizing every feature of his good looks.

As the days roll by, Marisol and Santé spend more and more time together at the dinner table. They are typically alone each evening from the time Senora Mendez retires to the living room until she returns to the kitchen around 9:30. Wednesday evenings are especially enjoyable since Senora Mendez leaves at 5:30 to attend a church supper where women gather to eat and make baby garments for the poor.

As Santé and Marisol become friendlier, he considers telling her about what happened in the desert. Still bothered by what he was forced to do, he continues to hold back, afraid both of frightening her and alerting the police if she were to tell others about the killings. Each time the subject comes up, he says simply that he had to defend himself several times during the crossing…and that the grandfather in the group never made it to the border.

Several weeks into the relationship, things suddenly take a turn for the serious. It is Wednesday night and Senora Mendez is getting ready to leave for church. Perhaps it is something she notices in Marisol's eyes or what she is wearing that prompts her to stop at the door. Squinting, she turns to her daughter, shaking her head. "That tank top is not appropriate when Santé is here. Go get a shirt and cover yourself…and while you're at it put on a longer skirt…(*pause*)…I may get back a little early tonight… just in case." Having said her piece, she heads out the door, not bothering to turn around. If she had, she might have seen a mischievous smirk on her daughter's otherwise unanimated face.

Back in the kitchen, Marisol takes her seat and resumes chatting with Santé. Again the subject turns to the desert and what happened there. This time Santé is ready to tell her the whole truth…on the condition that she keep it a secret between the two of them. She struggles to conceal her excitement. Outwardly she simply nods; inwardly she is about to explode. What moves her so dramatically is not the prospect of hearing the story but the fact that he now trusts her enough to tell it. Without warning she suddenly leaps up and takes off her shirt, flinging it onto her mother's chair. "It's too hot in here, don't you think, Santé?"

"I'm O.K." Santé responds, oblivious to her sudden change in mood.

Refusing to be disappointed, she grasps the table to conceal her trembling. "Tell me about the bandits," she says, barely able to speak. "How many were there?"

"Two…brothers, I think. One guy stabbed the old man while the second one was gettin' ready to rape the granddaughter. I was in the woods peein' so I was too late to help the grandfather, but I stopped the other guy."

"Oh my God…how did you stop him?"

Santé hesitates, studying her face carefully. "I used my macuahuitl…on his neck. He never got up again."

She gasps. "Your what?"

"It's a weapon…kinda like a machete, but with blades on both sides. My uncle made it for my birthday; it's a copy of what our ancestors used to fight the Aztecs. I have it in my closet…(*pause*)… want to see it?"

"Yes…(*pause*)…I think so."

As Santé leads the way down the corridor to his bedroom, Marisol hangs back, stopping in the doorway as he enters. She knows the room well; after all, she cleans it several times a week along with the rest of the apartment. But this time it's different. Never before has she been in the room while he was there. The atmosphere is electric; her heart is pounding. As he reaches into the closet to fetch the macuahuitl, she takes several steps inside the room, then stops. When he stoops to pick up the weapon, she takes a quick look in the mirror to make sure her tank top is covering everything. She is at once relieved and apprehensive. Her nipples are fully concealed as are the lower curves of her breasts but the cleavage above is palpable. She looks again, "Do I really want to show this much of myself?" Her head is spinning too fast to think.

When Santé stands up to show her the macuahuitl, his eyes quickly fasten on her breasts. Although he has seen his sister's breasts many times at home where the whole family shared a single room, he has always viewed them more as a curiosity than as something arousing. This is different. For the first time in his life, his whole body is flooded with the toxin of sexual desire…in this case a desire to touch and kiss what remains hidden just inches away.

The macuahuitl is soon forgotten as they sit together on his bed. She can hear his heart beating and waits demurely for his kiss. For weeks she has waited for this moment. Slowly she raises her head and looks into his eyes…then offers her lips. As he pulls her close she runs her hands through his hair, the soft, uncombed hair that she finds so beguiling. He responds by imitating her action…combing her hair with one hand as he caresses her cheek with the other. Like a stag in rut, he sniffs the air to test her readiness, then, assured that she is willing, presses his lips to hers.

His manhood is rock hard, pulsing with the need for release. With his mouth pressed tightly against hers, he slides his hand up her back and under her tank top. Her skin is warm and smooth. Back and forth under the fabric he massages her flesh, completely intoxicated but not yet daring to come full circle. If only she would take it off and let him see her flesh. He is so close, his lips twitching in anticipation. It is instinct that guides him now, all reason having been sacrificed on the altar of desire. Throwing caution to the wind, he brings his hand forward under the tank top…past her armpit…until he can feel the soft outer curve of her breast. Suddenly, without warning, she pulls back and slaps his arm. When he tries to continue, she slaps him again.

Confused and humiliated, he gets up and walks over to the chair in front of the small writing table. As he sits at the table, head down, she follows him with her eyes, adjusting her tank top as she watches. "Have I lost him," she asks silently. "He looks angry. But what was I to do? I want his love…yes… but I want his respect as well. So how can I please him without giving him the wrong impression?" She sighs now as the sight of him crumpled over in the chair tugs at her maternal instincts, releasing feelings that threaten to undermine all that she has been taught about the sanctity of marriage.

Silently she offers a prayer to the compassionate God she so ardently believes in…then looks out into the hall to make sure Mother hasn't come home yet. While Santé's head is still bowed, she pulls her tank top up over her shoulders and tosses it onto the bed. Now that the decision has been made, she can afford the luxury of a playful grin. Sneaking up behind him, she reaches down to touch his hand…then lifts it toward her chest, still holding it in her own. At first he is unaware of what is happening…pleased that she is no longer angry but curious as to what she is up to. Holding him by the wrist she lifts his arm still higher until he feels something soft and warm. With breath coming faster now, he rotates his palm so he can use his fingers to feel. Still silent, she leans forward and presses his hand to her breast, guiding his thumb and forefinger to her nipple. He turns his head, desperate to see what he now can feel.

"Come to bed with me," she whispers, scarcely able to believe her own words.

Santé's eyes open wide. As if by magic, all feelings of guilt, shame, humiliation and anger vanish instantaneously. Rising quickly, he takes her by the arm and leads her to the bed. Lying on her back with breasts fully exposed, she turns to him with open arms and smiles. He does not hesitate. Drawn to her nipples like a moth to flame, he grasps each one in turn with his lips and begins sucking. It delights her to see him so needy. Pressing down on her forearms, she lifts her chest to meet his lips, then falls back and closes her eyes.

He kisses her neck, then her chin, then her lips. When she moans softly, he places his hand on her leg and slides it up under her skirt. There is no immediate response. He slides it further, still without protest. When it reaches her thigh, she suddenly cries out, "No…not that…not until you tell me you love me."

Besotted with lust, Santé blurts out an ardent "I love you," oblivious to what he is saying other than he is aching to get inside her.

"Yes, but do you promise to marry me?" she responds anxiously.

"What?" he asks, stunned by this turn of events. "I know you for two months only…and you're just 16." When she fails to answer, he continues, "I want to go to college. Marriage means having babies and working hard to pay for family. That's not why I came to El Norte. I want to be an engineer. Besides, I promised my parents I send money each month as soon as I get a job."

She pulls away. "Then don't touch me again." With eyes flashing, she reaches for her tank top, covers her breasts and heads for her room. Still confused about what just happened, Santé gets up off the bed and closes the door. Standing there with head down, he struggles to make sense of the evening. "She wants to get married…that's crazy," he mutters. "She's sixteen and hardly knows me…(*pause*)…Maybe I should move…yes… that's the best way now. Tomorrow I'll start looking."

17

The Sheriff's Boy

Earl Culpepper eyes a third doughnut, then checks his paunch. "Maybe not," he says to Emma. "Just gimme a little more coffee." The ensuing lull in the conversation is broken when Eric speaks up. "I could use a little spending money, Dad. The $50 you gave me last week didn't go very far."

Earl starts to reach for his wallet, then stops. "Jesus Eric, school's been out for two weeks now and you still don't have a job. What are you waitin' for?"

Eric takes a quick look at his mother before answering. "I tried two supermarkets last week. They weren't hiring."

"Well, try somewhere else," Earl responds, his voice rising slightly. "Your freshman year in college is goin' to cost us a fortune. You gotta help a little."

Emma sits with hands folded, saying nothing.

Earl hands his son another $50. "Now look, this has gotta last you until you get a job. There have to be places that are hiring this time of year. Have you tried any of the resorts outside of town?"

Eric shakes his head, "How am I supposed to get there…walk?"

"Take your truck."

"I could…but that means gas….and there goes the $50 you just gave me. Besides I really need a new tire on my right front."

"O.K. I'll take you. Let me call the office and tell 'em I won't be in 'til noon. That should give us enough time to try several places. We can start with Tyler's Ranch and Spa out on Rt. 72. They hire kids every summer. I oughta know; I worked there one summer myself."

Eric looks at Emma and hangs his head. "That was a longtime ago, Dad. Things have changed."

"Let's give it a try. We got nothin' to lose."

As they approach the Ranch and Spa, Earl offers a little advice. "Tell 'em you've had some experience waiting on table. Mention the time when you did some bussing for a caterer….you know, at that Christmas party last year. Don't hold back. It's O.K. to exaggerate a little. Everybody does it. You have to make yourself look good."

Minutes later Eric comes out of the office with his head down. "No luck?" Earl asks.

"Eric shakes his head. "Nope."

"Well, don't give up," says Earl. "We'll try another one I know up on Addison Ave. Polly's Place I think it's called these days. Big restaurant crowd there, especially on weekends. They're gonna need some help."

When Eric emerges from Polly's Place with a similar look of dejection, Earl is quick to ask, "Well, what did they say?"

"Nothing. They've already got all the help they need for the summer."

Earl shows signs of exasperation. "You should've started earlier. I told you weeks ago this could happen…(*pause*)…By the way, what do you say when you go in? You know, the very first thing."

Eric hesitates, seeming to look for the right words. "Well, I say 'Don't suppose you need any help.' Somethin' like that."

Earl bites his lip. "Sounds pretty negative to me. If you say it like that, you make it easy for people to come back with, 'You're right, sorry'."

Eric shrugs his shoulders. "So, how would you do it?"

"You gotta be positive…make 'em believe that you can help 'em. Tell 'em you're good with customers…or that you work fast…or that you can do either bussin' or waitin' on table…whatever is needed. Smile a lot…make 'em think you'll be an asset to the place. Make 'em want you."

On his way to work later in the day Earl can think about nothing else. Over and over he asks himself what kind of business would hire an 18 year old kid for the summer. No new idea emerges… until he hears an ad for used television sets on his car radio. At the dinner table that evening he shares his inspiration with Eric and Emma. "O.K. Let's forget the resorts…it's probably too late for that now. How about an appliance repair service?"

Eric sneers, "A what?"

"You know…a place where they repair things like TV's, radios and CD players."

When Earl reaches for his coffee, Eric exchanges a wry smile with his mother. "I don't know squat about TV's, Dad. I can turn 'em on and off but that's it. I even have trouble with the remote."

"They might be willing to train you," Emma offers, warming to the idea.

Earl flashes a broad smile. "And I know just the place…it's run by a man who owes me a favor. I could've ticketed him last year when I caught him speeding on Maricopa Blvd. I don't know why I let him off the hook… guess I was just feelin' good that day. Anyhow, he owes me one…so let's get over there and see what he can do for us."

As Earl pulls into a space outside Maricopa TV Repair, Eric repeats his concern. "Now don't go tellin' 'em that I'm some kind of hot shot with appliances. I don't know shit about machines…except maybe for cars."

Earl winces. "Hey, watch your language…if you use words like that you're gonna come across like a hood. These folks might even be religious types. So, lay off the cuss words." At the office door, he whispers a final word of encouragement: "C'mon now, *make me proud of ya.*"

Earl yanks the door open and steps inside. Eric hesitates, then enters, his eyes immediately drawn to the girlie calendar on the wall.

"Hello, what can I do to ya?" comes the greeting from behind the desk. A second later, "Oh, it's you Sheriff, didn't recognize you without your uniform. Nice to see ya again."

"Hi Don. Good to see you too. This here is my kid, Eric. Eric, shake hands with Mr. Edmunds."

Eric, eyes averted, offers a limp hand.

Don withdraws his own hand quickly. "So, what brings you here, Earl… d'ya run out of bad guys to chase?"

"Eric is lookin' for a job…just for the summer….somethin' that will let him put a little money away for college in the fall."

"Oh, what college you goin' to Eric," Mr. Edmunds asks.

"A.S.U.," comes the laconic reply.

Turning back to Earl, "Well, Earl, I'd like to help but as you know business is real slow…not jis' here but everywhere else. It's the whole economy. TV sales are way down and that means fewer folks bringin' in their sets for repair… (*pause*)…Have you tried the resorts…they always hire kids in the summer?"

"Yeah, we tried that Don…but no luck. Lookit, Eric's a good worker, a quick learner…and besides…"

"I owe you…right?"

"Well, yeah, I guess you do."

Don sits back down and presses his hands together, as if in prayer. Turning to Eric, he asks, "Have you ever fooled around with radios or TV's…you know, built a little receiver yourself or fixed a broken one?"

"Nope."

Earl quickly interjects. "But he's a fast learner…did pretty well in high school."

Don looks at Eric, "Umm…you any good with your hands?"

Eric smiles slyly. "Yeah…jis' ask the girls at school."

Earl frowns. "That's not what Mr. Edmunds means, Eric. This is serious business, so show a little respect…(*pause*)…He's about to offer you a job, ain't ya Don?"

Don shifts in his chair and looks out the window. "Well, maybe we could give him a try Earl…give 'im some easy stuff to work on …nothin' that's gonna pay him a fortune though. You gotta realize that …"

"How much?" Earl interjects.

Don is about to call for his wife then changes his mind. "We could probably begin with $8 an hour; if he's really good we might move him up a bit…say, to $10."

Earl wrinkles his nose. "Eight bucks an hour? That's not even minimum wage, is it?"

Sensing support from his father, Eric adds, "My friends at school are makin' $15 an hour jis' mowin' lawns."

"Well, if he's as hard a worker as you say Earl, we might go as high as $10 an hour to begin with and a few bucks more later if he's really good."

Earl moves quickly to the desk for a handshake. "O.K. Ten bucks an hour now and $15 in a month if he's doin' a good job. Thanks Don. Now show him around the shop and get him signed up. I've gotta get back to the office and pretend to do some work."

As Earl heads out the door, Don gives his newest employee a closer look. Unlike his father, the boy is wiry, his lips thin and bloodless, his eyes constantly shifting…like someone looking for something to steal. He sighs inwardly. "I could regret this one…but what choice did I have? Earl saved me a $200 ticket last year…not to mention a black mark on my car insurance. I'll just have to put up with 'im for a month…then find some way to get rid of 'im."

He turns to confront his new employee. "C'mon Eric, I'll show you around." The two enter the shop just as Senora Edmunds appears in the office doorway. "Who do we have here?" she asks, not bothering to conceal her curiosity.

"Oh honey, this is Eric, our latest addition," comes the reply. He's Sheriff Culpepper's son. He's going to be with us this summer."

She squints and wrinkles her nose. "He is? We just took on the other boy; I thought we weren't hiring anymore."

"We aren't, but this is a special case. The Sheriff is an old friend of mine… so I thought it only appropriate that we give the boy a chance. I'll tell you later about what pay grade I've assigned."

His manner is unusually guarded, his speech uncharacteristically formal, conveying to his observant wife that the hiring was done under duress. She flashes a questioning look and disappears into the apartment.

18

Picking up the Scent

Three weeks later while cruising the streets of Phoenix, Sheriff Culpepper is passing his own house when he decides to drop in for a home-made lunch. Once inside the door, he is surprised to see Eric at the kitchen table chatting with his mother.

"Hey, how come you're not at work?" he asks gruffly.

Eric looks at his mother before answering. "I got fired…or laid off as the old guy put it."

"Fired? I thought you were doin' O.K."

"Guess not. He said I wasn't pulling my share of the load. Like I told you, I'm no good with radios and TV's."

Earl sits down at the table. "But he said they'd teach you. Christ, you've only been there for three weeks."

"Yeah. But I couldn't seem to learn anything. I'm no good at playin' with wires and transistors and tiny stuff like that. Some guys love it but I don't."

Emma interrupts to ask if Earl would like a tuna fish sandwich.

"O.K.…we got any pickles and chips?"

Without answering she heads for the kitchen.

"But you're good with cars," Earl continues, still struggling to understand this latest twists of events.

"Well yeah…cars and girls…that's about it."

Earl lets out a loud sigh. "That's not a helluva lot to be proud of Eric. So, how much have you saved so far?"

Eric hangs his head. "Not much. I had to get that new tire for my truck…and you know…lots of little things."

"For Christ's sake. School is only a month away and you haven't saved a thing?" He shakes his head in disbelief. "You're really lettin' me down….I hope you know that."

"Yeah."

"Well, I'm going over to the shop and find out what happened. The whole thing sounds fishy to me. After all, he promised to try you for a month and then give you a raise if you're any good. Remember?"

"That's what he said, yeah, but he doesn't want me anymore…(*pause*)…I can't go back there now."

"Well, maybe not, but I still want an explanation."

Within 15 minutes of finishing his sandwich, Earl is outside the shop. Not bothering to turn his engine off, he bursts into the office and hurls a question at Don who is reclining in his chair. "Watcha fire Eric for? You didn't even give the kid a chance."

Don drops back into his seat, fingers clutching the armrests. Taking a deep breath, he braces himself for the attack. "We did give him a chance, Earl," he whispers. "He just didn't have it. What I mean is, he was all fists and thumbs…even wrecked a few TV sets that I had to turn over to somebody else."

"I thought you were goin' to teach 'im."

"We tried. Like I said, the kid's got no knack for repairing things…and didn't seem all that interested in learning. In fact, his attitude was pretty negative. Nobody here seemed to like him, especially the guys who tried to teach him. So…we couldn't keep him. He was costing us money without giving us anything in return."

"But you owed me…or maybe you've forgotten that."

"I didn't forget Earl. It's just that business is business. I can't go on paying the kid for nothing. If I do that long enough, I'll go broke. You should know that."

Earl paces up and down the office, searching for something to say. As he looks into the shop, he spies Santé working at one of the stations. He stares, squinting. "Didn't I see that kid in here the last time I come in?"

"Which kid you mean?"

Earl points to Santé whose Latino ancestry is clear from his skin and hair. "You ain't hirin' aliens are you, Don? If so, you're in big trouble."

Don shifts uneasily in his chair. "Nah…that kid there…he's just learning the trade; he's not an employee. We're not payin' him beans. You can check the payroll if you want."

"You expect me to believe that? You're probably payin' him under the table. If so, we're gonna find out…and then you're in for a shitload of trouble." He turns to face Don again, "Maybe that station there was Eric's…but some poor bastard come along and agreed to work for peanuts….so you fired my boy. It's a goddamn shame. You're jis' contributin' to this whole fuckin' invasion that the rest of us are tryin' to fight. It's clear you don't give two hoots for your country, Don…(*pause*)…But you're not goin' to get away with it. One way or another, I'm gonna get to the truth."

At that moment Senora Edmunds enters from the apartment in back where she has been listening to the conversation. With eyes blazing, she strides across the office and stops directly in front of the sheriff. "Lookit Mr. Bigshot, you've got no right to question our employees unless they've violated the law somehow. If you try it, I'll report you to the Attorney General's Office."

Earl smiles. "I thought Don said the kid was not an employee."

"Well, he's not. I just meant that…."

(*Interrupting*) "Yeah, I know what you meant. The kid is bein' paid under the table. And that means you're breakin' two laws…you're not payin' payroll taxes on an employee and you've hired an undocumented alien. As you might guess, there are big penalties for both violations."

Senora Edmunds backs away toward her husband. From behind the desk, she raises her finger and blurts out, "You can't prove any of that, Sheriff."

"Don't worry, Paula, I'll find a way. You can count on that." Without further words, he turns abruptly and leaves.

19

The Library

Over the next few days Santé's relationship with Marisol becomes increasingly awkward…to the point that he begins looking for a new apartment in earnest. Under the watchful eyes of the mother, the two youths continue to exchange hellos and goodbyes at dinner time but avoid each other the rest of the time. Back in his room, Santé no longer wastes time imagining what it would be like to make love to her; she has become the enemy, a temptress who threatens everything he has achieved so far. It is about this time that he has a dream in which she appears naked in front of a small bird, holding a metal cage in her hand. Smiling, she opens the cage door and beckons the bird to enter. Tentatively the bird hops to the door of the cage and waits, enthralled by the sight of the girl with the slender body and soft, white breasts. As he totters at the entrance, she suddenly lunges and grabs him by the neck. The bird squawks and flaps its wings furiously in an attempt to get away. It is too late. He's pushed into the cage and watches as the door clangs shut, never to be opened again.

When Senora Edmunds hears that Santé is looking for a place to live, she offers him a room in her own apartment behind the shop. Santé agrees immediately and moves in the following week. While the arrangement is for room and laundry only, she makes it clear that he is welcome to join her and Mr. Edmunds for dinner as well. Her mood is ecstatic as she prepares his bed with freshly cleaned sheets and pillowcases. With her husband's help, a dresser is dragged down from the attic and placed against the wall. A small rug, purchased years ago on a trip to Mexico, fits perfectly at the side of the bed. All that is missing is a chair on which he can drape his pants at night. Once again Don comes to her rescue with an unused secretary's chair from the office. His wife spends hours making sure the room is perfect. When everything is finally in place, she heads for the doorway, only to return to fluff the pillows one more time.

Having Santé under the same roof changes Senora Edmund's normal routines. While she still spends several hours a day preparing the payroll and updating the accounts, she manages to be available whenever Santé returns to his room. When they talk, the conversation tends to revolve around his future plans, specifically his plans for college. She tells him that he must get his G.E.D. before he can even apply for admission. Having finished only ten years of schooling in Oaxaca, he will have to study hard to make up for the missing two years. Fortunately, she adds, the local library has copies of previous tests…but they are all in English, so there is little he can learn there until he's taken some language classes. Throughout it all, she walks a fine line between encouraging him to pursue his goals and reminding him how difficult it's going to be. He readily accepts her guidance and does not hesitate to show his appreciation, with both words and hugs.

"By the way," she says one night at dinner, "why don't you call me Paula…I think we know each other well enough for that."

In the days to come, he is surprised by how much she fusses over him. She tidies his room every day, washes and dries his clothes…even his underwear…makes his bed and invites him to dinner often even though their arrangement is technically for a room only. Despite his youth, he realizes how unusual the arrangement is and how lucky he is to have been taken under her wing. "She got to be everything a boy wants in a mother," he says to himself, adding, "all love and no scolding." In his letters back home, he is careful to leave out any details that might hurt his real mother's feelings. The $300 remittance he sends each month serves to relieve any lingering feelings of guilt.

On Saturday, he heads for the local library where he hopes to find copies of old G.E.D. tests…just to get a feeling for what lies ahead. He is met at the counter by a slender young girl with black wavy hair who asks if he needs any help. When her words come too fast, he smiles and asks if she speaks Spanish. She replies quickly, "Si. Yo lo aprendi cuando era nino por mi madre que crecio en Honduras." (Yes. I learned it as a child from my mother who grew up in Honduras). From that point on, they both speak Spanish. When he asks about English courses, she tells him about an E.S.L. class that meets at the library two evenings a week. He looks around to see if anyone is listening, then says, "My name is Asanté, but everybody calls me Santé. What's yours?"

She smiles and extends her hand. "Anna. It's nice to meet you Santé."

He stays for much of the morning looking for books to read and getting to know more about his new friend. Occasionally she leaves to help others find books or look up reference material...then returns to chat with the boy whose shy demeanor intrigues her. Usually they talk standing, but when no one else is around they sit together at a nearby table. In time he finds out that she is starting her senior year in high school and works at the library on Saturdays, hoping to make money for college next year. For an American, she is short, about the same height as Santé ...and petite. Her black hair is wavy and falls gently to her shoulders. To his way of thinking, aside from the waviness of her hair, she could be Latina or at least partly Latina. Her eyes are brown and her skin has a touch of bronze in it. There is nothing Spanish, however, about her last name...Erickson. Her father is Swedish, she tells him, indicating that the Latina looks come from her mother's side of the family.

He spends much of the following week thinking about returning to the library on Saturday. He is eager to tell Anna that, following her suggestion, he has enrolled in an English class and already knows how to count up to 100. In his mind's eye, he can already see her smile of approval, a smile that he likens to a seedling that carries in its core the promise of fully-ripened fruit. When Saturday finally arrives, despite her suggestion that he wait until he knows more English, he gets copies of the test and starts studying for his G.E.D.. Anna shakes her head in protest but continues to offer her support.

When Senora Edmunds finds out that he is working on both his English and a G.E.D., she goes out of her way to help. In order to be with him, she deliberately waits until he returns to his room before bringing in his clean laundry. Night after night they sit together on his bed, reviewing the lessons presented in class. A common exercise is to go around the room naming objects in English, then repeat the exercise with colors, animals, types of food and parts of the human body. Only subliminally aware of her motives, she develops a guessing game in which she touches certain parts of his body and tells him the English name. He is then expected to repeat what he has heard. She is especially thrilled to touch his forehead, his nose, his lips, and throat as the words are pronounced. The game continues when the roles are reversed and he is asked to do the touching. There is much laughing and giggling which helps to cover the unspoken pleasure she gets in being this close. Her secret hope is to have him touch her breast but he is too shy. She goes so far as to touch his chest, hoping this will make it easier for him to imitate her move when it's his turn. But he is too caught up in the lesson to fathom her real desires. Besides, he has already started to obsess over Anna.

For their first date he suggests a Spanish-language movie in town preceded by a trip to Taco Bell's for a dinner of tortas and burritos. With that in mind, he meets her at the library just as it is closing. Out on the sidewalk, the conversation turns to Mexico, Honduras and the plight of migrants in Arizona. Given their backgrounds, the subject is bonding. Half-way down the street, their hands accidentally touch. When he responds by pulling his back, she reaches out and takes it in her own. He looks away, his heart racing. Throughout dinner they play a similar game under the table as she rests her foot on top of his wherever he places it. Later, a similar sequence is enacted in the theater. When their arms touch on the armrest, he withdraws his only to have her reach over and return it next to hers. By the end of the evening there can be no doubt that both are smitten. A single, brief kiss at her door erases any lingering hesitation, leaving them unable to think of anything other than next Saturday. Inside the door Anna slips past her parents with an awkward wave; out on the street Santé stumbles toward home, oblivious to all but the memory of her lips.

In the weeks that follow both are careful to leave Saturday nights open. On the first few dates much of their conversation revolves around the sharing of personal background…his in Oaxaca, hers in Phoenix. Gradually a project of interest to both emerges …teaching Santé enough English so he can take the G.E.D. exam. He is an ardent pupil, eager to spend endless hours with a teacher who not only speaks beautifully but who knows how to make the process exciting for her student. She does it by personalizing each new word or phrase. Instead of having him memorize a list of things, she asks him to identify whatever they see on their walks…the sky, trees, automobiles, people's clothing. Then she asks him to say what color they are…or whether he likes them or not.

Sitting on a park bench one moonlit night, she decides to go further. "Do you love me?" she asks mischievously. When he answers in Spanish, she says, "No, tell me in English." He smiles and says, "Yes", which prompts a quick response, "What do you love about me?" He hesitates, then begins pointing first to her eyes, then her nose and lips, giving the English word for each. She is not satisfied. "A complete sentence, please," she says with a playful grin. When he complies, she immediately ups the ante. "O.K. so you love me. Now, what do you want to do to me?" As she says it, she cocks her head and runs her tongue across her lips. He is now at her mercy, unable to think clearly in either Spanish or English. Automatically he reaches for her shoulders. "The words first…in English," she says, no longer able to keep from laughing. "I want you kiss," he cries out, not bothering to check his syntax. "Not quite," she replies. "You can do better." As she waits for an answer, he begins to tremble visibly. First he squints, then twists his mouth into a scowl. Finally, driven by instinct alone, he grunts like a stag in rut, then reaches out and pulls her to his chest. When she tries to wriggle free, he presses his mouth to hers and holds her tight, refusing to budge until her lips open, signaling surrender.

The bench is now still. Locked in embrace even as others pass by, they slip into a realm where neither boundaries nor time exist. Here is only the kiss…no you, no me…no other to be possessed, no self to be wanting…no moon, no night…no church bells tolling the hour… just this.

The following week, when she expresses curiosity about where he lives, he invites her to see his room. Since there is only one chair in the room, they sit on the bed as they talk. This time they go beyond the naming of objects; verbs are the subject de jour…to have, to do, to want, to love. The lesson is continually interrupted with kisses, first hers, then his, until she falls back onto the pillow with arms outstretched. Santé acts quickly to slide on top of her. It is at this moment that Senora Edmunds raps on the door and hearing no response, enters with his freshly-cleaned socks and underwear. The sight of Santé lying on top of a girl startles her. When she goes to conceal a gasp, the laundry slips from her hands, falling to the floor. She apologizes, then bends to pick it up. As Santé scrambles to his feet, she mumbles something incoherent and leaves.

"What's wrong?" asks Don as Paula comes back into the living room. She takes a seat at the other end of the couch, saying nothing, but continues to stare in the direction of Santé's room. Her breathing comes fast now as feelings of love and betrayal fight for supremacy. Oblivious to what has happened, Don goes back to reading his newspaper. Screened from view, Paula lowers her head and closes her eyes. From deep inside, a question cries for attention, "How could he…after all I've done for him? Was I not enough?…Dear God, I could not have loved him more."

20

Anna's Family

"Well, we've finally gotten to meet you, Santé. I'm Anna's father. She's told us all about you…(*smiling*)…all of it good I might add. C'mon in and have a seat." The father's voice is warm and welcoming as he ushers his diminutive guest into the living room where they are joined by the mother who introduces herself as Esmeralda. Outwardly, the two parents could not be more different, he of Northern European descent, she obviously Latina.

Once everyone is seated and supplied with drinks, cheese and crackers, the subject turns to Santé's background and the broader subject of immigration. Although no details are either given or asked for, it is taken as fact that Santé has crossed into the U.S. illegally.

The father continues in fluent Spanish. "Santé, Anna tells us that you want to go to college here." His words have a patronizing quality similar to the way he speaks to students at the local college where he teaches sociology.

"Yes, Senor. I want to become an engineer."

The father nods and smiles. "I assume that you'll need some scholarship help. You're fortunate that the Supreme Court has ruled that colleges here cannot discriminate against undocumented applicants."

"Yes, Senor. I am very lucky."

Anna shifts uneasily. "Santé needs to get his G.E.D. first though, Daddy. He never got a chance to finish high school in Oaxaca."

The father peers over his glasses. "But how can he expect to do that if he can't speak English?"

Esmeralda fluffs her long, black hair and leans forward. "Anna says Santé takes English classes at the library…and she is helping him."

Mr. Erickson forces a wry smile. "A new language is not something you can learn overnight."

From across the room Anna offers her support. "It depends on the individual, don't you think? Santé happens to be very smart."

"I'm sure he is, but it still takes a long time. After all, English is not the easiest of languages to master. But learning a new language is just one of many hurdles to overcome. Finding a job, a place to live, paying for healthcare, furthering your education…they all take time. Most people who come here, whether legally or illegally, never assimilate completely. It is their kids who get Americanized…and that has its own tragic consequences."

"Tragic…in what way, Daddy?"

Mr. Erickson looks over at his wife and pauses. "Well, it doesn't always turn out this way, but very often the children grow up feeling ashamed of their parents. Thanks to their parent's efforts, the kids are better educated and speak better English than they do. Compared to their immigrant mothers and fathers, they also understand the American way of doing things better. They wear more American-style clothes; they shop at the malls; they play video games on their computers; they watch baseball and football on TV. Most important of all, they get better-paying jobs and can afford to live in bigger houses and drive newer cars."

Anna objects. "But wouldn't that make them feel grateful for all the sacrifices their parents made to come here? I certainly appreciate all that you and Mom went through to make such a nice home for me."

Mr. Erickson smiles at his daughter. "You are very appreciative, honey, but I think our family is not all that typical. After all, the Ericksons have been American citizens for generations. True, your mother was the first in her family to come here but she avoided many of the usual pitfalls of migration by marrying me. In a more typical migrant family, the mother and father are both from a foreign society…and to a great extent remain locked in that more primitive culture even as their children become Americanized. And that's where the tragedy begins. Parents and children gradually drift apart. Instead of feeling grateful to their parents for all their sacrifices, the kids end up feeling ashamed of them for their ignorance, their poverty, their poor English and backward ways."

Anna looks over at her mother. "I don't feel any of that. Knowing how hard it was for Mom to cross over and make her way in a new world with practically no help from anyone else…"

"But I had my brother, Anna," Mother interrupts. "Willie gave me a place to live and helped me set up a corner fruit stand so I could make some money. I don't think I could have made it without his help."

Esmeralda's eyes moisten as thoughts of her dead brother return.

Mr. Erickson rises and goes over to his wife. Still standing, with a hand on her shoulder, he looks at Santé. "Granted, things are hard for migrants these days…but a generation ago they were even worse."

Esmeralda reaches up and squeezes his hand. "When Anna's mother got here in the 80's," the father continues, still looking at Santé, "the Phoenix police saw it as their duty to protect the safety of naturalized Americans; immigrants without papers were left to fend for themselves. The drug dealers and racketeers, of course, thrived in this environment. What happened to Anna's mother is just one example of what took place all across the Southwest back then."

Santé straightens up in his chair. "What happened to your wife, Senor?"

"I'll let Esmeralda tell the story. Honey…"

Esmeralda drops her hands into her lap and sits up. Her face, naturally elegant in its symmetry and olive-skin smoothness, is twisted into wrinkles as she struggles to keep the tears at bay. Her hands tremble; she crosses then uncrosses her legs; her large brown eyes, helpless to conceal the feelings bubbling inside, shimmer behind pools of dark water. Without rising, she looks up at her husband, then over at their guest. "Santé, please don't let what I'm going to say discourage you from working hard to achieve your goals."

Calmer now, she pauses to recall what happened. "We came in a truck, all the way from Honduras, about a hundred of us crammed into the back of an 18-wheeler. I was one of the lucky ones: my brother, Willie, was waiting for me in Phoenix and took me to the trailer where he was living. There were 15 people living in that trailer…adults and children…some family, some friends. Most of us slept on the floor; we cooked and ate our meals outside around a fire pit. Those of us who could work went out each morning to a job. The men did gardening or worked in restaurants cleaning dishes; most of the women worked as housekeepers or babysitters. Thanks to my brother I had something better: I sold fruit drinks and pastries from a cart at the corner of Washington and Dewalt streets. I made the drinks and pastries at home and wheeled my stand to the corner every morning. It was really nice. People got to know me by name and came often to buy my things.

"I had been doing it for almost a year when a stranger came by one morning and said something that changed my life…and my brother's… forever." At this point Esmeralda stops and lowers her head. No one speaks. "He was Latino and spoke a kind of Spanish I had trouble understanding. He said he wanted to sell drugs from my stand…and would pay me a percentage of everything he made. When I finally understood what he wanted, I said 'No, I don't want to go to prison.' We argued for a while but I kept saying 'No'. He finally became angry and said that if I didn't help him sell drugs, he wouldn't let me use that corner to sell fruit and pastries. When I questioned his right to stop me, he grabbed my cart by the handle and knocked it over, spilling all the juices and cakes I had spent hours preparing. I screamed for help but he just laughed. I remember his words, 'You think the cops are gonna go runnin' after one Spic jis' 'cause he put the clamps on another Spic? Wise up honey…those guys with the badges and pistols work for the gringos, not for us.' With that he turned around and headed into town, but not before giving me a warning. 'I'll be back tomorra,' he said, 'Don't bother comin' here unless yir ready to do business with me. And that goes for every corner in this neighborhood. I've been assigned this area and nobody does business here without my say-so.'"

When Esmeralda pauses to catch her breath, her husband, still standing by her side, reaches down and strokes her neck. "That's when things really got ugly, isn't it?" he offers. "Yes," she replies, barely audible now. Wordlessly she shakes her head…as if trying to erase the past. "Maybe I shouldn't have told Willie what happened, but how else was I to explain that I couldn't go back to that corner anymore."

"You had to tell him," he replies reassuringly. "If you hadn't, someone else would have. You can't keep that sort of thing a secret."

"I knew that my brother had a temper but I never thought he'd do what he did. The next morning he insisted that I go back to that corner…cart and all…and wait for the drug dealer to come. The plan was for him to hide behind a big truck that was parked nearby…and come out when I gave a signal. The signal we agreed on was simple. As soon as the drug man approached me, I was to brush back my hair with my left hand…and keep doing it until I saw Willie come out from behind the truck. When I asked my brother what he planned to do next, he said he wasn't sure. He'd wait until he saw the dealer before deciding how to handle things."

At this point, Anna turns to Santé and whispers, "I never got to know my uncle. He died several years before I was born."

"Yes," says Esmeralda, responding to the whisper. "It's a shame because Willie would have been good to you. He loved children and he was always inventing games for the kids to play. He was kind to me too. Such a shame."

Mr. Erickson gives his wife's neck a gentle squeeze. "But tell Santé what happened when the drug dealer appeared."

Esmeralda sighs and takes a deep breath. "As planned, when I gave the signal, Willie came out from behind the truck. By the time he reached the cart, I could see that he had a stick in his hand. He first looked at me, then tilted his head toward the other man. When I nodded, indicating he's the one, he grabbed the dealer by the shirt and shouted something in his face…I can't remember what. But it was enough to startle the dealer who pulled a knife from his pocket and pointed it at my brother. Before I could call for help, Willie raised his stick and brought it down hard on the man's hand. The knife fell to the ground as the man screamed in pain. I knew enough to pick up the knife and get behind my brother. Right away the dealer backed away, mumbled some kind of swear word and fled down the street."

"But wasn't that dangerous for your brother, Senora?" Santé asks. "If the drug person was part of a gang, they might come after him."

"Well yes, Santé, they did come after him. I was afraid to go back out on the corner so I stayed home all the next day, helping with the kids. It was early in the afternoon when I heard a car drive up to the trailer. When I went to the window I saw four men get out and head for our front door. I yelled for Willie to run…but that was foolish of me since the trailer only had one door. Instead he went into the kitchen and got a large knife, then came back and locked the door. When I tried to phone the police, he pushed me aside and told me to go into the backroom and hide under a bed."

"I did as I was told. It was from under the bed that I first heard the knocking…then the shots…three of them. One of them apparently went through the lock, the other two through my brother, one in the middle of his chest, the other in his forehead. He was lying by the open door, the knife by his side, his face smeared with blood when I finally came out to see what happened."

"Mom, you never told me the whole story. Such a terrible way to die…and he was just trying to protect you."

"Yes (*weeping*). He couldn't stand being bullied by anyone, especially when I was involved. Even when we were kids back in Honduras, he got after anyone who tried to hurt me. I always felt safe while he was around… (*pause*)…until we moved here."

Santé asks, "Did you call the police?"

"Yes…but just as everyone told me, they only came once to see the body. They never even asked me what the dealer man looked like. I tried to tell them but I didn't know enough English back then to be of help. When I tried using Spanish, they said they didn't understand me and walked away…(*pause*)…The priest was the only one outside the family who came to the funeral."

No one speaks for several minutes.

"So what did you do after that?" Anna asks finally.

"I stayed in the trailer but didn't dare setting up my cart again. I was sure the drug man had friends who would come after me. I knew I had to make some money, so I answered an ad in the newspapers…an ad for a house cleaner. And that's the way I met your father."

Anna smiles. "I knew that you met through an ad but I didn't know everything leading up to that. So you started out as Daddy's house cleaner and…

"…ended up his wife. Yes. He saved my life. The person who was closest to me in the whole world was dead. There was no one I could lean on. If your father hadn't come along, I don't know what might have happened to me. He picked me up from the gutter."

Anna turns to her father. "So you felt sorry for Mom…especially after hearing about how her brother died?"

Mr. Erickson shakes his head. "Actually, she didn't tell me the whole story until after we were married."

"Yes," says Esmeralda, "I was afraid that it might frighten him if I told him my brother was murdered by drug dealers."

"I suppose it could have given me doubts," replies the husband, "but I think my concern for your mother's situation would have won me over in the end. I pride myself on my desire to help people who are in trouble…financially, legally or some other way. My parents were always reaching out to others and I have tried to assimilate their values into my own life. But sure, some of that concern played a part in falling love with your mother…although it's hard to say how much. Her beauty and personality were important too."

Anna's face takes on a strained look. "Do you think that same desire to help others was the reason you went into sociology?"

"Certainly. When concern for others is one of your primary values, it tends to affect everything you do. You can't isolate it…you know, apply to one person or one group of persons. If it's genuine, it can't help playing a part in all of your relationships."

"Even me?" says Anna, mischievously.

"Of course," he answers, taking her more seriously than she intended. "I am very concerned about you right now, Anna. You're at that stage in life when you want your freedom but you're not mature enough to act wisely… (*pause*)…There are things going on right now that I'm frankly worried about. For example, I don't like the idea of your driving around with Santé when he doesn't have a bona fide driver's license. That could get both of you in trouble."

"If we get married some day," Anna replies quickly, "he could get a driver's license, a passport, a Social Security number…lots of things like that."

The father stiffens. "I hope you're not thinking of doing something ridiculous, Anna. Use your head for God's sake. You've only known each other for a month."

Anna forces a weak smile. "It's been six weeks, Daddy."

Sensing the tension, Esmeralda issues a hasty call to dinner. "Anna, come help me serve. Everything is ready."

Throughout the meal of tacos doreados, arroz integral, ensalata and lemonade, Santé does his best to maintain a low profile. To this end, he says little and keeps his answers brief. Mr. Erickson, however, insists on making him the focus of attention. "Tell me Santé, have many of your friends in Oaxaca come to the United States?"

Santé hesitates, swallows his food, then answers carefully. "Yes, Senor, it is very hard to find work in Oaxaca. Here in El Norte there is good opportunity for jobs."

"I understand…but they're not coming for the jobs per se, are they? Isn't it really for the things that they hope to buy…you know, things like cars, clothes, a nice apartment, TV's and so on?"

"But Daddy, what's the difference?", Anna interjects.

Mr. Erickson stiffens. "The typical immigrant is not here because he's interested in a career…job satisfaction, self-fulfillment…that sort of thing. He's here for one purpose only…to make money so he can buy the things he's heard about on TV or magazine ads."

"I don't see anything wrong with that," says Esmeralda softly. "Do you?"

"Besides, Santé really does want a career," Anna adds. "The only reason he needs the money is to pay for college."

"And to send money back to my family," Santé says quickly. "They cannot pay rent and buy food without my help."

"Well, yes. I understand all that," Mr. Erickson continues. "But none of you are getting my point." Like the debater who is about to launch a winning argument, he leans forward, his lips curled into a self-congratulatory smile. "Santé may be an exception, but most immigrants come here…illegally I should add…because they crave the things they've heard about back in Mexico. Sure, they're frustrated and willing to make great sacrifices to get here. But what if they had never seen pictures of Americans driving beautiful cars or lounging outside their swimming pools? Don't you think they're frustrated because they've heard that other people have these things?"

Anna frowns. "I don't understand. What are you driving at?"

Mr. Erickson leans back in his chair. "There's a concept in sociology that goes by the name of 'reference group'. It's the people you turn to for opinions, for ideas about how to speak and dress, for notions of right and wrong…and most importantly for assessing your own status in life. In the past the typical Mexican used his fellow Mexicans as his reference group. When he did so, he saw lots of people just as poor as he was."

Not bothering to conceal her frustration, Anna interjects, "So, he didn't mind being poor. Is that what you're saying, Daddy?"

"Well, yes. You could say that. But look at the situation today. Somewhere in Mexico or Central America a boy walks past a store with a big TV in the window. Assume for a moment that he lives in a one-room shack with neither a kitchen nor an inside bathroom. All cooking is done outside over a tiny wood fire; all cleaning…utensils as well as personal hygiene…is done with cold water from a pipe located somewhere behind the house. Assume further that at night he sleeps on the floor, separated from the dirt by no more than a piece of cardboard carton. He stands there now, dazzled by what he sees on the TV screen…people sleeping on beautiful mattresses, cooking on electric stoves, drinking orange juice from refrigerators, eating ice cream and prepared dinners from freezers, driving to work in new cars with CDs playing, eating shrimp, steak and fresh salads in fancy restaurants. Compare all that now with a different boy…one who has never seen a TV ad…a boy of the same age who has no idea that El Norte and all its baubles even exists. I ask you…which boy is going to be more frustrated; which boy will be unhappier with his present existence?"

No one answers for over a minute. Anna shakes her head, then turns to face her father. "So, you're saying that the poor people of Mexico would be happy if they just stopped watching American programs on TV?"

"Well, I prefer to see it in more abstract terms. The frustration of Mexico's poor…the frustration that drives them to come here illegally…can be traced to the fact that they have chosen American culture as their basic reference group…a tragic choice in my opinion."

"When you say they've chosen Americans as their reference point, you mean instead of choosing other Mexicans?"

"Precisely. If they compared themselves to other Mexicans instead of to Americans, they wouldn't be so frustrated. It's all a matter of perspective."

"I'm not sure I agree with that," Anna replies tersely, "but even if you're right, what can we do about it?"

Mr. Erickson tightens his lips. "I don't think there's anything we can do about it now. It's too late. The genie is out of the bottle."

Esmeralda turns to Santé. In little more than a whisper, she says, "You haven't said anything, Santé. I'm interested in what you think of my husband's ideas."

Santé gulps before answering. "Well, I don't know Senora. In my family, we are hungry most of the time. We know that from our bellies. We don't need American television to make us want food. But maybe when it comes to cars and nice houses, the Senor is right. If we not know that other people have them, we might not think about them."

Mr. Erickson smiles. "I like Santé's reasoning. The reference group theory probably doesn't apply when you're talking about basics like food…things that you can't survive without. But even here, I think the group you usually compare yourself to can make a difference. For example, how long are you going to be satisfied with tortillas and beans when you hear about places up north where people eat meat three times a day. Sure, we all need food no matter what, but the kind of food we see others eating is bound to have an effect on how satisfied we are with what's on our own plate."

Anna rises and heads for the bathroom. At the doorway, she turns and hurls a final question at her father. "So you're saying…what…that the best way to keep Latinos from coming here is to stop them from viewing any TV programs, magazines, books or newspapers that show life in the United States. Keep the natives in the dark. Don't let them know there's a different and possibly better way to live up here. Who knows, they just might want it for themselves."

The father smiles but says nothing.

Esmeralda hurriedly offers dessert…a homemade flan…but there are no takers.

After a few minutes of awkward conversation in the living room, Santé thanks his hosts for dinner and prepares to leave. Just outside the door, he is surprised to feel Anna's hand on his arm. "Daddy can be a real stinker at times," she whispers. "I'm sorry you had to suffer through all that. But I wouldn't take it too seriously if I were you. It's the professor in him. He loves to theorize about life based on what he's read in books. Trouble is, his ideas don't have much to do with how people really live."

Santé rubs her hand in appreciation. "It's O.K.…he's a very smart man. I hope I can be smart too someday."

"Hmm. I think you're already pretty smart."

"Not really. I have much to learn."

"You're smart enough to know that I love you…yes?"

Santé smiles and pulls her close. "I am a lucky fellow. Someday you be my wife…yes?"

"I promise."

21

An Unexpected Ally

As Earl heads for the office door, his secretary, wary of his dark mood, asks, "Where you headin' this time, Chief?" Without stopping, he replies, "It's a personal matter. If you need me, I'll be over at the Maricopa TV repair shop." Head down, he slams the door and walks briskly to his cruiser.

On the way over, his driving is erratic, even reckless. At an intersection he narrowly misses a school bus as he races to beat a red light. He knows he should be a model driver but he can't help it. The only thing that matters right now is Eric and the Latino kid who has taken his place at the repair shop. "Just think," he muses as he weaves his way through traffic, "I give Don a break last year…probably save him several hundred bucks…and what's he do to thank me….he fires my kid and gives the job to some Mex who probably dropped outta school in fifth grade and can't speak a word of English. Goddamn it…it's traitors like Don that are ruining this country. How do we stop stuff like that? I dunno…maybe take his business away…or put 'im in jail. That would teach 'im not to go messin' around with migrants."

"Now, if I can just get my hands on some evidence…."

Meanwhile, Paula has been going around in a foul mood, unable to get anything done, either in the house or out in the shop. Twice this morning Don has commented on her petulance only to get upbraided for his remarks. "Whatever it is that's buggin' you," he snarls finally, "I wish to hell you'd take it out on somebody else." When she turns her back without responding, he heads into the apartment, leaving the shop to her. Alone finally, she goes behind the desk, sits down in the swivel chair, and folds her hands. She breathes slowly, hoping to keep the memory of last night at bay. Within seconds, images of Santé and Anna return to disrupt her peace. She can see them clearly all over again…Anna lying seductively on the bed, Santé hovering over her like a love-sick poodle. She sighs…how could he…?

Her reverie is suddenly broken as the Sheriff bursts into the office. "Where's your husband?" he asks in a loud voice, not bothering to preface it with a greeting.

"Out back," she answers, disregarding the coarseness of his question. They stare at each other without speaking before she asks, "What can I do for you, Sheriff?"

Earl hesitates before answering. Her demeanor strikes him as strange… somehow different…less hostile perhaps. This is not what he was expecting. On previous occasions she not only protested his visit but warned him she would go to the Attorney General's Office if he continued to harass them. There is no sign of that hostility now; if anything, her smile contains a trace of warmth. He ponders the situation for a minute, steps forward, then says, "Just thought I'd check in…see if they're any new developments."

Paula comes out from behind the desk to shake hands. "Well," she says, smiling again, "yes, a few things have changed. You know the boy we've taken on as an apprentice…he's doing just fine. We've decided to rent our spare room to him…at least until he gets on his feet."

"You're not payin' him anything I hope," Earl protests.

"Oh no. I think he has another job here in town…doing carpentry work or something. They must be paying him real good 'cause he just bought a used pickup. It's out in the lot right now."

"Sounds a little fishy to me," Earl responds. "How'd he save up enough money for a truck so fast?"

"I dunno. Probably put a few bucks down…and got a car loan for the rest. Or he mighta bought it from a friend…I haven't asked him."

Earl steps back as if to leave. "I hope he knows enough to get it inspected."

She looks around to see if her husband is listening from the doorway. Reassured that he isn't, she continues. "I'm pretty sure he hasn't. I looked this morning and didn't see any sticker on the windshield."

Earl's eyes light up. "How long has he had it?"

"He got it three days ago."

"By law, he's got 10 days," Earl replies, still curious about this abrupt change in her behavior.

"I don't think he even has a license," she adds, "unless he bought a fake one somewhere."

"Hmm," he says. "This kid could be headin' for a heap of trouble."

"I guess if he's driving without a sticker, you have the right to pick him up. And then…"

Earl interrupts. "You betcha. So…keep me posted. Call me if you see an inspection sticker on his windshield."

"I'll check every day."

Paula returns to her chair and sighs openly. The image of Santé in bed with Anna has receded, replaced now by a police cruiser with lights flashing…a pickup pulled over…a boy fumbling for his license. She smiles just as Don comes into the office. "You feelin' better?" he asks timidly. "Much better," she says. "Sorry I was so ornery before. It must have been something I ate last night."

When Earl still hasn't heard after a week, he leaves his cruiser at the station and drives his personal car to Paula's shop where he slides into an empty space in the parking lot. Sitting alone in the car, he resumes speculating on Paula's shift in attitude. "What the hell happened?" he asks, enjoying the luxury of such a question. "Maybe he stole something from the shop… or got caught goin' through her jewelry. I dunno…but something important happened to make her angry at him."

Checking his watch, he gets up and walks to the apartment door in back. Paula greets him with the same warmth as last time in the shop. When the

Sheriff asks about the Mexican boy's pickup, she shakes her head…"Not yet Sheriff, at least as far as I know…but he could be getting it inspected today."

"Do you know where he is right now? Earl asks.

"Most likely at the library…studying with his new girlfriend."

Earl is too concentrated on the inspection sticker to detect the sarcasm in her voice. Without any further questions, he turns, thanks her for the information and leaves.

At the library, Santé is anxious to tell Anna about the new truck. When he has finished describing it, she asks if he has had it inspected yet. He says no…and is surprised when she tells him there's a ten day grace period for getting a sticker. If he doesn't have it by then, he is in violation and can be picked up by the police.

"How many days has it been so far?" she asks, trying to conceal her anxiety.

Santé closes his eyes to count. "Oh God," he announces after an agonizing few seconds. "Today is the last day. I can't let 'em pull me over. If they catch me they'll find out I'm illegal and send me back to Mexico. I gotta go right now."

He leaps to his feet and heads for the door. "Wait," cries Anna. "Let me tell you where the nearest garage is. They don't all do inspections."

As he pulls out of the library parking lot, he is too frightened to notice the gray Buick following him. The only thing he is concerned with is getting to the garage before it closes. Over and over he checks his odometer to make sure he's not speeding. "Jis' another coupla miles," he whispers. "I'm almost there." Finally, he spots the garage sign. Just as Anna said, it's around the corner from Walmart, over on the left. Crossing over, he noses his pickup into an empty bay and goes looking for a mechanic.

Earl, just 25 yards behind, pulls up and parks across the street. As he sits there watching movements in and out of the two bays, thoughts of Eric return. "That sonofabitich Don…he never gave my kid a chance. I don't care what he says…I know goddamn well he kicked Eric out so he could hire that kid in the garage for $3.00 an hour. That's Don…anything for a buck…but maybe it's the whole goddamn country…I dunno…maybe I'm the odd man out. But if I can nail this kid for drivin' without an inspection sticker, then I can demand to see his driver's license. Once we haul him in, we can ask him all kinds of questions…like where he got the money to buy the pickup and whether Don checked his documents before hiring him." He pauses, eyes still on the garage, then breaks into a huge grin. "If we can get the kid to admit that the repair shop is payin' him, we can hit Don with a big fat fine. Once that prick has been convicted, he'll have a record and go to jail if he ever tries it again."

Satisfied with his line of reasoning, Earl settles back into his seat and lights up a cigarette. Within seconds the bay door rises and Santé emerges in his pickup. Without waiting, Earl turns on the ignition and prepares to follow. When Santé comes out onto the right-hand lane, Earl leans forward to check the pickup's windshield.

It's not what he was hoping for. There it is…a brand new inspection sticker near the bottom of the glass on the driver's side. The boy looks relieved as he makes a left turn and heads back to the repair shop. Earl slumps back into his seat, takes a final puff on his cigarette and throws the butt out the window. In a futile attempt to mask his frustration, he turns on the car radio. It's a mariachi song…replete with grito Mexicano yelling. In disgust he reaches for the knob to turn it off. The move is so violent that the knob breaks off and falls to the car floor. He kicks it to the passenger side and fills the air with a burst of ethnic slurs that can be heard half-way down the street. With a final shake of his head, he jerks the steering wheel to the left and heads out into traffic.

22

Trouble on the Highway

In a deserted parking lot across the street from the El Jardin restaurant, Santé and Anna are enjoying their first chance to be together in the pickup. "Shall we have some music?" Santé asks, caressing her cheek. "That would be nice," she answers. As they both reach for the radio, their hands meet. She entwines his hand in hers…and squeezes gently. Together they push the button…and fall back, unwilling to let go of each other. As their hands…his right, her left…come to rest on the emergency brake, Santé leans toward her shoulder, still uncertain what might be acceptable. Sensing his hesitancy, she places her free hand on his neck and pulls him toward her. Their lips are now just inches apart. Santé's whole body begins trembling at the boldness of her move. She feels his agitation and pulls him even closer. As their lips meet, she opens her mouth just enough to trace the curvature of his lips with her tongue. Stifling a gasp of surprise, he grasps her tongue between his lips and moans softly. She makes no attempt to pull away.

Suddenly the truck door is yanked open and Santé is dragged out onto the blacktop by a husky Hispanic man brandishing a knife. When Santé attempts to get to his feet, the man kicks him back down and tells him to stay there. Anna, still seated in the truck, watches in horror, torn now between wanting to help Santé and the desire to flee. She is shaken from her inertia when Santé suddenly yells, "The macuahuitl." Nothing registers until she remembers that Santé keeps his weapon on a rack just behind the driver's seat. Quickly she reaches behind her, grabs it by the handle and flings it out the door. It falls at the assailant's feet. When Santé dives for it, the man quickly steps on it, then reaches down to grab it for himself. In doing so he seizes the weapon at the wrong end. His cry fills the parking lot as the obsidian blades slice into his fingers. When the weapon falls to the ground, Santé sees his chance and lunges forward. The assailant, pressing his hand to his shirt to staunch the flow of blood, whirls just in time to deliver a kick to Santé's side. From the truck, Anna watches helplessly as Santé falls back, then curls into a fetal position, clutching his side. The man kicks the macuahuitl aside, then secures the knife between his teeth. Satisfied that the boy is no longer a threat, he reaches into his pocket for a handkerchief, wraps it around his bleeding hand and races for the truck.

As Santé looks on helplessly, the intruder jumps into the driver's seat and pokes the knife into Anna's side. She screams, then reaches for the door handle. Before she can escape, he hits the door lock next to the driver's arm rest and turns on the ignition. Within seconds the truck is careening out of the parking lot onto Highway 54, heading toward the Cactus Preserve just west of town.

Anna is about to cry out, "What do you want with me?" when she realizes the futility of her question and lapses into silence. "I'm going to be raped, that's for sure," she whispers to herself. "At least he's going to try. With his knife pressed against my side, what can I do?" Alternately frantic and determined, she gropes for a plan.

Tucked away in her purse is a cell phone, programmed to reach Santé at the touch of a button. If she has any chance of escape, this is it. To use it she will need to be alone, at least for a minute. The first step is to secure the phone. Without moving either head or legs, she reaches into her purse and pulls it out, turns off the ringer, then slides it under her dress. As if reading her mind, the driver turns toward her and shouts, "Gimme the purse." She hands it over and watches as he goes through the contents with his free hand. Satisfied there is nothing of value there, he tosses it out the window.

Shortly thereafter they make a left turn off the highway into a wooded area flanked by an official sign that says Maricopa Cactus Preserve. With their location now established, Anna silently rehearses what to say if she can break away. Alerting the police is not an option since that would mean involving Santé and his truck. Though innocent of any wrongdoing, he would be forced to reveal his illegal status and most likely get sent back to Mexico. No, there is only call to make. Silently she lips the words: "Santé, it's me…still in your truck. We're in the Cactus Preserve. Come quickly."

Back in the parking lot, Santé gets to his feet and races for the restaurant and a phone. But what can he tell the police other than the make of his truck and the numbers on his license plate? He has no idea where they're going other than west on Route 54. Still, it's his only chance to save Anna from being raped, possibly murdered. A few yards short of the restaurant door, he stops to catch his breath. As he stands there, watching customers come and go, he considers the consequences of what he is about to do. If the police find the truck, they will search for the registration and driver's license. One way or another Santé will be called in for questioning. When they determine that he is undocumented, he is certain to be sent back to Oaxaca. That means not seeing Anna again…and no more engineering degree. Sure, he can try crossing again but with two misdemeanors on his record, one for crossing illegally the first time and another for driving without a license, he will probably face jail time if he is picked up again.

In his frenzied state he stumbles over a ring of stones bordering a bed of flowers. As he does so the cell phone in his shirt pocket falls out. He shakes his head in amazement that he could have forgotten about something so important. Hastily he clicks on Anna's number and waits. The phone rings but there is no answer. He tries again. Same thing happens. His mind fills now with images of Anna's being stripped naked and violated. Then what …perhaps to cover his tracks the man will try to kill her. She will put up a fight, of that he can be sure…but to what end when he is so much bigger and armed with a knife?

In the car the man looks back to make sure he is not being followed, then heads for the darkest part of the Preserve, the part where dozens of giant saguaros are bunched together near a natural spring. He parks, then looks around to see if there's anyone else there. Reassured they are alone, he turns to Anna, "O.K., take off that blouse. I wanta see whatcha got underneath."

When Anna responds by clutching the blouse, he leans over and slices it open with his knife. The point of the knife cuts through her bra as well, leaving one of her nipples exposed. When he bends to take it in his mouth, she pushes him away, forcefully enough so that the back of his head hits the windshield. "Lookit, you little cunt," he shouts, rubbing his head, "you do that again and you won't get outta here alive. Now take off your skirt before I have to cut it off."

He is close enough now that she can smell the stale whiskey on his breath. Even in the dark, she can make out the contours of his face, can even see the whites of his eyes. He is probably in his forties, maybe fifties, definitely Hispanic. She listens carefully to his words, hoping to identify what part of Mexico or Central American he is from…but gives up when her knowledge of ethnic Spanish proves inadequate.

By now she realizes that fighting back physically is not going to work… not with this man at least. But there may be another way. Pretending to acquiesce in his demand, she begins pulling up her skirt. When it reaches her thighs, he moves closer, sliding his hand first up her leg, then to her knee. "That feels nice," she says in a hoarse whisper. "Don't stop." He smiles at this unexpected sign of surrender. Determined to conceal her fear, she smiles and readies herself for what is coming next. When, as expected, he pulls her panties aside and begins massaging her labia, she utters a soft lament. "My titties are feeling neglected."

He hesitates, one hand still gripping the knife. When she playfully cups a breast and offers it to him, he begins to withdraw his hand from her crotch. "Oh no," she cries, "I need both." As predicted, he drops the knife and does what she asks, using one hand to squeeze her breast while the other continues playing with her vagina. Although still a virgin, Anna instinctively knows how to fake arousal with her breathing. He is quick to respond. The minute he unbuckles his belt, she whispers seductively in his ear, "Wouldn't you like me to do you first?"

"Yeah, why not."

Inwardly trembling but outwardly cool, she forces her lips to say something she never dreamed possible. "Lie down on your back and I'll pull your pants off for you."

To a man who, unknown to any of his previous victims, uses force not as an end in itself but as a bid for affection, the warmth of her voice is irresistible. He does as he is told and lies back on the driver's seat with bare legs outstretched on Anna's lap. When he reaches down for the knife, Anna grabs his hand and places it on her thigh, then retrieves the fallen knife. When he tries to sit up, she moves his hand closer to her sex. He falls back, too intent on the pleasures that await him to worry about where the knife landed. As he lifts his hips in anticipation of entering her, she leans closer now, gripping the knife tightly in her right hand. Her breathing is rapid and heavy. When he hears it, he says playfully, "You're turned on, aren't you." Relieved that he can't tell the difference, she answers with a throaty 'yes'. To control her trembling, she squeezes the knife more tightly and raises it above his body. It is too dark for him to notice. No longer concerned about his safety, he guides her hand to his erect member and closes his eyes. She gives him a little squeeze.

Horror at what she is about to do raises questions about the ethics of self-defense, questions that are quickly resolved when she recalls how the positions were reversed just minutes ago. Still trembling, she fights back a tear. Then, convinced of his helplessness and at the mercy of her instincts, she lifts the blade high above his head and drives it into his outstretched neck.

As blood spurts from an artery, splashing her face and chest, she pulls away in horror, drops the knife and reaches for the passenger door handle. Once outside, she begins running toward the highway only to realize that she has left her cell phone in the truck. How else is she going to call Santé? She stands immobilized as fear and reason fight for control. When reason prevails, she runs back and opens the door. The phone is tucked into the crack at the rear of the passenger's seat. She reaches in to pick it up, then shudders when she hears him breathing. She looks into the driver's seat. To her surprise, he is sitting up and hanging onto the steering wheel. She turns and runs, clutching the phone in her hand. When she hears the truck door open again, she stops to look back. He is coming toward her, holding a handkerchief to his neck. She muffles a scream and stumbles forward. Racing toward the highway, her blouse half torn and bra hanging loose, she enters Santé's code on her phone and holds it to her ear.

Still outside the restaurant, Santé paces up and down, frantically searching for answers, his mind bobbing back and forth like a horse resisting a halter. A young couple stops to look, clearly concerned but hesitant to interfere. Sensing how he looks, he forces himself to slow down and take a deep breath. When a final attempt to call Anna fails, he decides to take his chances with the police. With the device in his hand and finger hovering over the 9, the phone unexpectedly rings. A startled look at the keypad tells him it's Anna.

Her breathing is labored. "It's me…don't hang up. I'm on the road coming out of the Preserve. He's chasing me. I stabbed him in the neck but he can still run. Oh Santé…he's getting closer. Should I try hiding in the woods? It's dark…maybe…oh, I don't know. I'm a mess…my clothes are all ripped and I'm covered with his blood."

Santé holds his breath before responding. "Anna, thank God it's you. I am so worried. But no, don't go in the woods. He'll hear you talkin' to me." He pauses to think. "If you make it to the highway, I can pick you up there."

"But how?" she cries, looking back at her pursuer. "Your truck is here in the Preserve."

"I'll get a taxi. There might be one outside the restaurant. Keep runnin', but don't hang up. I'll leave mine on too."

Scarcely breathing, he rushes to the front of the restaurant where he begins flagging down anything that looks like it might be a taxi. In less than a minute a real one pulls up at the front door and discharges two passengers. Santé immediately jumps in and pulls the door shut. When he sees that the driver is Latino, he blurts out in Spanish, "It's an emergency…head for the entrance to Highway 54, just north of Iona. My girlfriend has been kidnapped."

The driver wrinkles his nose. "Hey man, I don't want no trouble. Why don't you call the police? That's what they for, ain't it?"

Santé pauses for a few seconds before answering, then decides to take the risk. "I'm an illegal…Santé Aguilera…from Oaxaca …they'll send me back to Mexico if I ask for their help."

The driver nods. "O.K. Me Francisco. I know what you mean. That happened to my cousin…he got in a fight…(*pause*)… entrance to 54, right?"

"Yeah, the one goin' south. Just below Iona."

Before shifting into first, the driver turns to get a better look at his passenger. He's startled at what he sees. "Hey Santé, what's that thing you got across your knees?"

Santé smiles. "It's what I'm gonna use to take that guy's head off. Don't worry. I promise not to use it on you."

On the road out of the Preserve, two figures can be seen running…a girl in front with no more than half a blouse clinging to her chest, the other, twenty feet behind, a man holding a bloody handkerchief to his neck with one hand while gripping a knife in the other.

"Santé, he's still coming…but not so close now. I think he's losing blood. If I can just get to the highway, I can hitch a ride and… "

"No, Anna. That's too dangerous. You say your clothes are ripped and you covered with blood. You don't know who might pick you up. Wait for me…I'll be there in ten minutes."

Just ahead she can see the highway. She turns to take a last look at her pursuer and races the last 25 yards. Reassured that he is not gaining on her, she stops at the end of the road to catch her breath. It is still early evening and there are cars and trucks passing every ten seconds or so. Slowly she begins walking south along on the shoulder, turning every few seconds to see if her assailant is coming. When she sees him emerging onto the highway, she lets out a muted cry and begins to run again. He seems closer now; she can see the knife in his right hand. When she tries to pick up her pace, she stumbles on a discarded tire tread. Aware that her only escape lies in hitching a ride, she begins waving frantically to every car that passes. A Toyota RAV4 passes without stopping, then a Taurus, then an old Chevy pickup truck. Each time she waves, she is forced to slow down; each time she slows down, the man with the knife creeps closer.

Two more cars pass before an 18-wheeler honks and pulls over to the side of the road 50 yards ahead. Still clutching her cell phone, she races to reach the open door, pausing just long enough to read the writing on the side of the truck: 'Putnam's Furniture'. As she pulls the door tight, the man with the knife, now only 15 yards away, screams an obscenity. In a final paroxysm of rage he lunges forward, then falls to the ground, grasping his neck.

"Where you goin', honey?" the driver asks as the truck heads back onto the highway. "You don't exactly look like yir headin' for a party." His voice is warm, almost fatherly; his accent has the earmarks of a Mid-Western background. The effortless way he maneuvers the shift with one hand and the wheel with another suggest a man who has been driving the nation's highways for many years. Carefully he slides the truck into the right lane, forcing the stream of cars to make way. His eyes are aimed straight ahead which allows her to study his profile. She can see that his lips are full and sensuous, his nose bulbous…with hints of the purple coloring that comes with age. She guesses him to be somewhere in his early fifties.

Aware of her interest, he repeats his question. "I asked ya where yir goin'. It looks like you been in some kinda trouble."

"Yes," she answers. "I was attacked by a man back in the Cactus Preserve. I was lucky to get away…thanks to you. Now I should report it to the police…(*pause*)…Can you drop me off somewhere in town so I can take a taxi home?" As she speaks, she clutches the cell phone at her side.

He says nothing but continues to stare at the car in front.

"Well, can you?" she persists. "My parents will be worried if I don't show up soon." She struggles to appear cool but is betrayed by the wobbliness in her voice. As a man with a long list of conquests, he is not easily fooled. He smiles at her innocence. While outwardly concentrating on the traffic, he allows himself a private chuckle. "She might just as well have said it outright: 'I can tell you want me and I am scared.'"

When he finally turns to look at her, his eyes are fixed on her breasts. Unlike most males Anna knows from school, he makes no attempt to conceal his interest. Equally frightening, his breathing is now noticeably heavier. As he alternates between watching the highway and studying her breasts, his right hand, the shift hand, slides to the top of the gear box and remains there. Still, he says nothing. To Anna his silence is more menacing than if he were shouting at her. With an eye on his hand, now just inches away, she pulls the remains of her blouse together and inches toward the door. To be on the safe side, she reaches for her phone, turns it off and tucks it under her skirt. She has but one thought now…to get out of the truck and call Santé.

That opportunity comes minutes later when the driver pulls into an abandoned rest area. With the motor still running, he rolls down his window to look around. Convinced that no one else is there, he turns to Anna and grabs her by the wrist. When he tries to drag her into the sleeping compartment in back, she yanks her arm free and pulls the door open. Still clutching her phone, she steps down onto the running board and jumps out. A few feet away is a ditch, still muddy from the previous night's rain. She leaps over, then immediately dials Santé's number.

Santé's phone rings near the entrance to the Cactus Preserve. He presses the phone to his ear. "Anna…where are you?"

"Santé…I've just gotten out of a truck heading south on 54, a few miles below the Preserve. The man who picked me up attacked me. I managed to escape before he could pull me into the sleeping area. I've just crossed a little gully…it's all woods here…best I can tell, there's a hill just ahead… (*pause*)…Oh my God, he just got out of the truck and is heading this way. I can see his legs beneath the truck. Hurry Santé. He's coming after me."

"What kinda truck is it…like, how big?"

"Very big…an 18-wheeler I think."

"Whose truck is it…you know, is there a sign on it?"

"It says Putnam's Furniture. I don't know if there's any writing on the back though."

"O.K. I'm in a taxi and we jis' passed the Preserve Rd…gonna be there in a few minutes."

"Please hurry, Santé. I'm really frightened."

"I come pronto, Anna. But if he follows you into the woods, better we don't talk. He will hear you and know where you are."

"I'll whisper…please don't turn your phone off."

"O.K."

Within minutes, Santé spots the truck over in the rest area. He leans over and grabs his macuahuitl as the driver eases into the exit with lights dimmed. "Over there," Santé shouts. "Pull up just behind the truck." The minute the taxi stops, Santé jumps out and runs to the truck. When he sees that no one is there, he runs back to the taxi, asks him to wait, and heads for the hill. As soon as he crosses the ditch, he sets the macuahuitl down, then pulls the phone from his pocket and holds it to his ear. "Anna, I'm here. Where are you?"

"Thank God, Santé," comes the whispered response. "I'm part way up the hill. Over to the left of the truck. I can't see him but I can hear him coming."

"How close is he?"

"I think maybe 20 or 30 yards from where I'm hiding. I don't think he knows where I am yet. He seems to be looking all around. What should I do? Shall I stay here and hope he doesn't find me…or get up and make my way back down the hill? It's so dark now…I'd have to feel my way. I don't know."

"No Anna. Don't git up. If you come down the hill, he's gonna hear you. Right now he doesn't know where you are. So, stay there…Let me think."

(*Barely audible*) "O.K."

A minute passes without further communication. Then, suddenly, Santé is on the phone again. "Anna, don't speak. I know what to do now. Hang up but leave the phone on, then set it on the ground. When I call you, he's gonna hear the ring and start movin' toward you. Leave the phone there and start crawlin' down the hill toward the highway. I'm in the woods now…so I'll hear the ring too. I'll try to git to 'im before he finds the phone, O.K.?"

"Yes. But…"

"Hang up now."

When Anna hangs up, Santé immediately dials her number. From somewhere higher up in the woods, he hears the familiar ring tone and starts crawling toward it. He is not the only one to hear it. Surprised by this stroke of luck, the driver smiles at his quarry's foolishness and hurries toward the sound.

Ducking under branches and feeling his way in the dark, Santé moves quickly up the hill. When he's within a few yards of the phone, he stands and listens. The ringing has stopped, leaving the woods shrouded in silence. Then…from the left, several yards above him…comes the snapping of twigs. Someone is approaching, someone too heavy to conceal his footsteps. Who else can it be but the driver, headed toward Anna's phone?

Like a mountain lion stalking a new-born fawn, the unseen intruder drops into a slouch and inches toward his prey. From a few feet away, Santé pauses to listen, then crawls forward until the footsteps are just above him. As another twig snaps, Santé grips his macuahuitl and prepares to swing.

Assured that he has found the spot where the phone was ringing, the driver drops to his hands and knees and begins feeling the ground for her body. "Where are you little one?", he murmurs. "Don't worry…Daddy won't hurt you." He moves slowly in a circle, then back again. Still nothing… no hand or foot…not even the sound of her breathing. He cocks his head and waits for her to move. The silence is suddenly broken by a rustling in the trees just below…an animal perhaps…or maybe the girl…he cannot be sure. With senses heightened, he crawls to where the phone was ringing, then stops to listen. The only thing to be heard is the hooting of an owl deep in the woods. Then…to his immediate right, just a few feet below, there's a sudden breaking of branches. On guard, he rises to look. Still seeing nothing, he turns around to look in the opposite direction. He hears something…but it is a different sound…softer, barely audible. Something is moving near his feet, something small…it's too small to be a person…more likely a mouse or other animal…hardly a cause for alarm. Still standing, he breathes a sigh of relief and turns back to where he first heard the breaking of branches. Nothing but silence now. Convinced it was an animal, a deer perhaps that has moved on, he cups his hands and calls gently, "Little girl, where are you?" He holds his breath to listen for footsteps or a whimper. Nothing…no rustling of leaves, no heavy breathing.

He looks around again. There is less light now. As evening slips into night, it is harder to see anything at all. In the enveloping darkness, the trucker's resolve weakens. "Is she really worth all this?" he asks. "Yeah, she's pretty and would make a great lay, but I don't want to get lost tryin' to find her, not here in the middle of the woods. Maybe it's time to give up this little adventure and return to the truck." For the first time since leaving the truck, he can feel his heart pounding.

Once his mind has been made up, he turns, pushes a branch to the side and heads down the hill. His eyes and ears are on high alert; his mind clear and concentrated. When a twig snaps loudly a few feet in front of him, he freezes. It's loud enough to be a deer, but surely no large animal would let him get this close. What can it be…a human…the girl…someone else? "Who's there?" he shouts, making no attempt to hide the terror in his voice. No response…nothing. As he stares into the dark, the forest sinks into silence, pulling all sound into its maw. He turns to look behind him.

Suddenly the stillness is shattered as three razor-sharp obsidian blades cut into his right leg. He screams and falls to the ground, grabbing his knee. When he feels warm blood, he reaches for a kerchief and presses it to the cut. It is only then that he looks around for the offending animal…or rock…or piece of glass. He sees nothing. Completely mystified, he sits and begins rubbing his leg to assuage the pain. There is no other sound now but the rubbing. All desire for the girl has vanished…all images of her nude body…all stratagems for forcing her submission…all fantasies about winning her consent…yield to the recognition that he is alone in the woods with what could be a broken leg. His throat tightens, making it difficult to swallow. He twists his neck to look behind him…then listens again. Still nothing. He looks to his left, then to his right.

Then suddenly…there's a stirring in the trees a few feet away. He turns quickly toward the sound. It is too dark to make out the form. All he sees is a man's back…and something hanging from his hand. When the man disappears into the woods, the driver reaches down to inspect his leg. To his horror, the kerchief is already saturated with blood. Fearful now of losing consciousness before he can reach his truck, he ties the kerchief into a tourniquet. Rising slowly, he begins stumbling down the hill. Although the truck is no more than 50 yards away, he is too weak to reach it. No more than half way down, he collapses in the bushes, still clutching his leg. When he faints, the tourniquet falls to the ground, releasing a new spurt of blood. In and out of consciousness, he lies there throughout the night, not to be found until his truck is reported missing the next day.

As Santé makes his way down through the trees, he begins calling Anna's name. Within seconds she responds. "I'm over here. Where are you?" When Santé bursts from the brush, she rushes to him. Once in his arms, she whispers, "Are you alright…are you alright?" He nods and hugs her tighter. They kiss frantically.

"Where is the driver?" she gasps.

"He's still up there," Santé answers. "But I don't think he'll be coming down anytime soon. I got him pretty good with the macuahuitl. But let's get out of here."

"But how?" she asks. "Your truck is back in the Preserve."

Santé nods. "I told the taxi driver to wait…(*pause*)…I hope he's still there."

Gingerly they make their way down the rest of the hill. Relieved when they spot the black and white cab behind the 18-wheeler, they dash for the rear door and jump in. "Francisco, I got her and she's not hurt," Santé shouts as he slaps the driver on the shoulder. "This is Anna, my girl friend. Anna, meet my new friend, Francisco."

"Hola, Anna?" he replies, turning his head and offering his hand. "Glad you O.K. But where is the truck driver?" As he speaks, his eyes fall on her naked nipple. Before he can look away, she quickly pulls the torn blouse together and covers her breasts with both hands.

"Still up there," comes Santé's response. "It was so dark…I don't think he saw me."

Francisco nods his approval and starts the engine. "How you do it…how you stop him. Was it that thing…the thing on the seat?"

"Yes," Santé replies, reaching over to stroke his weapon.

Anna cringes. "What did you do to him Santé…or shouldn't I ask?"

Santé shakes his head.

"So Santé, where you want to go?" interjects the driver. We go anywhere you want…on me, as gringos say."

"I think my pickup is back at the Preserve…at least I hope it is. But I want to pay you…I have money hidden in the truck."

"No problema, Senor. We be there in ten minutes."

As they move to the northbound lane, Anna suddenly points to the other side of the highway, "There…that's where the man with the knife was when I got into the truck. He yelled something and then fell down. But he's not there now…"

"Maybe the police picked him up," offers Santé.

"I don't know," says Anna. "He looked like he was losing a lot of blood… (*pause*)…I hope I didn't kill him."

"Maybe he go back for pickup," adds Francisco.

"Oh my God, I hope not," says Santé. "He could drive away and we'd be stuck here."

 A few minutes later, the taxi enters the Preserve, heading for the spot where Anna was held captive. About half-way there, she suddenly shouts. "Over there, look…it's the pickup…off the side of the road."

Even in the dark, it's clear that the truck has slipped off the road and hit a small tree. Francisco brings the cab to a stop and all three get out to inspect the accident. To be on the safe side, Santé grabs his macuahuitl. As they approach the pickup, Anna shouts, "There's no one inside…he must have fled."

Santé moves around in front of the pickup. "Look, Francisco, it's the right front fender. It musta buckled in on the tire when he hit the tree." He lays the macuahuitl on the ground.

"No problema," says Francisco. "Together we bend it back so you can drive home."

While Anna continues to look around, the two men take turns pulling on the fender until it is clear of the tire. From their cursory inspection, aside from a slight dent in the front bumper, nothing else seems wrong with the pickup.

"You O.K. now, amigo?" says Francisco, heading back to his taxi. "But before I go, maybe you better see if engine runs."

"Don't leave yet," Santé responds. I want to get you some money. It's in the truck."

As Santé picks up the macuahuitl and heads for the driver's door, Anna circles behind the truck and approaches from the passenger's side. Just as she grasps the door handle, an unseen hand grabs her by the throat and yanks her back into the woods. When the intruder stumbles and loosens his grip, she screams. "Anna," Santé shouts as he races around to the other side of the truck. Before he can get there, she feels the point of a knife pressed against her side. She screams again. To confirm her suspicions, she twists her head to see his face. As she stares into his eyes, the man, now with neck wrapped in blood-soaked t-shirt, jabs the knife into her side again, this time piercing the skin. "Help, Santé," she cries, grimacing. Within seconds Santé comes careening around the pickup, holding his weapon high, ready to strike. He stops when he sees the knife pressed against Anna's side.

"Get out of the way…over there," the man with the knife says, pointing to the other side of the road. When Santé remains standing, he adds, "Get out of the way or I'll run this knife through her side." When Santé backs up, he shouts, "Over there…on the other side of the road." It is clear now that the man wants Santé far enough away so that he can get in the pickup and drive away, holding Anna hostage.

Santé is unprepared for anything like this. Up to now all he has had to do was swing his macuahuitl and watch the enemy fall to the ground. This man is more menacing. With his neck dripping blood and eyes glazed over, he looks desperate enough to carry out his threat. So close to death himself, there is little left for him to lose. Santé frantically combs his mind for a solution but finds nothing. While instinct tells him to strike, reason advises caution. Yielding to the latter, he lowers his weapon and steps back.

From the front seat of his cab Francisco watches with increasing alarm. He can't hear what is being said but is close enough to see that the situation is spinning out of control. Aware that he must do something, he quietly opens the cab door and climbs out. Still unseen, he drops into a crouch and slips into the woods with the intent of circling around in back of the assailant. When he gets within a few yards of the man, he stops to pick up a tennis ball sized rock.

When Santé sees Francisco about to strike, he reacts instinctively; his mouth opens wide, his eyes flash surprise…clear signs to the assailant that someone is behind him. The man turns, pushes Anna to the side, and raises his knife in self-defense. No more than a yard away now, Francisco, his arm cocked in readiness, stops as the knife is flaunted before him. Now it's Santé's turn. With Anna off to the side, he has a clear shot to the man's back. Like a leopard springing unseen from the grass, he leaps on his prey, knocking him to the ground…then wrestles the knife away. As the man struggles to get up, Anna wrenches free from his grasp. Francisco, still clutching his rock, crawls closer…then brings it down on the man's head. As all three scramble to their feet, the man's legs twitch for a second or two before his head falls to the side. To Anna's horror, blood begins to spring from his neck where she stabbed him earlier in the day. She looks away, then comes to Santé and wraps her arms around him. "What should we do? If we leave him here, he may die," she cries.

"True," says Santé …but…"

Francisco interrupts, "If you call police, they'll check on you…find out you not legal and send you back to Oaxaca."

Santé looks at Anna. "What you want to do, Anna. I'll do whatever you say."

Anna looks down at the man, then at Santé. "He might survive…it's possible."

"Maybe…but he's lost lotsa blood," Santé responds.

"I say leave him here," Francisco offers. "He not deserve to live, but we give him a chance."

The other two finally nod their agreement and move back onto the road. When they reach the pickup, they stand there holding each other without saying a word. Santé is the first to speak: "This is a bad night for you Anna… three times you was attacked…twice with a knife. I was afraid for you."

At his words, Anna begins sobbing. "Nobody has ever hurt me before… never in my whole life; it's so hard to believe…I was so frightened." As she speaks, she hugs Santé tighter…so tight that he gasps for air.

"Am I hurting you?" she whispers.

"Oh no," he replies. "I know you are frightened."

Anna looks up into his face. "If you hadn't come…on the highway and then here…I don't know what those men might have done to me. Thank you." When she offers her lips, they kiss…only to break away when they hear Francisco getting into his cab. Santé yells. "Hey, amigo, wait a minute. Let me get you some money." With that, he opens the truck door and reaches into a secret compartment under the driver's seat. Pulling out five twenty-dollar bills, he begins walking toward the cab. He's too late. As the cab heads for the highway, Francisco sticks his hand out the window and waves. "Adios amigos. Cuidado! (*be careful*) Someday you invite me to wedding, si?" Santé waves back, then heads to the pickup to rejoin Anna.

On the way back to her house, he asks, "How you gonna explain your blouse to your parents?"

Anna laughs. "I'll tell them you got a little out of control."

Santé frowns. "No, I'm serious, Anna. What you gonna say?"

"By the time we get to my house, my parents will be in bed. I'm old enough now so they don't stay up for me. Tomorrow I'll put the blouse in the trash…so…no problem."

"O.K. I feel better."

Anna giggles again. "So you noticed my breasts? I'm glad. But tell me, did you like what you saw?"

Santé's face reddens. He coughs. "I don't know what to say."

"You don't have to say anything."

He reaches over and puts his hand on her thigh. When she covers it with her own, he whispers, "I love you, Anna. Someday you will be my wife, yes?"

"I want that very much, Santé. But we both have to get more schooling first. You agree, don't you?"

Santé breathes deeply. "Yes, I will wait…but you mi carino now…yes?"

"Yes, Santé. I am your darling… now…and forever."

23

Paula

Several days later, a letter from Oaxaca arrives in Santé's mailbox telling of his brother's death in Chiapas. In the letter, Alma describes how Raul was thrown off the top of a north-bound freight train by bandits, only to die when his head struck a rock next to the rails. She ends by saying that the funeral will be held the following Friday.

By the time he gets the letter, it is clear that the funeral has already taken place. He is inconsolable. This is not what was supposed to happen. Before leaving Oaxaca, he had promised Raul that if things worked out in El Norte, he would help him get to Phoenix. The plan was to wait until Raul finished school in June, then come north following the same route Santé had used.

As he rereads the letter, Santé struggles to make sense of what happened. "Why did Raul try to come by hitching a ride on a freight train when I sent him money for a bus to Nogales?" Desperate for answers, he calls Oaxaca. The call goes to the local grocery store and is relayed to the Aguilera household. Alma, who has left Felipé for good and is living at home, tells him that their father kept the money that was intended for Raul's trip north and used it to buy an old Chevy.

Outwardly Santé remains calm; in his gut, he writhes convulsively as loathing for his father collides with ingrained respect. He is tempted to go home and confront him directly but backs off when he considers how his mother would react. In a traditional Zapotec family, hostility between father and son is simply unacceptable.   To display that kind of emotion openly would tear the family apart. There is but one option left; he must go to Chiapas and find out who threw Raul off the train. Forget the money; forget father's duplicity; find the man who killed his brother.

As his mind clears, he goes to his closet and picks up the macuahuitl. He grasps it by the handle, then tightens his grip. In his imagination, he pictures the train, the migrants riding on top, the bandits hiding, knives ready…

With heart pounding, he drops the macuahuitl and leaves for the office to tell Don of his brother's death and ask for a leave of absence. Don, quick to read Santé's emotional state, grants the request and wishes him well. Later the same day, he goes to the library and bids a tearful goodbye to Anna. After explaining the circumstances of Raul's death, he says that he needs to spend time with his family but fails to mention the macuahuitl or anything about revenge. When she seeks reassurance that he will return, he explains that he'll come back into the U.S. either by way of the desert or through a tunnel in Nogales. When she shows alarm, he promises to be careful.

Finally he goes to Paula and shares the letter with her. They embrace affectionately in the hall outside his bedroom. Neither is willing to let go. When he tells her how much she means to him, that he has come to love her as if she were his own mother, she begins to cry…secretly recoiling at the horror of what she has told the Sheriff.

After he leaves, she sits on his bed…talking to herself as she strokes his pillow. "How could I have betrayed him? He really loves me, I can tell. It's not as if I had been jilted…just that he loves another woman now… but it's a different kind of love, isn't it? I can offer him a mother's love… and he keeps telling me how important that is for him…so far from home now…no family around."

She grimaces. "It's unfortunate Anna's so young and beautiful. What boy wouldn't fall in love with her? Age certainly makes a difference. She's probably no more than 17 or 18…and can offer him something I am no longer capable of. But I used to be quite attractive myself…at least Don thought so. It's too bad that age makes such a difference in love.

"But I want to accept what has happened. I hate being jealous …it's demeaning. So how do you get over a feeling like that?" She tries one answer after another but rejects them all. Finally, she sees the light. "Obviously I have to stop seeing Anna as a rival and begin seeing her as a friend. Yes, that's it. Get close to Anna…learn to love her the way I love Santé. Make it a threesome where we are bonded together in love. My God, that *is* it. I've got to go see her and make her my friend."

Two days later Paula puts the plan into action. "So, where are you going so early in the morning?" asks Don as she heads for the front door.

"I think I'll head over to the library."

"The library? You've never done that before."

"Well, I'd like to read something on Mexico…get some historical background that would help me to understand Santé better."

"Hmm. I thought your feelings had cooled a bit. You've hardly spoken of him lately."

"Oh really? I still like him. I'm sorry he's going back to Mexico to see his family…but I understand. That was quite a shock for the Aguileras…you know, what happened to their son, Raul."

"Yes…a horrible tragedy. I just hope Santé doesn't run into any difficulties making his way back here."

"Well, he did it before. I'm sure he can do it again."

Paula leaves.

Upon entering the library she heads straight for the main desk. "Anna, that is you, isn't it? I'm Paula. We met once before…in Santé's bedroom when I was bringing him some clean clothes. It was probably not the best way to meet. I could tell I was intruding…so I left before we had a chance to talk."

Anna forces a smile. "I remember. I hope you didn't think we were doing anything inappropriate."

"Heavens no. I'm glad you had a chance to be together. It's only natural for two young people who like each other to want to be close. And Santé does like you. He's mentioned it several times. He can certainly use some friends…you know…being away from family like this."

Anna holds back. "Well, we're just getting to know each other. Nothing serious yet."

"I think it's great that you're helping him with his English. I do what I can, but we're not together all that often…mostly at night when I clean his room or return his laundry. And he's usually tired after a long day's work out in the shop…so we keep our sessions brief."

Anna nods without meaning anything special. Inside, questions are arising in her young mind. "What is this woman doing here, anyway? Why is she going out of her way to meet me? Why does she make me feel tense? Maybe I'm reading too much into this; there's nothing wrong with her coming here. After all, Santé has spoken of her many times…sees her as a second mother…a warm, kind person who does lots of nice things for him. So why am I curious…well, more than curious. Why am I suspicious? I'm not being fair, am I? Maybe she just wants to be friendly."

Try as she may, Anna can't shake the tightness in her stomach. When a man comes to the desk seeking information about some archived magazine articles, she welcomes the chance to turn her attention elsewhere. When she comes back to Paula a few minutes later, the knot in her stomach is still there. "All I know," she whispers to herself, "is that something inside me is saying 'be careful.'"

Sensing Anna's anxiety, Paula leans forward and smiles, "I think it would be nice if the three of us could so some things together, don't you?"

Anna squints, "Like what?"

"Well, maybe a night on the town together… you know, dinner at a nice restaurant followed by a place where they have music and dancing. I haven't danced in years but I could probably get back into it with a drink or two."

Stunned by the boldness of the proposal, Anna fumbles for a response. "Really, Paula. I don't know. Perhaps a meal at some restaurant nearby would be O.K. I can't answer for Santé, though. You'll have to ask him."

Paula, energized by the possibilities, draws her chair closer. "We could even take a picnic together or go for a walk through the woods. There's so much to see in Arizona. What about a weekend trip to a place like Lake Mead? Has Santé ever been there? They say it's really beautiful."

In her imagination, unseen by Anna, Paula visualizes the scenes she is describing. The first picture to present itself is of the three of them packed into the front seat of Santé's pickup…a not entirely satisfactory scene since Paula would be on the outside with Santé at the wheel and Anna in the middle. As she continues to talk, the image gives way to one in which they are all in Paula's car, an economy sedan with two separate seats in front. Paula is driving…Santé is in the passenger's seat…and Anna is in back alone. A much nicer arrangement. When the possibility of a trip to Lake Mead comes up, it is quickly followed by a detailed picture of a hotel room. In her mind's eye she sees the three of them entering the room together. As they file in, Paula turns to the other two with a suggestion. "Why don't Anna and I share one of the queen-sized beds while Santé takes the other?" When Anna hesitates, Paula hears herself whispering, "Your parents would probably prefer it that way, don't you think?"

Once that decision has been made, the fantasy continues. It is time for bed. So, what will she wear? What, in other words, would look best when she walks past Santé's bed on her way to the bathroom? Warming to the question, she begins imagining different types of clothing…first a floral, wool bathrobe that covers everything from top to bottom…a conservative solution…perhaps too conservative. Next, still fantasizing, comes a simple, cotton nightgown without any robe…a little more daring but hardly something that would draw attention. Finally she imagines a silk see-through gown drawn sufficiently tight to outline her ample breasts. "Now that would be an attention grabber," she mumbles to herself. Her chest begins to heave at the possibilities. Unaware that she is blurring the line between daydream and reality, she continues musing, "I don't have anything that revealing at home but I've seen catalogues that sell such things. I can order over the internet without Don ever knowing." Totally lost in fantasy now, she nods as if acknowledging the wisdom of her plan, then cups her breasts, lifting them slightly. The sensation of fullness brings a smile to her lips.

Anna stares, wondering what in the world is going on with this woman. Not knowing what more to say and unwilling to waste any more time, she excuses herself and retires to the back office. Before she is out of sight, Paula shouts, "I'll call you to make arrangements for our trip, O.K.?" When she receives no answer, she gets up and leaves.

Back home she is reassured when she sees the new inspection sticker on Santé's truck. Still worried about his lack of a legitimate license, she resolves to remind him that the police have no right to ask for his license just because he looks Latino. They must have some other reason like speeding or an accident.

That night in bed, she falls back into fantasy. "I can't wait 'til he gets back so I can ask him if he likes my idea of our doing things together as a threesome. I'm sure he will…after all, he told me he loves me. Yes, I know it's different than the way he loves Anna…but when you come down to it, it's not all that different…really." She sighs a soft, contented sigh. When Don, who is lying next to her, asks if she's O.K., she says nothing. Convinced that she's feeling lonely, he snuggles closer and wraps his arm around her breasts. This time she speaks, "Not now, honey, I'm not in the mood." When he is slow to remove his arm, she moves to the edge of the bed and closes her eyes.

Free again to lose herself in fantasy, she quickly returns to Lake Mead and the hotel room with Santé and Anna. After a beautiful day spent sailing and picnicking, all three are tired and ready for bed. It's time now for everyone to change into their bed clothes. For Paula this means changing from blue jeans and t-shirt to the much-anticipated see-through nightgown. In the bathroom she undresses slowly, then slides the gown over her head, pulling it down at the waist so that her nipples are clearly visible. Pleased with what she sees in the mirror, she opens the door and begins walking toward her bed. As she passes Santé's bed, she turns to look in his direction. He is staring at her. Their eyes meet in an unspoken declaration of mutual interest. "Just as I thought," she murmurs to herself, "He does find me attractive."

Her eyes open. Convinced that the fantasy is a harbinger of things to come, she permits herself a little giggle…one just loud enough to wake her husband. Don rubs his eyes and asks, "What was that all about?"

"Oh nothing, hon," she replies, not bothering to turn her head. "I'm just being silly. Go back to sleep."

24

Murder on the Rails

Santé decides that the safest way to cross the border into Mexico is by bus. Going by plane means that he would have to show some I.D.… most likely a driver's license…a fake one in his case which could precipitate an investigation and possible arrest. On the bus all he'll need at the border is a day pass which is easy enough to get. The Immigration Service, after all, is not concerned about Latinos heading back to Mexico. If anything, they wish them well and hurry them on their way.

The simplest route, he figures, is to take a bus to Nogales and then another down the west coast of Mexico through Sonora and Sinaloa all the way to Guadalajara. From there he can take an express carrier south past Mexico City to Oaxaca where he'll spend time with his family before moving on to Tapachula, the town near the Guatemalan border where trains enter Mexico from Central America. All he needs to do now is pack his bags and make a quick trip to the bank to withdraw some savings. If all goes well, he should reach Tapachula by Friday.

He arrives in Oaxaca early on Friday morning, physically drained and apprehensive about seeing his father. The meeting with Mama and Alma is an emotional one with lots of mutual hugging. The two women want to know all about Phoenix; Santé is anxious to hear all about Raul. When Papa overhears Santé complaining about the money sent for Raul's trip north, he storms in from the deck. "We're glad you're sending money," he shouts from the doorway…"but it's not up to you to decide how that money is spent. That's a father's responsibility. When you have a family of your own, you can make the decisions." Santé glowers, then lowers his head. When neither Mama nor Alma says anything, he looks up at his father and blurts out, "But is buying an old car more important than Raul's safety? I don't understand."

Father turns to go, then changes his mind. "I don't have to explain myself to you. I did what I thought was right…and that's it. I don't want to hear any more about it." He returns to the deck, slamming the door behind him.

Once tranquility has returned, Santé asks for more details about his brother's death. In response, Alma suggests that they go to the cemetery where Raul is buried. On the way over she takes his hand and squeezes. "He really loved you, Santé. The thing he wanted most in the world was to join you in Phoenix. That's all he talked about."

Santé bites his lips. "'Did he know that I was sendin' extra money so he could come by bus?"

"Yes. I told him myself."

"So, what'd he say when Papa used the money to buy a car? Was he upset?"

"I'm not sure. If he was, he didn't show it. But that's Raul. You could never be sure what he was feeling."

At the gravesite Alma tells Santé that Raul was with his friend Stefan when he was killed. "If you want more details, you should pay him a visit; he lives two blocks down the street from our house. I'm sure he'll tell you everything."

Later in the morning Santé goes to meet Stefan. The boy is thin like many teenagers and still has a lot of growing to do…certainly not the kind of kid who could hold his own in a fight. Adding to the image of frailness is his slumping left shoulder, a legacy according to Alma, of his fall from the train. When Santé offers to take him out for lunch, Stefan, who typically goes without breakfast, quickly agrees. At the restaurant he gives a graphic description of the events surrounding Raul's death. "There's a depot jis' outside Tapachula where trains comin' from Guatemala hafta stop before they go up through Mexico. That makes it a good place for migrants to jump on before the train gets goin' again. But you gotta watch out for the Judiciales…you know, the local police. As soon as they leave, you run alongside a boxcar or tanker and grab hold of the ladder. Once you git hold of a ladder, you hoist yourself up until yir foot reaches the lowest rung. Trouble is…if you reach the ladder with yir hand but can't pull yourself up all the way, you get dragged under the wheels. Lotsa kids lose their feet or legs that way. There's even a clinic in Tapachula for kids who got only one leg…or none at all."

Santé puts down his fork. "You say kids…is it mainly kids who ride the trains or are there grownups too?"

"Both. When me and Raul did it, there were a few guys in their 20's or 30's…but most were kids…you know…kids my age hopin' to join a relative in El Norte."

Santé sighs. "Like Raul. How about you…who were you going to meet?"

"My dad's in California…he's been there four years now…wants me and my mom to join 'im. He said to wait until he could send money for the bus…but my mom has a heart problem and had to go to the hospital. The doctors told her the problem was goin' to get worse if she didn't have an operation. That used up all the money Papa sent us…so I figured I better try it alone…on the train."

Santé nods his understanding. "Tell me, how fast are the trains goin' when you jump on?"

"Right after they start up from the depot, you can catch one goin' maybe 15 or 20 miles an hour. The other place to get on is a few miles up the tracks on a curve where the train has to slow down. All the tracks are very old…and so are the ties…doesn't take much to tip one of those tall boxcars over. They say it happens all the time."

"So, were you with Raul when he got on?"

Stefan smiles. "Yeah. I was right behind him. We both made it on our first try. But that's jis' the beginnin'. As soon as you get on, you hafta find a hidin' place cuz at the next checkpoint…the one at La Arrocera… the police come onto the train to look for kids stealin' a ride. Some kids jump off before the checkpoint and run through the woods to get back on further up the tracks; others hide. The safest place to hide is up on top of a boxcar. The ladders only go up so far so you hafta pull yourself up the rest of the way with your hands…and the migra don't like to do that."

"Is that what you and Raul did?"

"Yeah. When we got up there, we laid down flat on our stomachs so they couldn't see us. They caught some of the riders on the fuel tanker just ahead but we was lucky." He sighs. "At least until the bandits came on board later. We weren't so lucky then."

"Alma says you and Raul were both thrown off the train by men with machetes and knives."

"That's true. I guess they got on the train a few miles up the line. It was gettin' dark so we didn't see 'em at first. We was sittin' in a circle on top of the boxcar…maybe six or seven of us kids…when these two guys with machetes come up behind us. They started pointin' their weapons at us and yellin' for us to empty our pockets. A couple of kids got up and ran but there were two more bandits waitin' for 'em at the end of the car. I could tell that both men had knives and they weren't afraid to use 'em.

"After they went through our pockets lookin' for money, they made us all take our clothes off…'cept for our underwear. While we was standin' there shivering, they ripped open any hidin' places they found…like little pouches you mighta made with a needle and thread…stuff like that."

"Did Raul have any money to give them?"

"No…and that's what made them mad…or at least it made the leader mad. He come up from below jis' as we was undressin'. Any money the men with the machetes found, they turned over to him. When they told 'im Raul didn't have any money, he grabbed your brother by the shoulder and shook 'im real hard…then throwed 'im off the train. I knew I was gonna be next cuz I only had three pesos on me…so I jumped right after Raul got throwed off."

"How fast was the train goin' then?"

"We was pickin' up speed I could tell….dunno, maybe 30 miles an hour. Too fast, I know, cuz I landed hard on my shoulder…this one here (*shows Santé*)…and it still ain't right."

"And Raul?"

"When I got up, I went lookin' for your brother. He was lyin' on his side a few yards back down the track. Before I even got to 'im, I could tell he was out cold. When I got there, I shook 'im by the shoulder but he didn't move. Another kid come along about then and rolled him over on his back. There was no question about it; he was dead."

Santé exhales slowly. "Any blood?"

"Yeah…on his head. I think he landed on a big rock next to a tie. I was lucky to land on some dirt."

"So, what did you do…did you call anybody…the police…or someone else?"

"We jis' stayed there…me and this other kid…until a man come by lookin' for clothes and things tossed off the train…I guess he lived next to the tracks. He helped us get Raul to his house where he called the clinic I told you about. Two men in a pickup come a few hours later and took Raul away."

Santé bites his lower lip. "The clinic…yes…that's where Mama and Alma came to get his body. I guess there wasn't anything more you coulda done…(*pause*)…Anyway, I'm glad you made it in one piece. Does that shoulder of yours still hurt?"

(*Rubbing his shoulder*) "It got better after I took some medicine they give me at the clinic. They also showed me some exercises I could do to loosen it up but I still can't lift much with that arm. I don't think the pain is ever gonna go away."

Seconds pass without either one saying anything. Finally Santé breaks the silence with a question, "You mentioned the leader. What was he like? Does he have a name?"

"Oh yeah. Everybody calls him El Jaguar. They call him that cuz he looks like a jaguar…or at least he tries to look like one. You know, he dresses in black…both pants and shirt…and he wears a black mask. So, when he runs along the boxcars on all fours, he really looks like a giant cat. They say he runs faster that way than standin' up. Some kids say he was born in the forest…that his mother was a real jaguar and brought him up to hunt and kill like she did. I dunno if that's true…but he sure is scary."

"I thought jaguars were yellow with black spots."

"Yeah, but I guess there's some all black ones too."

"You say he wears a mask. That's pretty weird, ain't it?"

"Well, not if he wants to scare kids into givin' everything they've got. It works, I know. When you see him comin' at you on all fours with his yellow eyes glowin' and fangs showin'…you ain't gonna put up much of a fight. He even let his fingernails grow like claws so he can hold you down when he attacks. The thing is…you better have something to show 'im before he leaps. He don't like bein' stiffed. I seen 'im throw three kids off the train cuz they didn't have no money to give 'im. That's why I jumped."

Silence.

"How often do the trains come through Tapachula?" Santé asks.

"Every day I think…usually in the morning around 10:00 and then again around 6:00 at night…(*pause*)…You ain't thinkin' of gettin' on, are you?"

Santé squints, then looks away. "I dunno…maybe."

Stefan takes a deep breath. "Look, I don't wanna make you feel bad, but yir still a kid like me. You ain't no match for El Jaguar. He'll do to you what he did to your brother…maybe worse. I'm not sayin' that out of disrespect but jis' to warn you. He's not human; he'll eat ya alive."

"Maybe."

Stefan shakes his head. "Well, if you go, you better take a knife or somethin'…it might hold 'im off 'til you can jump."

Santé smiles. "I've got a little something back at the house."

"And wear a jacket or sweater. All of us kids froze our balls off when the sun went down…that's when the bandits like to attack…on the 6:00 train. It gets really cold at night…especially if the wind is blowin'."

"Good idea. Maybe I can pick up a jacket before I leave for Tapachula."

"You're in luck. There's a big sale on jackets at Milano…you know the clothing store next to the zocolo. They have a whole bunch of 'em. And for a few extra pesos, you can even get your name sewed onto the back. Everybody's doin' it. You can put anything you want on there…it doesn't have to be your real name. One kid…Rafael Garcia…he thought there was too many Garcias in town…so he had 'em sew on somethin' different…a name he jis' made up."

"Like what?"

"El Predator…crazy huh. But the other kids loved it. As soon as they saw it, they began rippin' off their real names and sewin' on new ones…like El Diablo *(the devil)*, El Rey *(the king)*, El Monstruo *(the monster)*….stuff like that…*(pause)*…I'm savin' up my money so I kin get one too."

Santé smiles. "And what name you gonna put on the back of yours?"

"I dunno. Maybe…*(pause)*…I'm not sure. Some kind of animal maybe… something that can kill a jaguar. Is there an animal that can do that?"

"I don't think so. But a man could probly do it…if he had the right weapon."

"Well, yeah…a person's name would be better…like somebody who wants to get back at 'im for what he done. Maybe I'd put El Vengador (*The Avenger*) on mine. What dya think?"

"I like it. But if you advertise yourself like that, you gotta be ready to back it up…you know…go after El Jaguar somehow."

Stefan hisses through his teeth. "No. I ain't ready for that. If I saw him comin' after me with that mask and all, I'd probly do what I did before… jump off the train before he got to me."

"That makes sense," says Santé. "Sounds like he's much bigger than you. You wouldn't stand a chance."

Stefan nods his agreement. "But Santé…if you want to use El Vengador on your own jacket…go ahead. It's O.K. with me."

"Thanks. I might do that. But look, I gotta go now…I want to talk to my family about all this before dinner. Maybe on my way back from Tapachula I'll stop and let you know what happened."

"That would be cool…if yir able to come outta there in one piece. But remember…a lot of kids don't make it back from Tapachula. The train can cut off your legs before you even get aboard…and if you're lucky enough to make it, you gotta deal with El Jaguar and the bandits. And there's the local police. If they catch you before the train comes, you know, hidin' in the cemetery or sleepin' in the grass, they'll shake you down for anything they find on you… then take you in…(*pause*)…Oh, I forgot…there's also the migra…they won't kill you but they'll book you for tryin' to migrate without papers…(*pause*)…It's really a jungle. Like I said, a lot of kids don't make it."

"I hear ya."

As Santé rises to leave the restaurant, he extends his arm toward Stefan as if to shake hands goodbye. Hidden inside his fist is a 500 peso note ($40 U.S.). "For your jacket," he says, opening the fist. "Thanks for all the info…and El Vengador." Before Stefan can answer, he pushes open the door and leaves.

Back home that afternoon Santé resumes his conversation with Alma and Mama. He shares with them some of the details he learned from Stefan but is careful to keep others to himself.

"So, now that you know all this," Alma says, "what's the point of goin' to Tapachula? Are you lookin' for more trouble?"

"I dunno," Santé answers softly. "All I know is that I have to go. I jis' have to. There's no point talkin' about it."

To change the subject, Santé takes out his wallet and hands three one hundred-dollar bills to his mother. Taking her hand, he says, "I didn't see any sense in sendin' it by mail since I was headin' down here anyway."

Mama takes the money but continues holding his hand. "We couldn't make it without you, Santé," she replies, tucking the money into her apron pocket. "We're just about out of everything. I'll go to Soriana's tomorrow. Alma, you wanna come with me? I won't be able to carry everything alone."

Before Alma can answer, father enters the kitchen and pulls up a chair. All conversation stops.

"You don't look too good," says the mother finally. "Anything the matter?"

"Bad news at the repair shop," he replies, glancing around the table. "Pedro said we need a new engine block. I guess it seized up when all the oil leaked out. There's gotta be somethin' wrong with the gauge or I woulda seen it."

"How much is that gonna cost?" Alma asks.

"Pedro said he could find me a used block…for about $9,000 ($750 U.S.)."

Mama stiffens in her chair. "Where in the word we goin' to get that kinda money? The three hundred dollars Santé just give me won't even cover rent and groceries for this month."

Father rises and walks over to his wife. "Three hundred dollars? Why is he givin' it to you? That money s'posed to come to me." He reaches out with his palm up. "Give it to me."

She looks frantically at Santé. When no response is forthcoming, she hands the money to her husband. "What are we supposed to do for food?" she asks, dropping her hands in her lap. "I was goin' to Soriana's tomorrow with Alma. And then there's the rent due on the first. We're already two months behind."

Papa turns to glare at Santé, then peels off one of the bills and hands it to his wife. "That'll buy food for a week; Santé can help with the rent. He's probly got a few more bills in his pocket right now…don't you Santé?"

Santé's throat tightens; he forces a swallow. "Yeah, I've got some money left (*patting his wallet pocket*) but I'm goin' to need it for Tapachula. And there's the trip back to Phoenix. I'll need somethin' for the bus."

Alma looks over at her brother. He's scarcely breathing.

Father's lips twist into a sneer. "What the hell you goin' to Tapachula for anyway? Raul's gone and there's nothin' you or anyone else can do about it. Yir wastin' your money on the dead when yir family needs it here."

Alma's eyes remain glued to Santé. He begins to squirm as thoughts of rebellion, painfully but successfully suppressed throughout childhood, creep to the edge of consciousness. He looks back at his sister, takes a deep breath, then turns to stare at his father. When he opens his mouth, his voice cracks; words split and break apart. "You want more money...for what ...(*swallowing*) ...to repair a car that you shouldn'ta bought in the first place...(*taking a breath*)...a car that we got no need for?" Surprised by his boldness, he allows his voice to grow louder. "You thought more about that car than your own son. Your selfishness got him killed before he had a chance to grow up."

His father's face turns white, his teeth bared like a tiger preparing to pounce. As he steps forward, Santé leaps to his feet, yelling, "You're a murderer...that's what you are. You're a murderer."

Father is now just inches away. He clenches his fist; his temples are visibly bulging. "You shut your damn mouth. You got no right to talk to me like that. Maybe it's O.K to talk back in Phoenix but it's still a sin in our family...a sin I'll never forgive you for. You're goin' to rot in hell for what you just said." When Santé continues staring, he steps back. "Go ahead... (*throwing his hands up*). Go to Tapachula. Throw your money away. Maybe you'll end up like your brother." As he heads for the door, he turns for a final thrust, "It's time you left anyway. Yir no longer welcome in this house."

Santé slumps in his chair. Mama, silent through it all, comes over and puts her arms him. "I know how you feel, Santé, but you shouldn'ta said those things. He's still your Papa."

Santé nods but says nothing. Slowly he rises and heads for the deck where he left his backpack. Alma follows him. Once outside, she closes the door and whispers, "You can stay here tonight…then leave in the morning before breakfast. Papa will never know."

"I've got to get down to Milano before they close," he replies. "Stefan said I'm goin' to need a jacket at night."

Alma grabs his wrist. "So, you're goin' to climb aboard the train…just like Raul did?…(*pause*)…You want the man who threw him off, don't you."

"Maybe."

Alma releases her grip.

"But look here," he says…(*reaching for his wallet*)…"take this for the rent. I'll try to send more when I get back to Phoenix."

Alma whispers a thank you and wraps her arms around him. "Please be careful, Santé. I've lost one brother; I don't want to lose another." With that, she opens the door and goes inside.

At Milano, Santé makes his way through a huge assortment of jackets… picking a bright orange one after concluding that if he is to make his presence known to the bandits, he needs to be seen. Disregarding the clerk's look of curiosity, he asks to have the name El Vengador sewn on the back; an hour later he returns to pick up the jacket and stuff it into his backpack. The only business remaining now is to catch some sleep on the deck back home. Early tomorrow he will take a bus to the capitol of Chiapas, San Cristobal…and from there transfer to Tapachula. If all goes well, he should reach his destination by that evening.

As he leaves the zocolo and heads back up the hill, an image of Raul being thrown from the train reminds him that things in Chiapas could easily go wrong…very wrong. To ease his anxiety, he reaches into his pack and grabs the macuahuitl by the handle. Reassured, he breathes a sigh of relief and picks up his pace.

25

The Train of Death

At the Tapachula bus station Santé learns that there are two roads leading to the train depot, a paved valley route that takes you past the cemetery and a dirt road, good for walking but hazardous for driving, that forms a semi-circle around the depot from above. He chooses the latter and sets out after a quick breakfast of eggs and beans. His strategy is to spend the day observing what happens when trains come in from Guatemala. According to Stefan, the first one should come through at 10:00; the second won't follow until 6:00 in the evening. Bandits can be expected on both trains but their leader, El Jaguar, usually appears on the evening one.

The dirt road he has chosen takes him up a hill before leveling off at the top; below, a stream cuts its way through dense underbrush. Further up the stream, the brush gives way to tracks and power lines, revealing a red brick station where a small group of men in uniform can be seen milling around. Santé takes a sip from his bottle of tea and stops to watch. It's 9:00 A.M. and the only railroad cars in sight are three fuel tankers pulled onto to a side track where they wait for an engine to continue their trip north.

As he scans the depot for signs of migrants, Santé suddenly becomes aware of footsteps on the road behind him. He turns in time to confront a young woman who is walking briskly toward him. Her tattered dress and worn rebozo suggest a life of poverty. Her face, probably once pretty, is severely wrinkled, her eyes red from crying. When she opens her mouth to speak, her missing front teeth confirm the impression of someone who no longer frets over how others see her. In her hand she is holding a basket covered with a piece of cloth. A yard or two away, she stops and smiles, then speaks, "Hola…I see you lookin' down at the tracks. You tryin' to find someone?"

Santé studies her carefully before answering. Given the reputation of the area, the basket represents a potential source of danger. Sensing his distrust, she comes closer and pulls the cloth away. In the basket are a dozen or more sweet rolls, still warm from this morning's oven. "You want one?" she asks. "I bake them every day for migrants; they ride the train from Honduras or Guatemala. They have nothing to eat for days."

Relieved at what he sees, Santé declines the offer but asks, "How dya give 'em the rolls? The tracks are down there (*pointing*)."

"Oh, you'll see. When the train comes in from the south, the migrants don't wanta get caught, so they jump off before they get to the station. They scatter like mice. Some hide in the tall grass; others run up this hill. As soon as the Judiciales leave, they jump back on."

"So you feed 'em when they're hidin'?"

"Yes. I take that path over there (*pointing*). I can tell where they are hidin' by watchin' the grass; when it shakes, I toss a roll in that direction. They always find it."

Santé grins. "You do this every day?"

"Almost. Some days I gotta stay home with my daughter…when she's sick or on weekends or when there ain't no school. Now that my husband is gone, I got no one else to take care of her."

Santé is quick to see her eyes moistening. "How long's he been gone?"

"He was killed down there (*pointing to the tracks*) last year. They say the bandits did it. They tried to take his money and he wouldn't let 'em. He was a gentle man…never raised his voice…but that money was all we had in the world…just enough to pay for a coyote. So, he fought back… (*pause*)…That's when they killed him…with a machete."

Santé is tempted to give her a hug when she begins sobbing…but decides against it in case she thinks he's up to something. He settles for a question. "Why dya come here and give away yir rolls when you could make money sellin' 'em in the market?"

She looks down into her basket. "It feels good. These people hafta bear so much…I wanta make it a little easier. That's all."

Santé smiles and nods his head.

"But tell me…what are you doin' here?" the woman asks. "You lose somebody too?"

"My brother…he was comin' to join me in Phoenix where I live now. He got thrown off the train and hit his head on a rock."

"I never heard that before. They throw people offa the train?"

"When the kids don't have money, the bandits get mad and throw 'em off."

"Don't they complain to the police?"

"My brother's friend…he jumped before they could throw him off…says the Judiciales are in on the whole thing. They let the bandits do their stealin'…then demand a percentage of the take."

She shakes her head. "You sure you won't have a roll…they's real fresh."

"They smell good, but I already et my breakfast. The kids comin' from down south are gonna need 'em more 'an I do."

At that point they both turn in the direction of a loud "Hoot". It's the incoming train. Another "Hoot" follows, then a sharp whistle. Sparks fly from the wheels as the train eases its way into the depot.

"I've got to run," she gasps. "They'll be jumpin' any minute now."

Without ever introducing herself, the woman hurries down the path and disappears into the tall grass. Seconds later, before the train comes to a full stop, Santé sees boys leaping from boxcars onto the roadbed and vanishing into the grass. The Judiciales see them too…and run to head them off. At least some do…the others, dressed in black uniforms and wielding clubs… climb up on the train cars and begin searching for illegal crossers. Within minutes, a dozen boys and two men are dragged from their hiding places and herded into a circle just off the tracks. A pickup, standing by for the occasion, backs up so that the captives can be loaded on. According to

Stefan, they will eventually be handed over to the migra for deportation back to Central America. The others are luckier; they are hiding in the grass, waiting for a sweet roll to come flying in their direction.

Soon after the Judicales leave with their quarry, the engine lets out a loud "Hoot" and begins to move again. As if choreographed, dozens of migrants, those from Central America, rise from the grass and go racing after the train. Santé fixes his eyes on three boys who are running alongside a hopper that's carrying coal. One after the other they reach up, grab a rung of the ladder, and hoist themselves up onto the coal-bed. None of the police remain behind to watch them. They are soon joined by a different set of migrants…those who have been hiding in the grass on the north side of the station. Since they did not jump from the train earlier, it is clear to Santé that these are not Central Americans but Mexicans who are just starting their journey. This is where Raul and Stefan must have boarded the train.

He moves a few steps to his right to get a better view of the unfolding drama. By now the train is picking up speed and the challenge of grabbing a ladder more difficult. One boy who looks no more than 14 or 15 manages to grab a rung but cannot run fast enough to hoist himself up. As Santé watches, he lets go and falls to the roadbed just inches from the train's grinding wheels. Within seconds, he is on his feet and running after the train. His friends, already aboard, wave to him, pointing to a curve just ahead where the train will slow down again. But it is too late. He is exhausted. As the train slips away, he falls to the ground, pounding his fist in the dirt. He has missed his chance. Perhaps he will try again tomorrow.

Santé covers his eyes, sickened by what he has witnessed. At the sound of footsteps he turns to see the woman with the sweet rolls coming back up the path; her basket now empty. She stops to talk. "It's scary, isn't it?"

When Santé fails to respond, she continues, "You never told me why you're here. You ain't thinkin' of gettin' on the train, are you?"

"I don't know," Santé whispers. "Maybe."

She looks him up and down. You ain't dressed like the others. You got a clean shirt and nice sneakers. If you wanna go north, why don'tcha take the bus? It's much safer."

Santé lifts his head. "Well, yeah, I could do that. But I'm not lookin' for a ride north. I already live there…(*pause*)…I come back to find out who killed my younger brother. I think it was a guy called El Jaguar…and…"

"El Jaguar," she exclaims, interrupting. "I know all about 'im; he walks on all fours and got claws that grab yir flesh. They say he was the one who killed my husband."

"But you said yir husband got killed with a machete. Somebody tole me that El Jaguar don't use a machete."

"True…but El Jaguar jumped my man and held 'im down. While he was on his back, another bandit hit 'im with the machete. At least that's what I was tole."

As the woman turns to leave, she says, "My name is Maria. I liked talkin' with you. If you wanna talk again, I come here most mornin's."

"Maybe I will. I'm Santé."

Santé remains on the road overlooking the depot after the woman has left. His mind is restive. "We are really different, this woman and me," he muses. "I'm here to make somebody pay for Raul; killing El Jaguar might not bring my brother back, but if I can do it, it'll make me feel a lot better. Now this woman…she don't seem to feel like that. Her husband got killed…maybe by the same man…but she don't sound all that angry…sad yeah, but not angry. So what does she do…she comes every day to feed the hungry migrants. She must feel sorry for them 'cause they're doin' what her husband tried to do. I feel sorry too…'specially when I see a kid fall down and almost get his legs cut off…but tossin' rolls to people hidin' in the grass ain't gonna make up for Raul's getting' throwed off the train…not for me, anyhow. For me it's gotta be more personal." With eyes still fixed on the tracks below, he reaches into his pack and takes out the macuahuitl. As he grips the handle, a faint smile forms on his lips. "I know what I need to do. I gotta get this Jaguar guy; that'll make it real personal."

The next train…the evening train…won't be coming through until 6:00 P.M. This gives Santé plenty of time to work out his strategy. From what Stefan and Maria have told him…plus what he has just witnessed himself…

he knows that first of all he's got to avoid the Judiciales. The way to do that is to hide in the grass with the other migrants. Next comes the hard part. "You hafta stay hidden until you hear a hissin' sound…that's when the train's gonna start movin' again. Next, look around to make sure all the Judiciales have left…then run for a ladder. A boxcar is best; you can't hide for very long on a fuel tanker or hopper. That's important if the police come on board at the La Arrocera checkpoint…which Stefan says they usually do. Once you get to the top of the car, take a position facin' the engine since getting' struck by a low-hangin' branch could knock ya off the train. Then wait for the bandits to come."

Satisfied that he knows what to do, he pulls the orange jacket from his pack, rolls it into a pillow and stretches out on the grass.

By 5:00 P.M. he is wide awake; he should be hungry but is too excited to eat. He looks first to see if any Judiciales have arrived at the depot. Satisfied that no one is there, he sneaks down the hill and takes a position in the tall grass just north of the station. He is not the first to do so. Although the day is windless, the grass a few yards away can be seen waving as youths eager to get a running start settle into their temporary homes. No one speaks. All eyes are pointed to the south where the train will emerge from Guatemala.

Suddenly the long-awaited "Hoot" fills the air, followed by a "Hiss" as steam bursts from the engine's boiler. Right on time, the train breaks into the clearing and slows to a stop just outside the station. It's only minutes now before it'll start up again…just minutes before the race begins…the race of nimble legs against what Stefan called El Gusano de Hierro (*The Iron Worm*).

Patience is crucial. The Judiciales must first be given a chance to catch a few migrants and send them back to Nicaragua or Honduras or wherever they've come from. Once the white pickup leaves with its load of detainees, the train will start moving again, creating a window of opportunity that will close quickly as the engine picks up speed. There's no more than a minute or two for migrants to jump up from their hiding places, run alongside a chosen car, and hoist themselves onto a ladder. From what Stefan has said, it is a race that not everybody wins. Those who reach the ladder but are not strong enough to pull themselves up risk being sucked under the train where their legs get cut off by the onrushing wheels. Some die there on the tracks; others are lucky enough to be found and taken to the clinic before they bleed to death.

The train begins to move. Santé, now wearing his orange jacket, waits until he sees two or three boys leap from the grass and run toward the train before following suit. Once on the roadbed, he picks out a boxcar and heads for the nearest ladder. To reach it he must run faster than the train… at least for a few yards. He imagines Raul calling to him from the boxcar. He raises his hand as if to wave back, then drives his legs faster, reaching the ladder just as his lungs are about to burst. Once his feet are set firmly on the lowest rung, he pulls himself up to the roof and then turns to face the engine. He is surprised to see that several others have already formed a circle a few yards in front of him. From their voluble chatter, it is clear that they are congratulating each other on having boarded successfully. Most of them are younger than Santé. He inches closer and tries chatting with one of the boys. A few stare at him but no one answers. Sensing that he is not trusted, he slides back to his original position and waits.

When the train slows at a second curve, Santé sees several young men, all armed with knives or machetes, climb aboard the boxcar up ahead. They go unnoticed by the boys who are still celebrating their victory over what the woman with the sweet rolls calls El Tren de la Muerte (*The Train of Death*). From his position to the rear, Santé watches as two of the men leap from their own boxcar onto the one he's sitting on. They quickly approach the circle of youths. One of the men is brandishing a knife, the other a machete. Awakening to the danger, the boys huddle together. The man with the knife, clearly Latino but speaking with a non-Mexican accent, orders them to empty their pockets. When the boys hesitate, he slashes at one, ripping his shirt. Facing the group as a whole, he yells, "O.K. All of ya…take yir clothes off or I'll do it with my knife." Slowly they begin to undress.

From a few yards away Santé watches with alarm but does not move. In his gut, away from prying eyes, a familiar feeling stirs, a feeling he associates with being bullied by Mestizos at school. When he sees the boy's shirt get ripped, he pulls the macuahuitl from his pack and places it in his lap. Slowly he inches forward. At first the bandits are too busy tearing apart pants and shirts to see him. Suddenly he's noticed. "Hey you," shouts the knife holder, pointing at Santé. "Git yir clothes off."

When Santé does nothing, the man with the knife repeats his order. Again Santé says nothing…but rises to his feet holding the macuahuitl behind him. The man comes closer, thrusting the knife forward. Santé waits until he is only a few feet away…then, gripping the macuahuitl tightly, leans forward and brings it down on his adversary's shoulder blade. Tremors from the crunch of blade on bone ripple up his arm, shaking it visibly. The night, silent up to now except for the engine's hissing, is pierced with shrieks of agony as the man teeters on the boxcar edge before rolling off onto the rails below.

The boys who have watched the scene unfold from a few yards away are stunned. At first no one speaks. When the other assailant, the one with the machete, turns and races to the opposite end of the car, they suddenly explode with a chorus of yelps. En masse they flock to their rescuer, eyes wide with joy and relief. Santé sits quickly, bracing himself for the onslaught.

When he turns to wipe off his weapon, one of the boys notices the back of his jacket. "El Vengador…what's that mean?" he asks.

Another boy, no more than 13, answers, "It means he's tryin' to get back at somebody…right?"

Santé nods.

The boy continues. "Who you tryin' to get back at…El Jaguar?"

Again Santé nods, saying nothing.

"You wanta kill 'im?" the boy persists.

Santé disregards the question. Instead he asks, "Was that him…the one who ran away?"

"Oh no," comes the response from a boy about Santé's age. I seen El Jaguar last time I was here…he's bigger than these guys…and wears a mask. A real scary dude. Me and my friend had to jump off the train when he come at us on all fours."

"Yeah," chimes in another boy, also a veteran rider. "You gotta be glad he weren't here tonight. He woulda cut ya ta ribbons."

"But how?" asks Santé. "They say he don't carry a machete."

"With his claws," the boy answers, relishing the chance to strike fear into his audience. "He digs 'em right into ya. They're sharper than knives."

"So why dya wanna get back at 'im?" asks a plump teenager sporting the beginnings of a mustache. "What he do to ya?"

Santé looks at the boy. "What's your name?"

"Beto," comes the response.

Santé nods. "Mine's Santé…(*pause*)…My brother tried to do what you guys are doin'. His name was Raul. He was gonna join me in Phoenix where I live. He never made it…got throwed off the train by El Jaguar and hit his head on a rock. They say he died right away."

"So that's why yir here," Beto continues, "to get back at El Jaguar?"

Santé nods again.

"What's that thing you got there…the thing you hit that bandit with?" asks a younger boy here for the first time.

Santé picks up the macuahuitl and holds it aloft so everyone can see it. "My uncle made it for me…as a birthday present. It's s'posed to be a copy of what people used in the old days…you know, when Zapotecs and Aztecs were fightin' each other around Oaxaca."

"Can I hold it?" Beto asks.

"Sure…but be careful," Santé says. "These here blades (*pointing*) are made from a really sharp kinda stone. You can cut yourself jis' by touchin' 'em."

The boys pass the macuahuitl around until it comes back to Santé. "You better not let 'em see it at La Arrocera," says Beto, referring to the checkpoint just ahead where the Judciales will be lookin' for migrants. "They'll steal it from ya."

"Or use it on ya," chuckles Damian, a frail-looking boy of 12 who has been caught at the checkpoint twice.

"So how dya avoid gettin' caught at the checkpoint?" asks Santé. "Where ya goin' to hide?"

Beto, who is emerging as the leader of the group, answers, "If you don't wanna to get caught, yir best bet is to jump offa the train before we hit the checkpoint and run through the woods behind the station…then jump back onta the train when it starts up again."

"Yeah," adds Damian, "but you gotta make it before the train hits the bridge about a mile up the tracks. Once it gets to the bridge it'll be goin' too fast to jump on."

Beto stands up to survey the surroundings. "Getting' through the woods ain't all that easy either. There's more bandits there…jis' waitin' to rob anybody comin' through. Sometimes you can outrun 'em; sometimes there's too many of 'em and they gang up on ya. If you get caught, you betta have a few pesos to give 'em or they'll get mad and cut ya with their knives."

As the train slows down, Beto inches over to the edge of the car and peers ahead. "There they are (*pointing to the Judiciales*). "Must be at least 20 of 'em jis' waitin' for us. Another hundred yards and we gotta jump."

As they prepare to jump, Damian comes over to Santé. "You want me to show ya where the path is? It's kinda hard to see from the tracks."

"Sure," says Santé. "I'll stay right behind ya."

One by one the boys leap from the moving train onto the roadbed. Within seconds they are charging toward the forest path that circles around behind the checkpoint. The race is on. During the few minutes the train is stopped, they must run a half a mile through the woods to where the path comes out at the tracks again. And then it's every man or boy for himself as the train picks up speed.

They've all boarded successfully back in Tapachula, so chances are they can do it again. But as Beto explained, it's going to be harder this time. Before re-boarding the train, they have to make it through a gauntlet of thieves waiting in the woods. Some never make it. They are held up long enough to miss the train or worse they are killed because they have no money. Others, aware of what lies in store for the penniless, simply turn around when they see a bandit and run back to the station at Tapachula in hopes of trying again another day.

Santé sticks close to Damian. They jump together and after dusting themselves off, head for the woods. Once they get there. they find the rest of the group bunched up along the trail. Just ahead is a man wielding a machete. Santé is close enough to hear him say there'll be no crossing "his" property until he collects 10 pesos from each person. He holds his machete high in his right hand as he speaks. A few boys give him what he asks; the rest, having already lost what little they had on the train, do nothing. They simply stand there, hearts pounding, aware that in a few minutes the train will be starting up again. If they are stuck here any longer, they will miss it and have to start over again in Tapachula. Mesmerized by the machete, now just inches away, they shrink back along the path.

Suddenly, Beto who is at the head of the line, sees Santé coming up the trail. "Santé…we need you up here," he shouts. As Santé moves forward, the group parts in the middle, opening a path to the man with the machete. Before he reaches the head of the line, Santé raises the macuahuitl high enough so that the man with the machete can see it. When the two men are no more than five feet apart, Santé carefully slides his hand along the obsidian blades…then displays the blood on his fingers. The bandit, clearly unnerved, retreats several feet but does not leave.

Beto sees a chance to add to the drama, "That blood is from the guy who tried to rob us on the train. He got his neck cut, right Santé?"

Santé smiles. "I think it was his shoulder."

Beto continues, "Anyway, he's dead now."

"Probly."

The bandit stares at Beto for a second, then lowers his machete. When Santé takes a step closer, the man turns and races up the path.

"I don't think they're goin' to give us anymore trouble," Beto says to the other boys.

"Maybe I should go as far as the train, just in case," says Santé.

"You mean you ain't getting' back on?" asks Damian.

"No," replies Santé. "I think I'll hike back to Tapachula and try again tomorrow. They guy I'm lookin' for wasn't on the train tonight."

"You mean El Jaguar? asks Beto, not needing an answer. "He should be there tomorrow night. They say he never skips two nights in a row."

"Unless he's dead," chimes in Damian.

Beto scoffs. "Fat chance of that. The guy has nine lives…just like a cat."

"Is it O.K. if I come with you," asks Damian, turning to Santé. "I wanna be there when you give it to 'im."

Santé hesitates. "Well, O.K.…but you gotta promise to stay outta the way. I don't want to see nobody else get hurt…*(pause)*…But you can help by pointin' 'im out to me."

"You ain't gonna need anybody to tell you that it's 'im," says Damian, eyes flashing. "When you see 'im comin' at you on all fours, you'll know who it is. Nobody else can run like that…at least nobody I ever seed."

The group, with Santé and Beto leading the way, continues on to the end of the path without seeing any more bandits. Once all the boys are safely aboard the train, Santé and Damian turn around and begin their hike back to Tapachula.

En route to Tapachula, Santé gets to know a lot about his new friend. He learns that this is Damian's fifth attempt to join his mother in Houston. The boy's mother left Chiapas six years ago after it became clear that she could no longer feed Damian and his younger sister Amanda. By that time the father had already left to start a new family with another woman. All alone and with the local economy in shambles, Mama decided that getting a job in El Norte and sending money back to Chiapas was the only way out…despite the terrible heartache it would create. So she left both children with their grandmother and set out for Houston, Texas.

Damian was O.K. with the loss as long as his Mama called often and promised to return soon. It helped that she sent presents for his birthday and at Christmas time. But when one and then two years passed without seeing her, he became depressed and began sniffing glue with his friends. It wasn't long before he was expelled from school. At home he began fighting with his grandmother who had problems of her own. Eventually things got so bad that she told him he could no longer live at her house. That was the day he returned from town to find the door locked and a box of his clothes set out on the porch. He was devastated. Now completely on his own, he took to sleeping in the shell of a partially-burned out house that still had a piece of the roof intact.

Damian proves to be surprisingly open with his feelings. He goes so far as to tell Santé that he has been having thoughts of suicide lately. Already frail, he has lost weight and developed a serious cough. Boys his own age who are still in school have begun to shun him. The only friend he has left is a boy who has been expelled for stealing food from the cafeteria. By his own admission the only thing that keeps him going is the thought of seeing his mother again.

Santé, who has been taking it all in, asks, "What dya do all day now that you're not goin' to school?"

"I sleep a lot, think about my mom, and sniff glue with my friend."

"What about food?"

"Grandma puts out stuff for me on her back porch. It's kinda like she's feedin' a wild animal she feels sorry for but doesn't want in the house… (*pause*)…but it's better than goin' hungry."

When they reach Tapachula, Damian asks Santé if he can sleep on the floor of his motel room. Santé, alarmed that the boy is becoming attached, says O.K., but reminds him that as soon as his business with El Jaguar is finished, he's heading back to Phoenix. When Damian begs Santé to take him to the U.S., Santé says he'll be going by bus to Nogales and doesn't have enough money for two fares. When Damian begins to cry, Santé promises to think about it.

Next morning, Santé is up first. In the shower he discovers that the only water coming out of the pipes is cold and rusty. He dresses quickly instead and leaves the motel to find some breakfast. After gulping liquid yogurt at a local grocery, he brings back a piece of fruit and sweet roll for Damian who is still asleep on the floor. By 9:00 they are both out on the street, headed for the train depot. The morning is cool enough for Santé to wear his orange jacket. Walking briskly, they take the same route that Santé took the day before...up the road where he met Maria...then down the hill and into the tall grass on the north side of the station.

For the next half hour they wait...watching carefully for the Judiciales and listening for the sound of the incoming train. Suddenly the train emerges from the woods, announcing its arrival with a loud "Hoot", followed by the hissing of steam and a burst of smoke. Just before the train reaches the depot station, migrants from Central America can be seen jumping off and running into the grass. As soon as the train comes to a stop, the Judiciales climb on board to hunt for any migrants who were too timid to jump. Once they have snared a few and confiscated their valuables, they leave for the migra deportation center. As the train starts up again, two dozen or more boys from the north side of the station break from the grass and streak for the cars. Damian goes first with his older friend right behind. Once he has caught up with a boxcar, the frail but lithe 12-year old grabs a rung on the forward ladder. Santé slows so he can catch the ladder at the rear of the same car. Soon both are safely aboard.

At least 25 other migrants, mostly boys, are already aboard. Damian wastes no time telling everybody what happened last night when the bandits attacked. As he fills in the details, heads begin turning to look at the mysterious teenager sitting off to one side. One of the more adventurous, an older boy with greased hair turned up in front, asks to see the weapon sticking out of Santé's backpack. Santé obliges...with his usual warning about the sharpness of the blades. As the boys take turns examining the strange weapon, Damian concludes his tale by acting out the final scene in which Santé brought the macuahuitl down on the bandit's shoulder, punctuating the act with a loud "thud". Amidst riotous cheers, the boys form a circle around the man/boy with the orange jacket. Some reach out to touch his arm or leg; others voice a sigh of relief. The more skeptical ones remain where they are.

When the train slows to snake its way around a curve, Damian spots two men climbing aboard the boxcar just ahead. He alerts the others who quickly rise and get behind Santé. The two intruders waste no time leaping from their boxcar to the one where Santé and the boys are sitting. The very speed of their approach indicates that they are up to no good. As they draw near, they reach into their belts and draw out knives. At a distance Santé watches carefully. Before the bandits can get close enough to attack, he stands up and raises his macuahuitl. The two men immediately stop in their tracks, mesmerized by the glistening of obsidian blades protruding from each side of the weapon…then turn around and flee. To Santé, it is clear they have been warned of his presence…presumably by the partner of the man whose shoulder blade he severed last night.

The boys celebrate with a whoop…some going so far as to embrace Santé from behind. Damian is ecstatic, "See…I told ya," he yells to the others. "They know what he done last night. They're too scared to try again."

"I'll bet their shittin' in their pants right now," offers one boy whose own underwear is a bit moist. "You see that guy's eyes when Santé lifted his weapon?" adds a second. "I thought they was goin' to pop outta his head like a coupla grapes."

The celebration continues right up to the time when they have to jump from the train at El Arrocera and race around to the other side of the station. Once they safely hit ground, they gather on the path and wait until Santé moves to the head of the line. Entering the woods as a group, they move slowly, being careful not to talk or make any noise with their feet. Not a bandit can be seen or heard. When the path comes out again near the tracks, it is clear that the threat is over. The boys are jubilant.

"I guess you scared 'em good, Santé," Damian whispers from behind.

"I dunno," Santé replies. "Maybe they're jis' waitin' in the trees until they think it's safe to attack again."

Damian shakes his head. "Could be. Maybe it's like with a snake...if you wanna stop it from bitin', you gotta kill it. And to kill it you gotta cut off its head...right?"

Santé turns as if to avoid answering, then changes his mind, "I thought you said he was a cat."

Damian chuckles. "Maybe he's a little of each."

Once they arrive at the tracks, they don't have long to wait before they see the train heading toward them. Just like it did in Tapachula, it sounds a warning "Hoot" as it picks up speed. Flush with renewed energy, the boys make a mad dash for the boxcar ladders. Santé and Damian wait until all have scrambled aboard safely before turning around and heading back to town. There is less said this time...and more thinking about what is yet to come. With each step Damian conjures up images of carnage, some more grotesque than others, all ending in the violent death of the masked cat whom they hope to meet tonight.

For Santé, the walk is a time to prepare for what is coming. This could be the moment he's been hoping for...a mano-a-mano meeting with Raul's murderer. But it's possible that El Jaguar won't show up...after all, by now he's been warned that there could be someone waiting for him...someone armed with a lethal weapon. So, what will he do? Up to now he's had his way with the migrants; they are young and unarmed...easy prey for a big, hungry cat. But things have changed. One of his gang has already been killed, another scared away. Clearly, it's not going to be as easy as it used to be...(*pause*)...Will he come anyway?

"I want him to come," Santé whispers. "He must come."

26

When Predator Becomes Prey

By 5:30 P.M. Santé and Damian are hiding in the grass again, waiting for the 6:00 to arrive from Guatemala. Up to now the routine has been the same as before…with a small difference; the other migrants are huddling closer. Some whisper "Hola" from their hiding places a few yards away. Others come over and introduce themselves to the man/boy in the orange jacket. Some want to examine the macuahuitl; all want to hear Damian's account of what happened on the morning train.

The train appears to be late, although no one knows for sure since they don't have watches. As usual, it hoots once before it stops and a second time as it prepares to start up again. All around Santé the grasses flutter as a dozen boys prepare to hitch a ride north. When the time comes to race for a ladder, they wait for Santé to climb up before following suit. Once all are safely on top, they quickly form a semi-circle behind the boy in the orange jacket…and direct their attention to the boxcar just ahead.

The train gradually picks up speed, soon reaching the point where it is too dangerous either to climb aboard or jump. In the semi-circle, all eyes are on the car just ahead, each boy wanting to be the first to spot the masked cat. For several minutes they wait, but no one appears. Then suddenly four men can be seen climbing onto the far end of the boxcar just in front; they are too old to be migrants. "Bandits," several boys shout. The intruders make no move but rather stand there, staring along the car roof as if trying to determine Santé's identity from a safe distance. Minutes go by as the two groups study each other.

Suddenly, the four men separate to make room for a fifth. He is taller than his colleagues, almost six feet tall, and wearing a black cloak. Santé squints to see his face; from this distance and with the sun setting, it is impossible to make out his features. Without moving, he leans forward and tightens his grip on the macuahuitl.

"It's him," shouts Damian whose eyes are better than most. "He's got a mask…it's black like the rest of 'im. I seed 'im before…it's him alright… it's El Jaguar."

A muffled moan goes up from the ring of boys behind Santé. When one of the boys reaches out to clutch Santé's shoulder, Damian pulls him back. "Yir gettin' in his way. Stay back." The boy, only eleven and making his first trip, begins to whimper. "Shh," whispers Damian. "Don't make no noise. It's goin' to be alright…you'll see."

All eyes are on the man with the black mask.

When El Jaguar turns to say something to the other men, they disappear behind him. He is now alone…and apparently unarmed. He stares at Santé from a distance…then slowly, step by step, makes his way forward. By the time he reaches the end of the car in front, his three-inch claws are clearly visible. To leave no doubt, he flexes his fingers and points both hands at Santé.

Through the slits in his mask he studies the group on the boxcar before him. What he sees whets his appetite. Convinced that he is facing a single adversary, he modulates his voice into a low, menacing growl and prepares to leap onto the car where Santé and the boys are sitting.

What he cannot see is the large branch jutting out over the tracks some fifty yards behind him. One of the boys sitting to the rear of Santé sees it and is about to yell when Damian yanks him backward and covers his mouth. El Jaguar senses trouble and turns quickly to look behind him. It is too late. As the train races forward, the branch, stretched out over the tracks and no more than a few feet above the train top, strikes him in the back and sweeps him into the space between the two boxcars.

The boys shriek their joy as the Jaguar disappears, headed for certain death on the rails below. Damian gets up and starts dancing; others quickly join in. Santé refuses the invitation but breathes a sigh of relief. Convinced that the danger has passed, he puts the macuahuitl back in his pack.

The celebration continues as the train rushes northward. Bits of potato, bread and tortilla are passed around as the boys, no longer silenced by fear, break into song. Moved by the excitement of his fellows, Santé adds his voice to the din. Hugs are shared all around…with Santé receiving the lion's share. Even the train seems to join in with a loud "Hoot" as it releases steam into the cool summer air.

Suddenly everything changes. Damian is the first to see him. From the space between boxcars…the very space that only minutes ago swallowed the man in black…a masked head appears, followed by a pair of hands and arms. Damian shrieks, "Oh my God!" as the giant cat, apparently returned from the dead, claws his way up onto the top of the boxcar where Santé and the boys are sitting. Terrorized by what they see, the boys stop singing and press in behind Santé. Santé stands and raises his macuahuitl.

Halfway down the boxcar, El Jaguar drops into a crouch then begins racing toward Santé on all fours. Petrified, the boys shrink further back. Santé braces himself for the attack. The cat, now no more than ten feet away, growls and flexes its claws. With macuahuitl held high, Santé stands ready. He waits until the cat springs toward him…then, grips his weapon and aims it at his assailant's neck.

It never arrives. Breaking through from behind, one of the bandits grabs Santé's arm, pulling him backward onto the boxcar roof. Still gripping his weapon but helpless to use it, Santé screams as El Jaguar sinks his claws into his chest, drawing blood. When Damian sees his friend pinned to the boxcar, he instinctively flings himself toward the bandit who is holding Santé's arm. Wrapping his frail arm around the bandit's neck, he pulls him backward just long enough for Santé to free his arm. As Damian and the bandit wrestle behind him, Santé, still on his back with El Jaguar on top of him, brings the macuahuitl down on his adversary's spine. Although short of a fatal blow, it pierces the skin, bringing shrieks of pain. Stunned by the blow, El Jaguar slides backward off his prey and stumbles to his feet. As he turns to run, Santé, still clutching the bloody macuahuitl, lifts himself off the boxcar and gives chase.

Behind him a small uprising is in full force. Emboldened by Damian's heroics, the other boys have thrown themselves on top of the bandit, forcing him onto his back. Multiple fists, still small and undeveloped, fly at the intruder like a swarm of angry bees. Pummeled into semi-consciousness, the man is pushed to the edge of the boxcar and rolled off onto the tracks. A hiatus in the sound of wheel on rail tells of his grim fate.

Shouts of the boys' victory reach Santé as he races toward El Jaguar. Although bleeding from multiple chest wounds, he holds his macuahuitl high, buoyed by the hope that revenge is just yards away. Up ahead, El Jaguar stumbles toward the end of the boxcar, hesitates, then leaps to the next car where he crawls for a few yards before forcing himself to stand again. Once on his feet, he reaches around his back to rub the massive cut to his lumbar. Sickened by what he feels, he sags, then falls again. From his knees, he casts a quick glance at his pursuer, rises, and hurries on.

From ten yards behind, Santé, recognizing that his quarry is crippled, slows his pace to conserve his strength. By now his shirt is soaked with blood where El Jaguar's claws have ripped open his skin. Gripping the shirt with his free hand, he presses it against his chest to staunch the bleeding. It helps, but he's starting to feel weak. It is clear that if he loses much more blood, he's going to faint.

Back on the other car, the boys watch with morbid fascination as predator and prey, roles now reversed, leap from car to car, one bent over at the hip, the other clutching shirt to chest. In an adjoining field a farmer drops his work to look up as two figures, silhouetted against the darkening sky, re-enact the tale in which Achilles, enraged at the murder of his friend Patroclus, chases Hector around the garrison at Troy before disemboweling him.

Still leaking blood, El Jaguar stops at the edge of the last boxcar and looks down; ahead is a hopper carrying coal. He turns for a glimpse at Santé who is only a few yards behind…then rips off his mask and jumps. Even as he falls, he senses that the end is near. With no strength left and too realistic to expect mercy, he resigns himself to death. By the time Santé arrives at the edge of the hopper, the cat is lying face down on the coal. Santé pauses for a second…then jumps in after him.

When El Jaguar fails to move, Santé turns him over. His skin, up to now hidden by the mask, is light, even sallow…definitely more Mestizo than Indian. His eyes, small and beady, sink lifelessly into sockets too large for his narrow face. Beneath his full black mustache, his lips part to reveal one missing tooth and two that are severely chipped.

Sensing Santé's presence, El Jaguar opens his eyes…than looks up at his pursuer and sneers. "Yir bleedin' to death," he whispers hoarsely, his eyes aimed at his adversary's chest. When Santé fails to respond, he adds, "Too bad about yir brother…he weren't too smart…shoulda had some money on 'im." The words strike Santé like a kick to the groin. His lips curl. From deep inside, a voice screams for justice. He opens his mouth to speak but the words, too fevered to articulate, never reach his lips.

He drops the macuahuitl. As he looks down at El Jaguar, his body tenses with a surge of energy. The burst is so sudden, so powerful as to defy explanation. Bewildered, he flexes his shoulder muscles and takes a deep breath. As he does so, an image flashes into consciousness…the image of a woman in Oaxaca who was photographed lifting a truck by its front fender when her two-year old daughter got pinned under its wheels. He smiles at the memory. Without a word, he grits his teeth, then nods his head in silent affirmation.

Oblivious to the loss of blood, he bends over and grabs El Jaguar by the shirt and pants. As his victim begins to squirm, Santé lifts him to his knees, then to his waist. Dangling in mid-air, El Jaguar flails desperately with both arms and legs. Santé takes a final breath and summons the whole of his strength. Bracing himself on the coal, he raises the cat's body all the way to his chest…holds it steady for a moment…then hurls it over the side of the hopper. As it sails through the air, a creaking of the rails below warns that the train is passing over a bridge. Too exhausted to see where the body lands, Santé closes his eyes and collapses onto the macuahuitl.

For the last five minutes the boys have watched from a distance…right up to the point where both men jump disappear into the hopper. Because the hopper is lower than the boxcar, they are unable to see what is happening until Santé stands up and lifts El Jaguar to his chest. Transfixed, they stare in disbelief as he hurls the full-grown man over the side of the hopper…

then wait for the thud of flesh against the railings below as the body twists grotesquely before falling into the river.

Without pausing to celebrate, the boys rush en masse to the hopper where Santé is lying face down on the coal. Revived by their cheers, he struggles to his feet and hugs each one in turn. Still groggy, he unzips his jacket and rolls up his shirt. The boys nearest to him let out a loud moan. Around his nipples there are a half dozen deep claw marks, some of which are still bleeding. When he starts dabbing the wounds with his shirt, one of the older boys brings out some rags from his pack; another offers several yards of string for holding the rags in place. When everything has been secured, Santé rolls his shirt back down and announces the treatment a success.

Together they hunker down in the coal bed, bunching close for warmth against the coming cold. As the train hurtles northward, an unanticipated calm envelops the riders. Over and over they rehash details of what they've seen but still have trouble believing. Each struggles to preserve the memory of what happened. No one is untouched.

As the train approaches El Arrocera, the group gets ready to jump. One by one they land on the roadbed and race for the path at the entrance to the woods. There are no bandits to be seen there or anywhere inside the forest. Some of the boys hoot and holler; others whistle or dance; all are delirious. When it comes time to re-board on the other side of the station, many seem reluctant to continue without Santé. Even when Damian explains that there is nothing to worry about now that the snake has been decapitated, some of those present mumble openly about the dangers that lie ahead. The parting is difficult for Santé as well. When he tries to say goodbye, he is nearly knocked over as a dozen exuberant but anxious boys fight to get the last hug. With Damian at his side, he waits until all are safely on board before waving back. Satisfied that he has done what he could, he turns and heads back to Tapachula.

On the way, Damian stumbles, then falls to the ground, clutching his arm. As Santé helps him to his feet, he asks what's wrong. After considerable prompting, Damian admits that the bandit he was wrestling with cut him with a knife before the rest of the boys jumped on. When he tries to minimize the injury, Santé insists that the boy lean on him the rest of the way to Tapachula.

They head directly to the clinic where both are admitted and receive emergency care for their wounds. Because Damian's condition is more serious, he is told he must stay for several days until the cut to his arm begins to heal. Santé, with a clean set of bandages on his chest, is free to leave. At Damian's bedside he promises to send money for a bus to Nogales as soon as he gets back to Phoenix. Their final hug seems to last forever. On his way out the door, Santé, who hasn't cried since early childhood, feels tears on his cheek. When he reaches to wipe them, he smiles at his discovery. They are not his own.

27

A Talk with Javier

Before leaving for Phoenix, Santé returns to Oaxaca to say goodbye to Mama and Alma. His mother, who hasn't slept well since he left for Tapachula, is relieved to see that nothing bad has happened to him. Alma, equally anxious but eager for details, wants know what happened on the train but covers her ears when he gets to the fight with El Jaguar. "I'm just glad that Raul's murder has been avenged," she explains. While the three talk in the kitchen, the Father listens from outside but is careful to avoid any direct contact with his son.

Throughout the discussion, Santé appears to be frustrated…a feeling evident to Alma not only in the staccato cadences of his speech but in the total absence of a smile. She can see the hesitation but is unsure whether it comes from his earlier confrontation with Papa…or something deeper. Sensing her brother's need to share his feelings with someone, she suggests that he pay a visit to his Uncle Javier before leaving Oaxaca. Santé agrees.

Later in the day he hikes over to Javier's apartment and knocks on the door. The traditional bear hug comes so quickly he doesn't have time to protect his chest. Javier, reacting to the grimace on his nephew's face, offers a hasty apology. "Sorry, didn't mean to crush you like that. What happened? You get hurt in Tapachula?"

After sitting down, Santé gives his uncle a detailed report of events…from his first encounter with the bandits up to the moment when he threw El Jaguar off the train.

"Well, he got what he deserved," Javier says. "An evil man for sure…but tell me, was the macuahuitl helpful? Sounds like you had to use it more than once."

"Yeah, many times…not jis' on the train but before that…like when I crossed the desert. I don't know what I woulda done without it."

"Let me take a peek (*pointing to Santé's backpack*)."

"Sure (*handing the weapon to Javier*)."

"Looks like the obsidian's been nicked in a few places. How dya do that?"

"Bones, probably. I got El Jaguar on the back and another guy on the shoulder…that was on the train. Earlier I had to use it on a coupla bandits who attacked us in the desert…oh yeah, then there was a trucker chasing my girlfriend in the woods…got him on the leg."

"My God, Santé, when I made it for you, I figured you'd probably hang it on the wall somewhere. I had no idea that… (*whispering*)…Did you kill anybody?"

"I'm not sure about the trucker…but yeah, the others…they all died."

Javier gulps. "Are you in any kind of trouble…you know, because of that?"

"Not that I know of. On the train, the only ones who saw what happened were the kids I was ridin' with. They was pretty happy to see it happen… anyway, they're half-way to the U.S. by now."

"How about in the desert…any witnesses?"

"Well yeah…a family…mother and daughter…but I did it to protect them, so I don't think they're gonna turn me in."

Javier rubs his chin. "Well, how do you feel about all this…any guilt or remorse?"

"Not really. Not that I enjoy killin'…but somebody had to do it. They was all evil men who were preyin' on kids and old people…people who couldn't defend themselves…(*pause*)…The macuahuitl sort of evened things up."

Javier chuckles. "You remind me a little of Emiliano Zapata…you know, defender of the weak and helpless. Are you following in his footsteps?"

Santé shakes his head. "Not really. I was jis' tryin' to get to the U.S. so I could get a job and help my family. I didn't go lookin' for no trouble. It came to me."

"Well, it's easy to feel like Zapata…wanting to help people who are having a hard time. We're surrounded by families here in Oaxaca that live from day to day, never sure where their next meal is coming from."

"Well, yeah…you're right…I know lots of families like that. Those kids I met on the train for instance…they wanna go north to see their parents or to send money home, but they can't afford the bus…so they hop on a train and take their chances with the bandits. A lot of them don't make it…they lose a leg or arm…or like Raul…get throwd off the train. What I don't understand is why they got such a bum deal. I mean…is it their fault they was too poor to take the bus? It really isn't, is it?"

When Javier says nothing, Santé continues. "Take the kids up in Phoenix…they've got everything…beds and refrigerators, good food, new clothes, bikes, baseball gloves, video games, iPods for music, TV's in their bedrooms…everything. Most kids I've met up there learn how to drive when they're 15 or 16; some even have their own cars in high school. And get this: their parents don't pull 'em outta school in 9th grade so they can earn money for the family; they encourage 'em to finish school and maybe go on to college…*(pause)*…I dunno…it jis' doesn't seem fair…you know, that people down here have so little when it's not our fault."

"I've got no answer for that one, Santé."

"I don't understand it. How come people don't get what they deserve…you know…if you work hard, you should make good money; if you fool around and goof off, yir gonna stay poor. Isn't that the way it's s'posed to work?"

"I don't think there's any particular way it's 'supposed' to work, Santé."

"Why not? It don't seem right that some people have to live in dirt-floor huts and go without clean water or electricity jis' 'cuz they was born in a city like Oaxaca. Maybe if everybody in the world was poor, it would make sense. But it's not like that. Up in Phoenix there's lots of people who have beautiful houses, fancy cars, and refrigerators filled with good things to eat. Now I ask you…do they really deserve all that nice stuff…did they do somethin' special to earn it…or was they jis' lucky to be born in Phoenix and not Oaxaca?…(*pause*)…What I'm sayin' is…do people get what they deserve…or is it all jis' a matter of luck…good luck if yir born in Phoenix, bad luck if yir born in Oaxaca?"

"That's really hard to say…maybe some of each. I don't know."

Santé, clearly dissatisfied with the answer, shakes his head. "Take my family…Mama and Alma work night and day but are never able to make much money. I'll bet that if they was livin' in Phoenix, they'd be doin' pretty well. Now, is it their fault that they was born here and not in the U.S? Is it their fault that they was born in a place where no matter how hard you work, you jis' can't get ahead?…(*pause*)…Those kids up in Phoenix… the ones that have everything…how'd they get it all…did they earn those TV's and iPhones in some sweat shop…did they have to fight desert snakes and bandits before they got all that stuff…or was it all jis' handed to 'em?"

From the look on Santé's face, Javier knows better than to intervene.

"I can understand if one kid pulls himself outta poverty by workin' hard and gettin' educated while his brother stays poor 'cuz he'd rather buy a car and chase girls. That makes sense. But take two kids the same age… both poor but smart and hard-workin'. One is born in Oaxaca, the other in Phoenix. Don't they both deserve a chance to get ahead…to move up in the world? But we all know what's gonna happen…one's gonna get rich and live in a big house, the other's lucky if he don't end up sleepin' on a dirt floor…(*pause*)…I ask you…is that fair?"

By now Javier has heard enough. "Whoever said life had to be fair?" he asks, not waiting for an answer. "Think of the Aztecs who innocently offered presents when Cortez marched into Tenochtitlan…and then watched while their people got slaughtered and their whole way of life destroyed. Or consider the West Africans who were caught by slave traders and hauled across the Atlantic to Virginia in chains? Do you think they deserved that fate? And while you're at it, ask the Sioux Indians up north about fairness as they watched the invading Whites butcher their buffalos and drive them off their land. It didn't matter how hard the Aztecs, Africans or Sioux worked or how virtuous they were…or even how faithful they were to whatever gods they believed in. In the end they still got screwed… (*pause*)…That's just the way life is."

Santé slumps back in his chair, saying nothing. What he just heard is too new, too strange to evoke an answer. He was hoping, even expecting, that Javier would argue that life was basically fair, perhaps citing examples of how, in the long run, people get pretty much what they deserve. But that's not what he just heard. His uncle, whom he has always respected, said the opposite. He claimed not only that life was inherently unfair but that we should accept that fact and move on. "But that's crazy," Santé says to himself. "How can you agree that some people get more than they deserve while others get less…and then say that's the way life is…that you jis' have to accept it? That sounds like yir givin' up…throwin' in the towel. That don't sound right to me. There's gotta be some other way."

Javier is aware of his nephew's dilemma and moves quickly to change the subject. "Tell me, have you found a girlfriend up there in Phoenix? I've heard that there are lots of pretty ones…some probably eager to find a handsome Latino boy like you."

Santé smiles at the thought, relieved to take his mind off heavier questions. "I found one…and she's very pretty. Maybe we gonna get married some day."

"What's her name?"

"Anna. I met her in the library where she works. She's helpin' me with English. She says I learn fast."

"How's her Spanish?"

"Real good. She learned it from her mother who's Honduran …came here in a truck many years ago. I met the mother and father last month at their house. The father is very smart. I don't think I understood everything he said."

Javier rises. "Well, I hope everything works out for you. After all you've been through, you certainly deserve a few breaks."

At the door, Santé turns and smiles, "But you said we don't always get what we des...."

(*Interrupting*) "Forget what I said. Just enjoy what comes your way."

"O.K. Goodbye for now. I will write you from Phoenix."

"Bye, Santé."

28

The Tunnel

A few hours listening to other crossers in the Nogales bus terminal is enough to tell Santé which of the three tunnels running under the U.S.-Mexican border is the safest to use. It's the one migrants refer to as "Highway #2". Like the others, it's a giant culvert, almost five feet high, whose function is to drain water away from the hilly residential and commercial areas on either side of the valley. On the U.S. side the tunnel comes out in a field behind an abandoned parking lot which the Border Patrol inspects several times a day, looking for crossers. Fortunately, Santé is told, they are much less likely to do so at night.

While soliciting information, Santé falls in with a small group of migrants… mostly older Mexicans and their children. Some have crossed this way before and have important information to share. Among other things, they say that the Border Patrol has tried to slow the flow of crossers by erecting a metal gate midway through the tunnel…at the point that divides the U.S. from Mexico. According to more than one informant, however, it can be broken easily. More of a problem they say is a gang of teenagers who live and sleep in the tunnel and, like the trolls of Scandinavia, demand payment from anyone who tries to cross *their* property.

One thing Santé likes about the group he has attached himself to is that they have no coyote. They are brave enough to try crossing alone, thereby saving thousands of dollars and avoiding the risk of being abandoned. The down side, of course, is that once they make it through the tunnel, they will be completely on their own as they fan out to Phoenix in the West or Houston in the East. Each member of the group has a plan for traversing that part of the trip; some will walk until they're a safe distance from the city, then hitchhike the rest of the way; others plan to call relatives who will pick them up in a car outside Nogales. All have been told to avoid the buses in and around the city which are a favorite hunting ground for the Border Patrol.

The group agrees to meet at the Mexican entrance to Highway #2 at 8:00 P.M. With nothing better to do, Santé roams the city streets until he feels tired, then heads for a restaurant. After gulping down a large torta milanese with salad, he returns to his motel for an afternoon nap. Soon after 6:00 P.M. he is up and ready to go.

By 7:45 everyone is at the entrance. There are now eleven in the group…six men, two women and three young girls. For most, this is their second or third trip through the tunnel. Joaquin, a squat Mexican of Mixtec heritage who is traveling with his wife and daughter, warns the newcomers that it's going to be anything but pleasant. In a hushed voice he explains that he made it all the way through last month only to be apprehended on the U.S. side as he emerged from the tunnel.

His warning proves to be accurate. The tunnel itself is about 40 yards long. Because it gets no sunlight, it remains dank and clammy. Pools of water serve as traps for young rodents and smell of putrefying flesh. With Joaquin's flashlight showing the way, the group moves into the tunnel and heads for the metal barrier half-way through. As they step gingerly around the fetid water, they keep their eyes peeled for signs of the teenage gang known to inhabit the area. Fear ripples through the group when Joaquin points to a pile of soggy blankets heaped on a stretch of dry land. Multiple footprints in the sand confirm the presence of other humans. Everyone is told to speak only in whispers.

Ten yards further into the tunnel, just beyond the point where Highway #2 intersects with a smaller culvert coming from the East, Joaquin signals the group to stop. Directly ahead is someone holding a flashlight. When Joaquin, hoping to avoid detection, turns off his own light, the person up ahead comes closer, scanning the area with his own torch. As he approaches the migrant group, whispers can be heard. He is not alone.

When he is no more than ten feet away, he lowers his light so that the migrants can see. What they see is a young man of about 18, surrounded by seven or eight other teenagers. The boy in front, known as Christian to his friends, is brandishing a large kitchen knife. He is the first to speak. "If you wanna get through here you gotta pay a fee…$50 U.S. a head," he says. His Spanish is street Spanish, easily recognized as Chiapas. A younger teen named Hugo moves quickly to Christian's side. "Hey," he says, staring at Joaquin, "that chain around yir neck looks like gold." Without waiting for a response he reaches out and yanks it off Joaquin's neck. Joaquin's wife, Sofia, who is standing beside him, begins to tremble. "That's from his mother," she whimpers, "and her mother before that. Someday it's goin' to be for our children."

"Lookit, bitch," says Hugo, taking in a breath to elevate his diminutive size. "You wanna get to El Norte? Then stop yappin' about the chain and gimme the money in yir bra. I can see that yir storin' more there than your tits."

Unseen is Santé who remains in the shadows over to the right, his head lowered slightly to avoid touching the moist roof of the tunnel. From his vantage point, he can see what is happening without being seen himself. In many ways, the scene resembles a theater. In the midst of blackness stretching in both directions of the tunnel, a tiny stage stands illuminated, drawing all eyes to its unfolding drama. As Santé watches, actors young and old move in and out of the light, performing their parts in turn.

Behind their leader, feral children no longer claimed by their parents, trade shouts of encouragement, exulting in the helplessness of their prey. Some wield sticks and make menacing gestures.

The crossers, partially blinded by the light and weary from sleepless nights, stare blankly at their captors. This is hardly what they expected. Instead of kinship with their similarly dark-skinned relatives, they find callousness, the hallmark of those who having been cast aside early in life, have given up the quest for love and resigned themselves to a world where power is all that matters.

Slowly Santé slides toward Christian who is now holding a knife to the chest of the man next to Joaquin. The man, a stocky Guatemalan in his mid-forties, aware that his wife and children are crouching behind him, grips his walking stick tightly, then, casting caution aside, raises it over Christian's head. He is too slow. Before the stick can reach its target, the boy's knife penetrates his chest, sending him screaming to the ground.

Santé sees it all. As the Guatemalan twitches in a pool of blood, he moves closer. His heart is pounding, his breath labored. It is too late for caution. Holding the macuahuitl in his right hand, he steps unseen from the shadows and advances toward the light. Christian is too busy gloating over his easy victory to see what is about to happen. Noiselessly, Santé proceeds to within a few feet of his adversary, raises his weapon and brings it down swiftly on the boy's neck. At the last second Christian catches a glimpse of the obsidian blades and turns his head away. The move, while understandably instinctive, has the unintended effect of exposing still more of his neck. As the macuahuitl slices through the boy's flesh, severing arteries and vertebrae, his head falls to one side, partially separated but still hinged to his body. A collective gasp fills the tunnel. In horror, the thieving teenagers turn and run for the exit, not bothering to see if the man with the strange weapon is following. Christian is dead within seconds, his dismembered body left to rot in the tunnel.

Before leaving, Santé stoops to press a piece of cloth over the cut in the Guatemalan's chest, then lifts him to his feet. With help from men on both sides, he begins to walk. Slowly, the migrants, stunned into silence by what they have just witnessed, follow the fleeing boys out of the tunnel into an empty parking lot. The only cars there are old, beat-up models with For Sale signs stuck to their windshields. Nearby, the streetlights are on; a few pedestrians can be seen heading for the shopping district. After hugs and well-wishes, newly-made friends make their farewells and go their separate ways, some east toward Houston and the Carolinas, others west toward Phoenix and Los Angeles.

Santé is the last to leave. Before looking for a public phone, he brushes the dirt from his pants and pulls a clean shirt from his backpack. As Javier warned many months ago, with the Border Patrol searching for "illegals," it is important to avoid looking like a "wetback." Once he has found a phone, he stops to consider the time. "Probably around 9:00," he muses… not too late to call."

"Hello," comes the voice, warm and welcoming.

"Anna…it's me."

"Santé…oh my God…where are you?"

"In Nogales…can you come and get me? I can't take a bus…the Border Patrol are everywhere."

"Of course…but I'll have to ask my parents first. My father may need the car in the morning."

"No problem. It's only two hours…but don't hurry. I know you don't like to drive at night."

"Alright. But how are you? It seems strange not hearing from you for days. I've had all kinds of fantasies. Did you find the man who killed Raul?"

"Yes. I tell you everything when we get together. Do you know the big shopping area in Nogales…the one right next to the border? I wait for you at the Mobil gas station…it's on that street…somewhere in the middle…I forget the name."

"I'll find it. Can you hide somewhere until I get there?"

"It's dark. I stay in the shadows until you come."

"O.K.…(*pause*)…Do you still love me?"

"Silly girl. Of course I love you. I think of you all the time."

"Hmm. I like that. Please don't stop."

"O.K. Bye, Anna."

"Bye carino."

29

An Orange Jacket

At the regular morning meeting in Sheriff Culpepper's office, the main topic of conversation is a recent newspaper story about a Mexican boy who crossed illegally into the U.S, then returned to Chiapas to avenge his brother's murder. No names are given …just the fact that he wore an orange jacket with the name El Vengador (*The Avenger*) sewn on the back. The story is based on interviews with migrants who made it to the States before being picked up by the Border Patrol. They agreed to talk to the newspaper as long as their names were withheld.

Tom Flaherty, the visitor from Border Patrol, is the first to comment. "They say he took out several bandits with some weird kind of machete his uncle made for him."

"Yeah, I forget the name of it," adds Walt Baker, an ardent anti-immigrationist, "but they say it's really deadly. Took one bandit's head right off."

"Whew!," exclaims Jim Jaccoby. "I mean the kid's got guts. He's only 17 or so but he didn't hesitate to go after the head honcho…you know, the guy who threw his brother off the train."

Tom is quick to respond. "Oh yeah, the one known as El Jaguar. They say he wore a black mask and had huge claws...even ran like a giant cat. I guess he scared the shit outta those kids…no wonder they gave 'im whatever money they had."

Ted Polk, who usually sits at the back of the group and says little, hops down from his desk. "The article said he was so scary that kids actually jumped off the train when they saw him comin'…even when the train was racin' along at 30 or 40 miles an hour. Can you beat that? Some of them got hurt real bad…I guess a couple even got killed."

Tom nods enthusiastically. "Yeah, but what really strikes me is the courage of the kid in the orange jacket. Let's face it…he goes down there all alone and takes on a whole gang of bandits…some of them armed with knives or machetes. And then he goes after the leader…an older, bigger man… the one who murdered his brother. He refuses to quit until he's made this guy pay for what he did."

"What's really hard to believe," adds Jim, "is how he picks this Jaguar guy up from the coal bed after chasin' him from car to car…and then, holding him chest-high, throws him off the train. Maybe the kids made that part up… I dunno. It sounds too good to be true."

"I don't know," says Walt. "If you're really fired up…as this boy musta been…you can do almost anything. I've heard stories like that before."

"Yeah, but c'mon," says Emiliano, the only college graduate in the group, "the kids said that this Jaguar guy was tall…probably weighed at least 175 pounds…maybe 200. How can you pick up a load like that when you got blood pouring outta your chest? It can't be done. The kids musta made it up."

"Well, remember," says Walt, "we're talkin' revenge. That's a pretty powerful motive, wouldn't you agree? Besides, the boy in the orange jacket was powerfully built. At least that's what the other kids said."

Through all the comments, Earl sits quietly, letting images of El Jaguar, the boy in the orange jacket, and the train flicker across his mind. Unlike the others in the room, he hasn't read the article. At first he doesn't pay much attention to what is being said. His thoughts are still on Eric and how he's going to pay for next year's tuition at A.S.U.

As more details of the carnage in Chiapas emerge, he begins to listen carefully. Still, he says nothing. It's not until he hears how the boy in the orange jacket picked the Jaguar up and tossed him off the train that he becomes engrossed. Once alert, he sits up in his chair and starts putting the story in perspective, "Who the hell is this kid, anyway?" he asks himself.

"He's only a teenager but he goes down to Chiapas on his own…armed with nothin' but a homemade machete…and takes on a whole gang of bandits …including their leader. O.K.…so he was an illegal crosser…but Christ, you gotta admit the kid's got balls. And he's only 17…same age as Eric."

Without speaking, he shakes his head in admiration. "I would love to have a kid like that," he muses. "Who wouldn't? He crosses illegally into the U.S.…that part I don't like…but he's got the heart of a warrior. Somebody killed his brother and he's not goin' to let 'im get away with it…even if he dies tryin'. That takes guts. How many illegals would risk everything they achieved up here…a job, money, a nice place to live…and go back to where they came from in order to confront a murderer? Not many, I tell you. No…this kid's got heart…lots of heart."

Still listening, he tries to form an image of the kid in the orange jacket. According to what he has just heard, the boy is short, broad-shouldered, muscular, and bronze-skinned like an Indian…with black hair and brown eyes. He knows this much…but still has trouble picturing him. Each time he tries, he sees a face…but it's Eric's face instead. The skin is pale, the eyes narrowed to a slit, the lips frozen in a perpetual smirk…more bicycle thief than warrior. Earl recoils in horror. "What's goin' on here?" he asks. "Why do I keep seein' Eric? Is there somethin' I wanta say…or am I feelin' guilty because I admire this other kid?" He takes a deep breath. "O.K., so I would love to have a son like this other boy…but that doesn't mean I'm ready to trade Eric in for a stranger. The two are different for sure…but…"

His thoughts continue to drift aimlessly as the discussion comes to an end. As the others rise to leave, he bids them goodbye but refrains from commenting on the article…leaving the impression that he doesn't share their enthusiasm for the story. Several confront him with raised eyebrows, waiting for a sign that he too is impressed. It never comes. For the others there's no conflict; it's easy to admire a heroic deed from a distance, even when an illegal crosser is involved. For Earl it's more complicated. There's family to be considered. "Am I being disloyal to Eric?" he asks, "when I marvel at what this Mexican kid did? Let's be honest. He has the courage I was hoping to find in my own boy, but Eric turned out different…good with girls and cars apparently, but not much else. Maybe it's my fault…

or maybe his mother spoiled him…I dunno. But yeah, I would love to be this other kid's father…go huntin' and fishin' together…watch him play sports…be at his side as he grows up. Now, does that make me a bad person? I dunno. Maybe."

The very next day Earl hunts down a copy of the newspaper that featured interviews with crossers from Chiapas. He reads it over and over until he has memorized every bit of information about the boy at the center of it all. When no one is around, he closes his eyes and replays each scene in turn like a movie. He sees the boy hiding in the grass, climbing on the train, killing a bandit, racing through the woods, confronting the Jaguar… and then, believe it or not, tossing the monster cat overboard. With each playing of the movie, the boy becomes more real…and more deeply lodged in the Sheriff's psyche.

Slowly he sheds his misgivings about wanting a son like the boy in the orange jacket…even allows himself the luxury of picturing the two of them sitting down and talking together somewhere in Phoenix. To enjoy the fantasy, however, he must forget that the boy may have crossed into the U.S. illegally and, technically, should be sent back to Mexico. He is helped to forget this inconvenient truth by the way his co-workers reacted to the newspaper article. "After all," he muses, "if people in my own office aren't letting their jobs get in the way of admiring the kid, why should I?"

He's aware that he still has a job to do, however, and that includes helping the Border Patrol, I.N.S. and I.C.E. catch undocumented crossers. Reminded of his duty, he leaves the office and heads over to the Maricopa TV Repair shop to check on Don and Paula. He is particularly interested in getting any new information Paula might have on the boy they're training…the 'apprentice' who just bought a pickup and waited until the last day to get it inspected. From what she told him a couple of weeks ago, the Mexican certainly sounds like he crossed illegally. If so, it's just a matter of time before he slips up and gets caught.

At the shop he nods briefly to Don before looking around for Paula. He doesn't have long to wait. When she hears people talking, she enters from the apartment and gives the Sheriff a wave, but doesn't go so far as to shake hands. Earl scrutinizes her face closely, looking for signs that she still intends to cooperate. When he doesn't see what he's looking for, he concludes that it's probably because of Don's presence. He can be patient.

The Sheriff starts with an innocent question about business. Gradually the discussion moves to the question of what should be done about the growing number of undocumented aliens. Paula listens but adds nothing. While Earl and Don play verbal cat and mouse, Earl manages to glance inside the work area where a dozen technicians huddle over their TV's and radios. Each time he looks, his eyes wander to the back of the shop where he last saw the apprentice at one of the work stations. "Apprentice, my ass," he says to himself as he leans forward. "I know goddamn well they're payin' 'im…and payin' 'im half of what they paid Eric for the same job."

Incensed by what he knows to be true, he steps into the work area to get a better look. Suddenly he stops, rubs his eyes and looks again to make sure he's not mistaken. "For Christ's sake," he mumbles, "that kid…the one in back…he's wearin' an orange jacket." He turns immediately to Don. "Who's the kid in back…the one with the orange jacket? Is he new?"

Don takes a deep breath. "No, that's the kid we've been training for the past month. He just got back from a vacation. I guess he needed a break; he's a real hard worker."

Earl steps back into the office. As both Don and Paula watch with alarm, he stumbles into an empty chair and lets out a loud sigh.

"Anything the matter?" Don asks.

Stunned by what he has seen, the Sheriff struggles to conceal his confusion. Aware that he must say something, he begins a sentence, then stops halfway through…clears his throat…finally whispers, "I hope you're not payin' that kid anything."

"Of course not, Earl," Don responds. "He'll be leavin' when his trainin' is over…probably in another month or two."

No one speaks.

Earl flashes a questioning look at Paula…then gets up and stares into the shop again. "What's that on the back of his jacket?" he asks, pointing to the same boy in back. "It looks like there used to be some letters there but somebody tore them off; all you can see is the outline. From here, I can't make out what it says… (*pause*)…Do either of you know?"

Don shifts in his chair. "Ah, no, Earl…I've got no idea. Probably some soccer team logo or maybe the name of a shop where he used to work… (*pause*)…Why are you interested?"

Earl considers mentioning the newspaper article but changes his mind at the last minute. His heart is pounding as he turns and heads for the door. Paula steps forward to confront him, "Aren't you gonna say goodbye, Sheriff?"

"Oh yeah, bye" he replies, not bothering to look her in the face, "Forgot you were there, Paula…gotta get goin'…see you later."

At home that evening, Sheriff Culpepper leaves the dinner table early and retires to his tiny office to answer a question that has bugged him all day. As soon as he's settled into his chair, he reaches for the English-Spanish dictionary on the desk. "Avenger…that's the word they mentioned in the article," he says softly. as if someone might be listening. "How do you say that in Spanish?" As he thumbs through the dictionary, Emma suddenly appears at the office door. She stands there, staring at her husband, saying nothing.

"What do you want?" Earl barks, awakening to her presence.

(*Softly*) "Well, you got up early from dinner…so I thought it must be something important."

Earl follows her eyes to the dictionary he is holding. Her stare seems accusing…even though no crime has been mentioned. "So, what's wrong with looking up a word?" he asks, unaware how defensive he sounds.

"Oh," she replies, "is that all? What's the word? I remember a little Spanish from high school."

Earl answers by slamming the dictionary shut. Without looking at her, he snarls, "If I need any help, I'll ask you."

She presses a finger to her trembling lips…then heads back to the kitchen.

Earl waits until she has left before resuming his search. "Ah, Vengador," he says, having found what he was looking for. "So, 'The Avenger' must be 'El Vengador' in Spanish." He stops to recall the back of the jacket. "Not sure about the first part…but I think there was a capital V in there, followed by some smaller letters. Jesus Christ!" he cries, rising from his chair. "Could it be? Is this the kid they talked about in the newspaper article?"

In the days to come, what started as a guess becomes a certainty. He can think about nothing else. At home he remains as tight-lipped as ever…perhaps more so. At work, he answers any residual questions about the newspaper article with a shrug of indifference. Secretly, he begins laying plans for a get-together with the boy. But is that possible? After all, he's the Sheriff of Maricopa County. He's supposed to check up on suspicious individuals…snare them when they falter…not socialize with them. His desire is too strong, however, to be thwarted by an inconvenient bit of reality. "I'll find a way," he muses. "Somethin' will turn up."

The following day he is cruising the streets of Phoenix, still agonizing over his dilemma, when a desire for some music asserts itself. He reaches for the on-off button only to find that it's missing; the bare spindle is too slippery to turn. In disgust he leans back in his seat and hits the accelerator. The car bolts forward, nearly hitting a truck coming in from the right. He swears at the driver but does nothing. A block or two down the street he spots the garage where he waited for the 'apprentice' to get his pickup inspected. Suddenly the scene comes back to him…the frustration, the anger, the Mariachi music…the violent twisting of the knob. "Ah, yes," he sighs, leaning over to pick it up, "I gotta get that fixed."

On his way home that night he gets what he would later call the inspiration of a lifetime. It comes to him while sitting alone in his office re-reading the newspaper article which he keeps hidden in a locked box. "Why not go into the repair shop where the kid works," he reflects, "and have 'im work on my radio? I can even pull out a wire or two to make the job look worse." When he hears Emma's footsteps in the corridor, he quickly closes the box and slides it into the desk drawer, confident that the problem has been solved.

He awakes the next day with a kind of energy he hasn't felt for decades. Bouncing from bed, he races into the shower and turns the knob to cold, leaving it there until he can't stand it any longer. When Emma calls him for breakfast, he bursts into the kitchen, still combing his hair. "No uniform?" she asks as she pours his coffee. "Got other business," he snaps. "Oh, and I'll need the Buick today." Minutes later he is on his way into town. He waits until he is sure the Maricopa TV & Radio shop is open for business, then heads for the office.

As he enters, he is aware that a little explanation is in order since he has never appeared this early before. "I've got some business at the D.A.'s office later this morning," he offers. "Thought I better come in before you get too busy." He goes on to reassure Don that he is not here on official business. "The radio on my Buick is busted," he says. "I tried to fix it myself but ended up breaking the knob off. It's the kind of thing you guys are good at… right?"

Don smiles. "Well, Sheriff, I would hope so. I can put Ross on it right away. He's just finishing up a TV repair."

Earl bites his lip, then exhales slowly. "I'd like a chance to meet that new kid you've got out back…you know…the one with the orange jacket. Can you put him on it?"

Don smells an attack and moves to parry the thrust. "What dya want him for?" he asks, scowling. "I've got plenty of other guys with experience on car radios. After all, he's only an apprentice."

"Let's forget the 'apprentice' crap, Don. I know goddamn well you're payin' 'im. I just want to find out who he is…where he comes from…what route he took to get here…stuff like that…(*pause*)… Lookit…just let me talk to 'im and I promise not to make any trouble."

"But if he's illeg…"

"No matter. A promise is a promise. "

"You won't pull him in?"

"Nope. Just want to talk to 'im."

”But why? What's so special about this kid?”

“I don't know. He just seems like a good source of information. Maybe he can explain some things the rest of us don't understand…like why migrants risk their necks to get here when they know we don't want 'em.”

Don shrugs his shoulders. “Well, O.K. Earl…but I'm going to hold you to your word. No arrests…no matter what.”

“Don't worry…just go get 'im. Tell 'im I've got a problem with my car radio and keep the rest of what I said to yourself …(*pause*)…and for Christ's sake, don't tell 'im I'm the Sheriff.”

30

First Meeting

Earl arrives at Maricopa TV & Radio Repair ten minutes before his appointment. With nothing better to do, he begins fiddling with the radio…and in the process manages to break a second knob. As he combs the floor looking for it, the office door opens, then closes. He rises to his feet just in time to see a dark-skinned, broad-shouldered teenager coming toward him. Earl extends his hand.

"Hi, I'm Earl Culpepper," he says. "Don tells me you're pretty good with car radios. Any truth to that?"

"Well, I learn," the boy answers, taking Earl's hand. "Senor Edmunds… he teaches me a lot. My English still not very good."

Earl's eyes scan the boy's frame…taking in his bronze complexion, straight black hair and stocky build. "What's your name?" he asks.

"Asanté…people call me Santé."

"Nice name. Did Don tell you about my radio?"

"He say you have busted knob…maybe some wires loose."

Earl chuckles at the unintended ribbing as he motions Santé to take a look inside the car. The boy slides into the driver's seat and begins unscrewing the radio faceplate from the dashboard. "Already I see two wires come loose…maybe more." He looks up at Earl who is standing by the door. "How this happen? Maybe somebody try to steal your radio…and then give up."

"Yes…something like that."

When the radio is all the way out, Santé tucks it under his arm and heads back into the shop. Before he has gone very far, Earl asks, "Is it O.K. if I tag along? I'd like to see how you work. Maybe I can learn something."

Santé stops, surprised by the request. "It's O.K. with me if Senor Edmunds say yes."

As Santé heads for his work station, Earl broaches the subject with Don. "Well, yeah, I guess so," the owner says. "It's a bit out of the ordinary but I don't see any harm in it…(*pause*)…But what are you hoping to find, Earl?"

Earl smiles. "Who knows…I may be looking for a new job after next year's elections."

"Don forces a grin. "O.K.…but remember your promise."

"Don't worry. I'm just gonna watch."

At Santé's work station, Earl takes up a position on the left…close enough to see what the boy is doing but not so close as to get in the way. Neither one speaks for a minute or two. Earl finally breaks the silence with a question. "Where did you learn about radios? Did Mr. Edmunds teach you all this or did you know it before you came here?"

Santé hesitates. Still apprehensive about the stranger's motives, he keeps his remarks to a minimum, "When I was in school, I fix my parent's radio… then my neighbor ask me to work on his. Pretty soon I make enough money to buy my own tools."

Earl is about to ask where he went to school but decides against it. "I don't want to sound like the Immigration Service. Let him tell me when he's ready." He's aware that to get what he wants in this relationship, he needs to be careful; he needs to show first of all that he's harmless…then secondly, that he wants to be friends. For guideposts he turns to lessons learned from the criminal interrogations he's conducted over the years. The keys come quickly. If you want to get someone to open up, you first have to win their trust. With Santé this means moving slowly…avoiding questions about Mexico…like where he was born…how he got here…and so on. Concentrate instead on the present…find out about his likes and dislikes, his hobbies, how he spends his leisure time. As he begins to relax, and only then, ask about the future…where he's headed…his ambitions …possible plans for a career.

Satisfied with his strategy, he continues. "Do you like working with machines?"

"Oh yes. They no give you trouble. Always the same…no surprises."

Earl smiles his approval. "Your fingers seem to know exactly where to go inside the radio. You're like a surgeon."

Santé looks embarrassed. "No understand, Senor."

"I mean…you treat the radio like a person…the way a doctor treats a patient. You're tryin' to find out what's makin' it sick so you can fix it."

Santé laughs. "Si Senor…but big difference…here no blood…just grease."

(*Laughing*) Earl pats him on the shoulder. Convinced that the boy is relaxing, he decides to go deeper. "You're still pretty young," he says. "Do you have any plans for the future or are you content to stay where you are?"

Santé suddenly goes pale.

Sensing the boy's anxiety, Earl tries again. "What I meant was… what do you want to be when you grow up? What do you want to do with the rest of your life?"

"Ah…I understand now. I want to be engineer…go to college and learn. Fixing radios is O.K. now but as engineer I have more success."

Santé works quickly. On two occasions he leaves for the supply room to get new parts…some new wires and later a replacement for a damaged transistor. While he is gone, Earl looks around the shop. There are 10 or 11 other workers, all white, many in their 40's or 50's. When he gets their attention, some wave back, others merely nod. All are aware from previous visits that he is the county Sheriff. It is clear from their smiles that they expect something interesting to happen. Although they keep such sentiments to themselves, they've been hoping to see the 'apprentice' arrested and deported to Mexico. Some even have children or cousins waiting to take the boy's place.

Within 45 minutes, Santé holds the radio up and declares the job done. All that remains is installing it in the dashboard. On the way through the office he stops to let Don know how the job is going. The owner looks pleased and gives him a pat on the shoulder. When Earl follows, Don waits for a sign that the Sheriff is satisfied with his "investigation." No sign is forthcoming. Without further words, Santé and Earl head out to the car where Santé slips the radio into the dashboard and fastens the faceplate. Once the last screw has been tightened, Earl leans over to shake his hand. "Hey. Thanks for a great job. I enjoyed watching you."

Santé takes his hand. "Maybe you try it now. See if O.K."

The two switch places. Earl settles into the driver's seat, turns the radio on and picks a station at random. When a mariachi tune blares forth, he quickly turns the volume down and nods to Santé. "It's perfect…just like new."

As Santé turns to leave, Earl looks carefully at the back of his jacket. This time there is no question…the thread holes clearly spell El Vengador. His head spins at the discovery. Quickly he gets out of the car and takes the boy by the shoulder. "Santé …what do you do on your days off?"

"Me, Senor? I play soccer on Saturday. We have our own field in East End…used to be cornfield but we clear it. Now we have six teams…a whole league…so three games every week. We even have uniforms…and a referee."

Earl nods approvingly. "I never played soccer myself…just a little what we Americans call football…you know, goalposts instead of nets. But I would like to come and see you play." He stops…aware that for the first time he has openly acknowledged that Santé is from Mexico or Central America where soccer is known as futbol. His breathing stops as he waits for the boy's reaction.

Santé squints…apparently searching for the right words. Finally he asks, "I like you Senor Culpepper, but why you want to be my friend? I am nobody."

Earl bites his lip. He is aware that his behavior…in particular the invitation to get together over the weekend…makes no sense without reference to the newspaper article. It's time for a decision…either back off or tell the truth. To continue his bid for friendship he must confess that he knows about Sante's feats in Chiapas and that he is impressed with the boy's courage. Without a second thought he plunges ahead.

"You are far from nobody, Santé. On the contrary, you are very special. Why do I want to be your friend? The answer is simple…I admire what you have done. I wish I had a son like you." He cringes…dreading the response.

"How you know about me, Senor?"

"From a newspaper article I read…the one that had interviews with kids who were with you on the train in Chiapas."

Santé scratches his ear. "But how you know that's me?"

"The orange jacket with the letters on back."

Santé looks down, saying nothing.

"You are El Vengador, aren't you?"

"Are you policeman?"

Earl stops to think. "In my job, yes, I am the Sheriff of Maricopa County. But here with you, I'm just Earl Culpepper…a man who wants to be your friend."

Santé stiffens, his muscles visibly tensed for a getaway.

Earl moves quickly to allay the boy's fear. "I would love to watch you play soccer. We could even have lunch afterwards… somewhere near the soccer field." When Santé hesitates, Earl continues, "I don't care whether you're here legally or illegally, Santé. It doesn't matter. If you want to keep certain things to yourself, that's O.K. with me. I won't ask."

Santé looks behind him like a fugitive planning his escape route.

"Santé," Earl says. "I know you're worried, so hear me out. I left my uniform back home this morning so I could approach you man to man.

Forget that I'm the Sheriff; it doesn't apply here. Besides, I can't turn you in even if I wanted to; you haven't done anything wrong. If I wanted to arrest you, I'd have to wait until I caught you speedin' or breakin' some other law…(*pause*)…and I certainly wouldn't waste my time watching you fix my radio."

Santé permits himself a smile.

"So, how about it? Can we get together on Saturday? Tell me where the soccer field is and I'll be there."

Santé drops his shoulders and nods O.K. "The field is in back of cemetery…on Alcala Avenue. You know Alcala?"

"I'll find it. What time is your game?"

"Maybe around 11:00. Depends on how long early game lasts."

"O.K. I'll see you there."

Before leaving home on Saturday morning, Earl checks his encyclopedia to brush up on soccer terminology. Armed with the names of each position, he heads to the soccer field behind the cemetery. There are no bleachers; the handful of people who have come to watch are either sitting in lawn chairs along the sideline or up on a grassy ridge some 20 yards from the field. It appears that the early game has ended and participants in the second contest are out on the field practicing. Having failed to bring a chair, Earl picks an empty spot up on the ridge and sits down. His eyes immediately go searching for Santé.

Half of the players are wearing white uniforms, the other half green. As he scans the entire field, he kicks himself for not asking Santé what color uniform he will be wearing. He looks instead for a boy of Santé's height and build. When that narrows the field to a half a dozen, he waits until he can see their faces. It is not until the game actually begins that he identifies Santé…number 9 on the white team. According to the encyclopedia, that number is traditionally worn by the center forward…the most prolific scorer on the team. He smiles at his discovery. "Of course," he mumbles. "Who else?"

By the time the game ends two hours later, Earl is ready to get up and walk around. His seat is moist from the morning dew and his legs aching from sitting so long. All discomfort is forgotten, however, as he rushes onto the field to congratulate Santé who scored two of the team's four goals. "A great win," beams the Sheriff as he slaps Santé on the back, "And those two goals of yours…things of beauty."

Santé smiles as he brushes back his hair. "Yes, we win, Senor. But the other team good…they make two goals. Maybe we lucky."

"I don't know about luck, Santé. You guys looked awfully good out there… especially in the third period when you scored both of your goals… (*pause*)…You ready for a little lunch? You gotta be hungry after runnin' up and down the field for two hours."

"Si, Senor…very hungry…but I must say goodbye to my teammates first. Is possible I meet you here in ten minutes?"

"Sure…I'll stay right here."

At lunch, Earl quickly becomes aware that he will have to carry the brunt of the conversation. While not totally reticent, Santé prefers to answer questions rather than ask his own…at least at first. Having rehearsed his role carefully before coming, Earl starts with the least intrusive questions… with plans to go deeper as his friend opens up.

"So where dya learn to play soccer so well, Santé?"

"In school we have a team…but mainly on street with other kids."

"To be chosen as center forward. you gotta be pretty good, right?"

"Well, we have many good players on our team…that's why we best in our league."

The waitress arrives to take orders. Santé chooses the burrito in green sauce and ice tea; Earl settles for a hamburger and Coke.

"You like Phoenix, Santé?" Earl asks, shifting the subject.

"Very much, Senor," the boy answers. "People here very nice. No fighting."

Earl smiles. "You know, you can call me Earl. I'd like that."

"O.K., Senor Earl."

"How dya find that job at Maricopa TV and Radio? Sounds like a natural for you."

"I fool around with radios at home…so I know a little when I look for job. Senor Edmunds…he give me little test to see how much I know."

Earl can feel goose flesh rising as he digests this latest information. To confirm what he already suspects, he plunges ahead. "I hope they pay you a decent wage."

"Is enough to pay for room and board…and my pickup."

In view of Eric's brief stay at Maricopa Repair, Earl is tempted to ask how much Santé is being paid, but chooses to let the subject drop. Instead he takes a different tack, one laden with its own dangers. "Do you have any relatives here in the States?"

Santé stops, takes a bite of his burrito, then looks across the table at his friend. The silence that follows is testimony to his lingering wariness. He breathes deeply…then, without looking down, pushes the plate to the side. Across the table Earl squirms in anticipation. The boy's eyes tell all; a decision is coming.

Santé clears his throat and leans forward. "No relatives here, Senor Earl… but big family back in Oaxaca where I grow up… Mama, Papa, sister, older brother, uncle, and five cousins. And a younger brother, Raul, who is dead."

"Yes," says Earl solemnly. "I know about Raul from the newspaper article. It must have been pretty hard on you seeing that you were so close."

Santé gulps and shields his eyes. "He wanted to come here…live with me. I sent money for bus…but he wanted to ride the train. So foolish."

From the newspaper article Earl is aware that the story is more complicated than that…and that Santé is probably too ashamed of his father to fill in the details. Rather than press the matter, he changes the subject. "How many years of schooling did you get in Oaxaca?"

"I drop out before 10th grade...after we sell our little farm and move into city. My Papa...he not find job there...so we live on what Mama and Alma earn from making clothes. Not enough to pay rent and buy food...so I come here to make money and send some home for my family." Wondering if he has said too much, he looks into Earl's eyes, searching for signs of disapproval. When he finds softness instead, he relaxes. "What you think Senor Earl...is good story for movie?"

Earl chuckles. "Well, perhaps. I hope it has a happy ending...like boy goes on to get college degree and become a famous engineer. Something like that."

It is Santé's turn to laugh. "Maybe we make movie together, Senor. You be cowboy, I be Indian...Indian becomes engineer and builds big barn for cowboy."

"Just a barn? How about a private road to my mansion? Or a bridge over my private lake?"

"I work on it, Senor."

As they move on to desert, Santé opens up even more. Convinced of Earl's intentions, he begins talking about his home life in Oaxaca and how hard it was to leave. Prompted by his friend's questions, he shares some of the troubles he had in crossing the border. At first he provides a general outline; later he fills in the details...being attacked by bandits, fleeing from the Border Patrol, a confrontation with El Chacal, his return to Chiapas to avenge Raul, and finally the ambush in the tunnel.

Through it all Earl listens carefully, posing a new question whenever the boy comes to a stop. By the time lunch is over, he has a pretty good idea who he is talking to. Nothing he has heard detracts from the image he formed from the newspaper article. "This kid is really somethin'," he muses. "He's got everything that's missin' in my own son. He's not afraid to take chances...he's got guts...he looks after other people...and above all, he's honest about himself. Those are the very things I tried to instill in Eric...but, for one reason or another, they didn't take. Maybe I tried too hard. I don't know."

As they walk out of the restaurant together, they agree to meet again next Saturday…first the game, then lunch…same place, same time. Back in his car, Earl lets out a loud "Wow". "I'm one lucky sonofabitch. The kid trusts me…he knows I'm the Sheriff and he still tells me how he crossed here illegally. I guess I played it right." As Santé's image returns, he grins and revs up the motor. Back on the highway he turns on the radio and picks a station at random. It's a program of Mariachi music. This time he sings along.

31

Surveillance

As the weeks go by, Emma becomes curious about the soccer games Earl goes to on Saturday morning. What makes it particularly strange is that he has never shown interest in soccer before. When three weeks have passed and her curiosity turns to alarm, she shares her concern with Eric who decides to find out for himself what his father is up to.

On the following Saturday morning, he gets into his black pickup and tails his father as far as the soccer field where he discovers the truth. It's not another woman as both he and his mother suspected; it's another boy. He stays in his truck throughout the game, with one eye on his father, the other on the playing field. At the end of the game he watches his father and a Latino boy of about 17 or 18 leave the soccer field together and head for a nearby restaurant. Eric follows at a distance. For an hour and a half he remains parked outside the restaurant. It is not until the two emerge and continue chatting on the sidewalk that Eric can see their faces. While he's too far away to make out the boy's features, he can tell that he's smiling. Perplexed by what he sees, he slumps back in his seat. His thoughts race: maybe it's official business or he's getting' ready to arrest the kid. He straightens quickly, however, when he sees his father pull out a camera and take a photo of the boy. This is hardly official business. He watches with sullen disbelief as the two shake hands…then wave goodbye.

As Eric prepares to leave, feelings of abandonment compete with the thrill of catching his father in a compromised situation. "Just think what people will say," he muses, concentrating on the latter, "when they learn that the Sheriff of Maricopa County is socializing with an illegal alien. This could mean big trouble." His only thought is to get home quickly and share the information with his mother.

Back in the kitchen Eric makes no attempt to hide his bitterness. As anticipated, his mother is consoling; she is also relieved that no other woman is involved. With her blessing, he decides to begin following this new boy… and perhaps find out something that will change his father's feelings.

In the days that follow, Eric gives up any pretense of looking for work. It is now only two weeks before the fall term at A.S.U. begins; he must take advantage of this window of opportunity. At the very least, he needs to find out where his father's new friend lives and works. "Just who is this boy?" he asks over and over. He has no particular plan in mind…just a need to know more about him.

Throughout the week, he tries to lose himself in video games but the days refuse to hurry. By the time Saturday arrives, he is frantic. The minute his father leaves the house, he follows him to the soccer field and takes up a position on the street next to the field. The rest of the routine is familiar. After the game, he waits until his father and the boy leave the field and head for the restaurant; then he settles into a parking space less than a block away. Hidden from view, he lights up a cigarette and fixes his eyes on the restaurant door. By the time his targets emerge an hour and a half later, his nerves are on edge, his throat raw from smoking. He waits until they wave goodbye and return to their separate vehicles. As soon as the Latino boy reaches his pickup, Eric rolls down the window, tosses his cigarette and turns on the ignition.

Fifteen minutes and ten blocks later he is surprised when the white pickup he is following turns into the Maricopa TV Repair parking lot. He is even more surprised when the boy gets out and disappears into the apartment in back. While he still can't see his face, he suspects that it's the kid who was being trained earlier as an apprentice. Still in his truck, he lights up another cigarette and waits until he is sure the boy is not coming out. When an hour passes and nobody emerges, he figures that since the shop is not open for work on Saturdays, the kid must be living in the owners' apartment. His heart jumps at what this means. He starts up the truck and races home to convey the news to his father.

At dinner Eric brings up the subject of his father's latest talk with Don. "Are you convinced that he's not hiring illegals?" he asks, struggling to conceal his own news.

Earl seems surprised at the question. "Why do you ask?"

Not one to be caught off guard, Eric responds with a well-rehearsed fudge. "Well, I went over there yesterday to pick up a backpack I left behind and saw a Mexican kid working at my station. That got me thinkin'….maybe that's why they let me go….you know, 'cause they wanted to hire this illegal kid. I figured you'd wanta know about it."

Silence.

Eric sets his fork on the plate and leans forward. "I mean…it's bad enough to hire illegals in the first place but to fire an American so they can bring in an alien who'll work for peanuts…well, that's goin' too far, isn't it, Dad?"

When Earl still fails to respond, Emma becomes nervous. "You've got to do something about it, Earl. We can't let Don and his wife get away with this. At least go over there and find out about this Mexican boy. Is he working for them or is he just learning the trade? If he's on their payroll, they're breaking the law and should be reported. Don't you agree?"

Earl shifts uneasily in his chair. "I don't think that's why Don let Eric go. It was more a matter of him not learning fast enough…and not having the right attitude. In other words, he thought Eric was lazy. My guess is that the Mexican kid was workin' there even before Eric got fired…(*pause*)… Maybe they **are** payin' him under the table; I don't know. But it's not worth a special trip over there to find out. Right now I have more important things to do with my time."

Eric winces, then looks over at his mother before rising from the table. When he senses his father staring at him, he drops his head to hide his moistening eyes. Emma's face reddens as she turns to face her husband, unconscious that she is biting her lip. A pool of blood spreads across one side of her mouth, but goes unnoticed until she wipes her lips with a napkin. Still, no words are spoken. When Eric goes to his room, husband and wife sit silently, staring out the same window. They are only a few feet apart but to each it feels like opposite ends of the continent. She checks her lips again. Assured that the bleeding has stopped, she picks up the dirty plates and retreats to the kitchen.

Alone at the table now, Earl sinks into reverie. With eyes half-closed, he wanders back to the soccer game and the look on Santé's face when his second goal went into the net. He can still see the sparkle in his eyes, the determination in his jaw…best of all, the way laughter spilled from his lips at lunch when he described how the kick felt. Earl closes his eyes now, smiling at the memory.

When he opens them again, he is facing Eric's chair. He has to catch his breath as an image of his son appears where Santé's face stood a minute ago. Eric's skin is a listless white, bordering on gray, testimony to his aversion for the Arizona sun. His eyes are more like slits, not fully open as if he were hiding something. Contributing to a similar effect are his lips… bloodless and thin…so thin in fact that they disappear when his mouth is closed. His smile, rare as it is, borders on a grinning smirk, a gesture that is useful when he wants to show disdain for someone without appearing impolite. All in all a weak face, Earl concludes, a mask of sorts, the kind you wear when you don't want anyone to know what you're thinking.

Earl rubs his chin and blinks his eyes all the way open. "And yet the girls at school find him attractive," he muses, "if you can believe what he says. But maybe he made that up. I don't know what to believe now…except that he's not the son I've always wanted. He's got none of the strength that I see in other men in my family. I hate to think what our relatives back in Alabama would say if they knew how Eric turned out. He's no Culpepper for sure."

Still staring at the empty chair, his thoughts return to Santé. "Now take Santé…there's a kid who's got everything you could want in a son. I don't think he was makin' anything up when he told me how he got here. He comes all the way to Arizona from Southern Mexico, crossin' the desert at night with all them rattlers around…fights off a couple of bandits while he's protectin' a family…finally gets here in one piece. Then he goes back when he hears his kid brother got thrown off a train in Chiapas…avenges the boy's death by cuttin' down the murderer with a home-made machete. As if that isn't enough, he has to use it again when a gang of teenage thugs ambush him in the tunnel at Nogales. Holy Jesus…how many kids do you know with the guts to go through all that…and come out as humble as Santé?"

Back in his room, Eric starts putting the pieces together. "Dad knows real well that this boy is here illegally. He's not going to confront Don about it 'cuz he likes the kid…likes him enough to go watch him play soccer every Saturday morning…and then take him out to lunch." When he starts to feel dizzy, he sits down on the bed, head in his hands. "Did he ever do that kind of thing for me? Never…not once. O.K. so I'm not that interested in sports…but we coulda gone shoppin' or taken a walk together…at least had lunch at some restaurant. Doesn't he owe me that much?"

Still trembling, he wipes the tears from his cheek. "But there's more to it than that. The Mexican is not only here illegally; he's the one who took my job. Don would never have fired me if the new kid hadn't come along and offered to work for half of what I got. And Dad knows it. As the Sheriff of this County, he should go in there and have both Don and the kid arrested. It's his duty! So what's he do instead? He takes the kid under his wing… goes to his soccer games, treats him to lunch…even takes pictures of him."

He pauses to take in some history. "Out in the living room there are plenty photos of me when I was a child…but not one since I was ten years old. Not a single one. Why? Did he stop liking me when I got to be eleven? Did I change into something he couldn't stand? It's strange that Mom doesn't feel that way. She's always loved me…no matter how old I was. I can't imagine her going off to some kid's soccer game and leaving me home alone. Even when I've gotten into trouble at school, she's never deserted me. Dad is way different…if I get into trouble, he jumps to the conclusion that it's my fault." He closes his eyes, then tilts his head as a strange new thought arises. "Maybe he's not my real Dad. I never thought of that before…but it makes sense. Maybe Mom had an affair with some other man and never told Dad. So he got stuck with somebody else's kid and didn't find out about it until I was eleven; that's when he turned his back on me. I gotta ask Mom about it. She'll tell me the truth. I'll talk to her tomorrow morning after Dad leaves for work." Buoyed by this new possibility, he crawls under the covers and falls asleep, unaware of the dark feelings stirring deep inside.

32

Bristlecone Drive

As Santé leaves Anna's house and heads for his truck, he is unaware of the black pickup parked down the street…and the person watching him from inside. For two hours Eric has been waiting for this moment. If he were asked why he was there, he would claim that it's to gather information on the Mexican boy…but his recent fantasies suggest that there may be more to it than that. At the very least he is aware that the boy who presumably took his job at Maricopa TV has become an obsession. For several days now he has found thinking of anything else impossible…even college which is due to begin in a couple of weeks. He has obsessed about other things in the past…usually girls at school…but this is different. These thoughts are dark and frightening…thoughts that won't go away despite repeated attempts to suppress them.

As he watches Santé get into his truck, a dream returns…a dream in which a teen-aged boy, feeling cast aside when his mother unexpectedly gives birth to a second child, waits until his parents are off shopping, then takes the baby and stuffs it into a trash can where it freezes to death. The dream is terrifying in its vividness. "Being jealous of a new brother is understandable," he says, shaking his head upon wakening, "but how could any kid ever go that far?"

As he ponders the question, he is unaware of ominous impulses swirling deep inside. His heart is pounding; he can feel the sweat on his brow; he's starting to feel sick to his stomach. He knows he is on edge, but in his innocence can only ask, "Where the heck did that dream come from? It doesn't make any sense."

When Santé pulls out of the driveway, Eric begins to follow.

Once he is out on the road, Santé breaks into a huge smile as he replays his goodbye with Anna…a scene in which they kissed so long that they both fell to the floor laughing. As he steers the pickup into the right lane, other memories of the evening return…holding hands while talking about college, a serious talk about marriage…even a discussion of how many kids to have. He has never been this happy…never in his seventeen and a half years has he had so much…a beautiful girlfriend who loves him, a steady job working with TV's and radios, a comfortable place to live… even a new friend who comes to his soccer games. "Ah," he sighs, "I wish Raul was with me…so sorry he's not alive to see El Norte…so strange to have no family here."

Thoughts of a future with Anna soon return, sweeping away the last strands of sadness. To celebrate his happiness, he turns on the radio and begins singing. When singing proves inadequate to his mood, he starts keeping beat with the music by tapping the horn. After a few minutes of enthusiastic beeping, he glances at his rear-view mirror to make sure he's not bothering anyone. He's surprised to see another vehicle; it's a black pickup, about 20 yards behind him. It's not often that he sees vehicles here in the early evening…other than an occasional delivery truck taking the back route to a town up north. Buoyed by the lingering scent of Anna's perfume, he forgets about the pickup and returns to thoughts about college and family.

The road he is on, Bristlecone Drive, continues on the flat for several miles before beginning a descent into the canyon. Prior to the descent, there are warning signs along the ridge alerting drivers to the steep drop-off just beyond the shoulder. Having traveled the road many times, Santé is aware of the danger and takes his foot off the accelerator. Just coasting now, the pickup slows to 30 miles an hour. He taps the brakes to be sure they're working and turns on his headlights in case someone is coming up the hill. When the road curves sharply to the right, he slows down to 15… then picks up speed when it straightens again. Visibility is becoming more difficult now as dusk envelops the road, obscuring the white line between lanes. He turns off the radio in order to concentrate on driving. Still uneasy about the vehicle behind him, he takes his eyes off the road momentarily to look in the rear-view mirror. The black pickup is still there, but closer than before. His lights are not on.

Ahead is the steepest part of the road, shooting straight downhill for two miles before swerving sharply to the left. As he readies himself for the descent, Santé checks his speedometer: the gauge says 25, a little too fast. As he slows down, he steals one last glance at his rear-view mirror…then shudders. There is no one there.

Before he can figure out what happened, he senses someone coming up on his left. He turns quickly…just long enough to recognize the black pickup. The driver is a young boy, his mouth slightly open, his eyes intense and fixed on Santé. Alarmed by the closeness of the pickup, Santé waves him off, then moves slightly to the right. Instead of withdrawing, the other driver follows suit, closing within inches of Santé's left front fender. When Santé shouts an obscenity, the other driver smiles and gives him a finger.

As he closes on the white pickup, Eric tightens his grip on the steering wheel. At this distance, there's no longer any question in his mind: the boy in the white pickup is the 'apprentice' he knew from Maricopa TV & Radio. As he stares fixedly at the Mexican, studying the expression on his face, he can scarcely breathe. He has no plan, no carefully worked out goal; the only thing he is sure of is what he feels. By now the rage locked deep in his gut…a rage previously sensed but not yet acknowledged…looms at the very edge of awareness. He trembles at its power. Suddenly, the trash-can dream returns…but cast in a different light. It is less alien, less menacing than before. Where earlier he had sickened at the thought of fratricide, he now sees the reasonableness of the brother's response. "After all," he muses, "the boy's place in the family was taken over by a newcomer. He got pushed aside. No wonder he did what he did."

As he replays the dream, a burst of energy ripples through his body. For the first time in recent memory, he feels vindicated in his grief. Freed from moral censure, he shouts his joy into the night. "The boy in the dream is right; I would do the same thing." As dream and reality become fused, the scene shifts to the present. Now it is the boy in the white pickup who has invaded his family. He stares again, chest heaving, then points his finger at the Mexican. His whole body is trembling. "It is you who has to go," he shouts hoarsely. Reassured that his cause is just, he aims his truck directly at the Mexican. He holds the steering wheel steady until he can hear the two fenders touching…then turns to see the terrified look on the boy's face.

By now they are half-way down the hill; less than a mile ahead is a sharp turn to the left. It is clear to Santé that unless he straightens out, he'll spin off into the canyon. In desperation he honks his horn repeatedly, then hits the brakes and yanks his steering wheel to the left. It is to no avail; the pickup keeps sliding to the right. As both vehicles near the edge of the road, his immediate thought is that their fenders have accidently gotten locked. He glances over to the other driver, expecting to see a similar look of consternation. His fear turns to horror when the boy in the pickup flashes a grin. Santé's eyes widen in disbelief. "You crazy," he shouts, clenching his fist. Seconds later the black pickup pulls away and goes racing down the highway.

As his own pickup teeters on the shoulder's edge, Santé steals a look into the canyon hundreds of feet below where yellow rocks reflect the sun's dying rays. Frantically, he floats a prayer to Dios, his Father and Protector. Nothing changes; the pickup keeps sliding. There is no escape now; he can't stop what's happening. His dream of marriage, career and kids is about to end. As shadows creep across the canyon floor, the road suddenly drops out from under him. Yielding to gravity, he sails into space, twists against the wind, then plunges like a tethered kite whose tie to earth has been severed. As he falls, he has a vision. The scene is a college graduation ceremony where diplomas are about to be awarded. Anna is at his side. She smiles and squeezes his hand. He squeezes back…and then all goes black.

33

After the Funeral

Earl arrives home from Oaxaca late on Friday afternoon. At the door Emma greets him with outstretched arms but settles for a brief nod. In the living room conversation is cool and halting. She asks nothing about the funeral; he offers nothing. When he finally looks up at her, she reads in his eyes a mixture of sadness and anger. His lips are tight, his eyes quick to turn away. When he heads to his bedroom, she starts to follow, then changes her mind and returns to the living room.

At dinner that night Emma keeps looking at Eric, as if trying to support him with her eyes alone. Earl finally breaks the silence as he addresses his son. "Have the State Police showed up yet...you know, in regard to the Mexican boy's death?"

Eric lifts his head. "No."

Emma bristles. "Why should they? Eric had nothing to do with it."

Earl breaks into a wry smile as he turns back to his son. "So Eric, you're goin' to deny that you knew the kid and that you were up there that night."

When Eric says nothing, Emma sits up in her chair. This time she stares directly at Earl. "There's no sense in getting Eric involved if there's nothing the police know that can connect him with the Aguilera boy. There were no witnesses that night so where are they going to get Eric's name? And even if someone comes forward to identify his truck, he can always admit that he was present and that his truck was involved...but that contact with the Mexican was an accident. How can they prove otherwise?"

Earl nods, then pushes his plate away. Without saying anything, he sits back in his chair and looks out the window. Inwardly his thoughts begin to sort themselves out. "I guess I have a decision to make…and not a lot of time to make it. Do I go to the police and report what I know…or not?" He may not know it, but that decision, still hidden from awareness, has already been made. All he can be sure of as he gets up from the table is that a certain peace has fallen upon him. After days and nights of inner turmoil, it comes as an unexpected blessing. He acknowledges the feeling now with a wan smile as he heads for the door. Still seated, Emma sees the change in his face and is frightened. She reaches for Eric's hand.

Early the next morning Earl enters the Phoenix Police station and tells what he knows. Three days later Eric is arrested and charged with vehicular homicide. A hearing is set for September 20th.

At work, Earl's changing attitude shows up during the morning's discussion with his colleagues. It's not that he says anything different…but more the way he looks. To others in the room, he seems uncomfortable…restless in his chair, unconsciously squinting, even biting his lip occasionally as if trying to hold back a remark. His subordinates, some of whom have worked in the Sheriff's office for years, are no longer sure what it's O.K. to say and what it's not. Not surprisingly, the group breaks up early.

Pablo, a 25-year-old Latino fringe member of the group, is usually hesitant to speak up during discussions on the grounds that his views, generally sympathetic to migrants, will only distance himself from his co-workers. He is seen, incorrectly, as shy by the others, but accepts that tag as an alternative to being shunned. When he senses a new openness on his boss's part, he stays to talk after the group breaks up.

Once he and the Sheriff are alone, he pulls up a chair and gets right to the point. "Chief, you say nothing today. What make you change? Nobody understand you anymore."

Earl musters a smile, then stiffens in his chair. Before he answers Pablo, he reviews his alternatives. He is aware that he can get into trouble by saying too much. Given the sensitivity of the migrant issue, his relationship with the whole law enforcement community is at stake. His job as Sheriff could even be on the line. At the same time he owes it to Pablo to tell the truth. After all, the man already suspects that his boss has undergone a change of heart; he deserves an honest answer. And then there's Eric's upcoming trial to be considered. Who knows what kind of information is going to come out there? Pretty soon everybody is going to know about his friendship with the boy from Oaxaca. "What's gonna happen then?" he asks himself. "I know goddamn well what's gonna happen. The shit is gonna hit the fan. People are gonna get real angry. Then there's the ethical issue. Is it even right for me to remain Sheriff of Maricopa County? After all, I got elected because I promised to be tough on illegals."

"Let's go across the street for some coffee," he says to Pablo.

Once the two men are seated in the café, Earl lays his hands on the table and looks straight at his partner. "Somethin' weird is happenin' to me, Pablo, and I don't know what to do about it."

"I could tell somethin' was goin' on, Chief. I noticed you been different ever since you read the article about that boy in Chiapas."

"Yeah, that's where it all started. The article got me thinkin'…but Jesus, I had no idea I'd actually be meetin' the kid face to face. And I sure didn't figure that I'd end up treatin' him like a son…goin' to his soccer games, takin' him out to lunch, getting' to know all about his life in Mexico."

"Sounds like you really liked him, Chief. A real nice kid, was he?"

"Yeah, I liked him alright…maybe too much. Makin' friends with Santé has already cost me my family. My wife and I aren't speakin' anymore and my son…well, he's off in another world…(*pause*)…Who knows, losing my job may be comin' next."

"I hope not, Chief…but I think I know where you're at. It's the old rock and hard place problem, ain't it?"

"Meaning?"

"Well, tell me if I'm buttin' in…but this is the way I see it: the rock is your friendship with this Mexican boy. This is the first time in your life you ever got close to an immigrant. They look different up close, wouldn't you agree…real human like?…(*pause*)…Now, the hard place is all the ideas you still got in your head about immigration…you know, how Latinos are

takin' away our jobs, floodin' our schools, forcin' us to learn Spanish…
stuff like that. You're stuck in the middle. Before all this happened, you
was lookin' at Mexicans with one eye only…the eye that looks South and
sees a horde of dark-skinned, illiterate peasants comin' this way, threatenin'
to break through the gate and destroy our way of life. But now you seein'
through your other eye too…the eye that looks at migrants as individuals
and sees people you might really like, folks like Santé, folks you admire
for their courage and goals…(*pause*)…Am I right, Chief?"

Earl bows his head. "Maybe…(*pause*)…I guess so."

"Maybe you just gettin' ahead of the curve. You know what I'm sayin?"

"What dya mean?"

Pablo straightens up and looks directly at Earl. "People are angry now at
all these Latinos comin' up here…you know, uninvited. I understand that.
There are so many of them that folks haven't had time to get used to it.
In a few years that could change. People are gonna realize that migrants
make good citizens. Lookit…anybody who's willin' to hike across the
desert at night dodgin' snakes and bandits…or crawl through tunnels
filled with other people's shit…they gotta really want to be here. That's
real motivation, ain't it? When we talk about so-called 'aliens', we're talkin'
about folks who are willin' to put their lives on the line to get here. Sooner
or later the gringos are goin' to wake up to the fact that these crossers make
good citizens. With the way you took to this Santé kid, you seem to be
movin' in that direction, Chief. That's what I meant when I said you was
already ahead of the curve."

Earl tightens his lips. "But let's face it, Pablo, some of these crossers are not
all that desirable as neighbors. They've committed crimes back home; they
may even be totin' drugs."

"True…and we have to find ways of filterin' 'em out."

"And there are others who come here just to make money for their families
back home. They stay long enough to make a bundle and then disappear.
You can't really say they want to become part of our world."

"Well, O.K., I agree. But we need those temporary people too, don't we? They're willin' to do jobs that Americans look down their noses at…pickin' up trash, mowin' lawns, cleanin' houses, workin' in slaughter houses. So what if they do send some of their pay back home…ain't they still doin' us a favor by comin' here and doin' our dirty work for us? We really need people like that, don't we?"

The waitress, clearly Latina, arrives to ask if they are interested in anything else…another coffee, a sweet roll or dessert. When both men decline, she lays the check on the table…exactly in the middle. Earl immediately pulls it in with one hand while reaching for his wallet with the other. "Interesting discussion, Pablo," he says. "You've given me a lot to think about." As the two men rise to leave, Earl pulls out a twenty-dollar bill and places it under his coffee cup…then heads to the cashier's station to pay the bill. On the way out the door, Pablo smiles and gives him a nudge. "Beau geste, Chief."

Earl smiles. "You speakin' French now? What's next, Russky?"

34

The Trial

When a grand jury finds sufficient grounds to indict Eric, a trial is set for October 15th. As the proceedings open, Eric is accused of vehicular homicide with intent to kill. If convicted, he faces 20 to 25 years in prison. Convinced that he is vulnerable to attack, Lloyd Harris, his attorney, has advised him not to testify. The 12-member jury consists of both men and women, mostly middle-aged and older, with a sprinkling of Hispanics. The judge is Samuel Foster, a man of 30 years experience who is known throughout the state for his no-nonsense (some would say authoritarian) approach to courtroom procedure.

In the days leading up to the trial, the Sheriff is an emotional wreck... dragged down by days of soul-searching and nights without sleep. He is also 13 pounds lighter. Without consulting his friends or therapists, he has come to the wrenching decision that he will testify for the prosecution... even though the defendant is his own son. While the state plans to call experts to give evidence regarding vehicular damage, speed, and impact at the time of collision, the Sheriff will serve as their main witness.

Leonard Oswald, the lead attorney for the prosecution, is a 30 year-old Harvard Law School graduate who was assigned the case because of his success in a previous assault trial involving the governor's nephew. It is an open secret that he will stand up to anyone and has political ambitions of his own. The Sheriff, who is on speaking terms with Oswald but dislikes his abrasive manner, shudders when he hears about the assignment. The prospect of seeing Eric torn apart on the witness stand is chilling...even if his son is guilty. He is relieved when he hears that Eric will not be testifying.

Once he is sworn in and identifies himself, the Sheriff is asked to describe what he saw in his driveway when he got home on the evening of August

17th, the day after the victim's death. He starts by talking about the black spray paint he saw on the right fender of Eric's pickup. Knowing the answer in advance and anxious to capitalize on it, Oswald then asks if the witness bothered to examine the fender more carefully.

Earl nods. "At first I was concerned that the paint didn't quite match the original. I remember thinkin' how difficult it is to get a perfect match with jobs like this. It wasn't until I knelt down and ran my fingers over the paint that the truth hit me. That's when I saw a few flecks of white paint lodged in one of the dents that ran the length of the fender. I remember yelling 'Oh my God…what the hell is he up to? Was he up on Bristlecone Drive last night? Did he have something to do with Santé's death?"

Oswald looks at the jury, then turns back to his witness. "So, let's be clear about this, Sheriff. Before you came home that evening, you already knew about the Aguilera boy's death."

"Yes. I saw it on the morning news in my office."

"O.K. So when did you put the pieces together, that is, when did you connect the spray paint on Eric's fender with the news about Asanté's death?"

Earl sighs as the details come back. "Right after I saw the white paint on his fender. When I went inside and confronted him, he finally admitted that he was up on Bristlecone Drive the previous evening and had contact with the white pickup. It was an accident, he claimed. He said that he was headin' down the hill gettin' ready to pass the white pickup when he saw an 18-wheeler comin' up the hill toward him. When the white pickup refused to pull over or drop back, he had no choice but to push it onto the shoulder. But he had no idea that it went over the cliff. That's what he said."

"Did you believe him?"

"Not really."

"Why not?"

"Well, when I asked him what he was doing up on Bristlecone Drive at that time of day, he couldn't give me a good answer."

"What did he say?"

"He said that he was up there to 'view the sunset' or somethin' like that. I asked him if he was with a girl…you know, someone who could verify that he was there…and he didn't answer."

"So you drew the conclusion that he was lying."

"Probably lying, yes."

"Objection," shouts Mr. Harris, the young attorney who recently graduated near the top of his class at Wyoming Law School. "This whole story is hearsay, your honor."

"Objection denied," replies the judge without hesitation. "The witness is not trying to prove the truth or falseness of anyone else's remarks. Please continue, Mr. Oswald."

Mr. Oswald approaches the witness stand. "If you think that your son deliberately ran the victim off the road, can you provide us with any facts that might explain why he did it?"

"Objection, your honor," cries the defense. "Mr. Oswald is asking the witness to speculate on the defendant's motivation."

"Yes (*turning to Mr. Oswald*). Be careful. You may ask the witness what he knows to be true from his personal observation…but not what he thinks about the defendant's motivation."

Oswald responds with a barely-concealed smirk, then turns back to the witness. "Sheriff, have you observed anything that might shed light on the defendant's behavior the night of August 16th?"

Earl looks first at Eric, then Emma. "Yes. At the breakfast table a few weeks ago, Eric admitted that he had followed me to the field where I watched Santé play soccer. He saw me talking with Santé right after the game; he also saw us go into the restaurant together. In other words, he knew Santé. He knew who it was that I went to see on Saturday mornings."

"Did he have any other contact with the Aguilera boy that you know about?

"I think so. He said that he saw a Mexican boy at the Maricopa TV and Repair shop where he had worked for a few weeks. Apparently he went over to pick up a backpack he had left behind after the owner fired him. He said that when he looked into the shop area, he saw the Mexican working at the same station where he used to work. I learned later when I went over there that it was Santé."

"How did he act when he told you this?"

"He was very upset…asked me to do something about it…you know, go over there and make a big stink…arrest the boy for crossing illegally, arrest the owner for hiring an undocumented worker."

"So, he had every reason to be jealous. He not only saw you being friendly with the Aguilera boy but must have figured from your absence every Saturday that the relationship had become a serious one. Later, to make things worse, he found out that his rival was the very boy who had replaced him at the Repair shop…(*pause*)…Putting all the pieces together, Sheriff, does it make sense to you that your son was hurting?"

"Absolutely."

"And that his pain was powerful enough to make him want to hurt the Aguilera boy…perhaps even get rid of him?"

Mr. Harris jumps from his chair. "Objection, your honor. Counsel is playing psychologist. All this talk about the defendant's feelings is pure speculation."

"Objection sustained," says the judge. "The jury will disregard counsel's comment about the defendant's motivation…(*pause*) …Now. If there are no more questions for Sheriff Culpepper, the defense may cross examine."

Mr. Harris takes a deep breath, shuffles some papers, then walks up to the witness stand. "One simple question before we move on, Sheriff. You say that Eric told you he saw the Aguilera boy at Maricopa TV and Radio

Repair the day he went to pick up his backpack. Now, are you familiar with the layout at the shop?"

"I've been there several times."

"Do you know which work station Eric was referring to when he said he saw Aguilera?"

"Yes. It's in back…but you can see it from the office."

"Is the station facing the office…or is facing the other way. In other words, when you look into the work area from the office, do you see the individual's front or is it his back?"

Earl pauses before answering. "His back."

"So, how could Eric have recognized Aguilera from looking at his back alone? Isn't it possible that the person at Eric's former workstation was someone other than the victim…another Hispanic, perhaps?"

"Well, yeah…it's possible, although it's mainly Whites who work there. But the way Eric got upset tells me it was the same boy he saw with me at the soccer game."

"That's theoretically possible, or course, but it hardly constitutes proof that the two boys were one and the same."

"I still think it was Santé both times."

"Of course, that's your position, isn't it?" Harris pauses, turns to look at the jury, then takes a step closer to the witness. In a carefully modulated voice, he asks, "Would it be fair to say that you hate your son, Sheriff Culpepper?"

"Not at all. I loved him…after all, he was our only child."

"I notice that you used the past tense; you used to love him. But what about now?"

Earl looks out at the courtroom; his eyes come to rest on Eric.

"I've lost a lot of respect for him, but he's still my son."

"You didn't answer my question, Sheriff. Do you love him now?"

Earl shifts in his chair. "I don't want him to go to prison…but…"

"But what…?"

"If he did run the Aguilera boy off the cliff, that's where he belongs."

"That's still to be decided, isn't it, Sheriff? So, in the meantime, let's get back to the details. Tell us what you actually saw and heard the day you discovered Eric painting the fender of his truck."

"Like I said, it's when I was comin' up the driveway. I saw Eric bendin' over spray-paintin' his pickup."

"The whole truck?"

"No, just the fender…the right front fender."

Mr. Harris flashes a boyish grin. "Tell me Sheriff, have you ever seen your son working on his pickup before?"

"Yes…a coupla times. Once he was changing the oil…then there was the time he was puttin' in a new tail pipe. Oh, and he changed batteries once too."

"So, would you agree that it is not strange to see your son doing things to fix up his vehicle."

"No. Like I said…"

(*Interrupting*) "We heard what you said, Sheriff. My question is simply this: if he did have an accident in which some of the paint on his fender got scraped off, would you find it strange to see him spray-painting that fender?"

"No…but I don't think it was an accident."

The judge leans over. "Stick to the question being asked, Sheriff. You are not being asked for your opinion on what happened that night."

Earl shrugs his shoulders. "O.K. I wouldn't find it strange to see him spray-paintin' his truck…and I didn't find it strange that afternoon 'til I got close enough to see a few flecks of white paint underneath."

"So, as soon as you saw the white paint, you jumped to the conclusion that your son murdered your Mexican friend. A rather hasty conclusion I should think. But isn't the white paint on the defendant's fender consistent with the fact that the two trucks accidentally collided?"

"Maybe…until you consider the other stuff that was going on."

Mr. Harris shakes his head and returns to his bench. "That's all for this witness, your honor."

Judge Foster turns to Mr. Oswald. "Please call your next witness."

Fred Wilkerson has been brought in to testify in his role as an expert on vehicular accidents, especially those involving large insurance claims. He is a man in his forties, tall, blonde, with narrow, steel-rimmed glasses, suggesting that he spends a lot of time reading fine-print documents.

Mr. Oswald asks a few introductory questions, then gets right to the point. "We have heard a witness testify that the defendant told him an 18-wheeler was coming up Bristlecone Drive at the very time he was attempting to pass another vehicle. Are you familiar with Bristlecone Drive, Mr. Wilkerson?"

"Yes. Just to be sure, I went out to inspect it yesterday."

"O.K. In your role as an expert on transportation, does it appear possible to you that a truck that big could make it up a road that steep?"

"No. Even if it were only half-full, it couldn't make it."

"Not even using the lowest gear possible?"

"No, not even then. There's no 18-wheeler I know of that has that much horsepower."

"Thank you."

Judge Foster leans forward. "Mr. Harris. Do you wish to cross-exam the witness?"

Harris walks to the stand so quickly he stumbles.

"Are you alright, counsel?" the judge asks.

Harris grabs his leg, then turns to the judge with a smile. "Ah, yes, thank you…(*pause*)…Now Mr. Wilkerson. You've said that no 18-wheeler could possibly get up a hill as steep as Bristlecone Drive with even a half a load."

"Yes."

"How about if the truck was completely empty? Could it make it then?"

Suddenly Wilkerson's smile turns to a frown. "That's hard to say," he says, scratching his neck. "Depends on the truck I suppose."

"Thank you. That's all, your honor."

The judge turns to Mr. Oswald. "Do you wish to rebut?"

"Yes." Oswald rises slowly, his smile reaching from one cheek to the other. After a quick look at the jury, he poses his question. "Drawing on your extensive experience with vehicles, Mr. Wilkerson, what would you say is the fastest an *empty* 18-wheeler could travel up a hill like Bristlecone Drive?"

"Up a hill that steep…I'd say about 20 miles an hour…at the most."

"Slow enough, then for a passer coming down the hill to get back into lane."

"Well, yeah…assuming the guy started his passing move early enough…you know…near the top of the stretch. Once he sees the truck, he should have plenty of time to get out of the way."

"Thank you. That's all, your honor."

Judge Foster bangs his gavel. The court will adjourn until 2:00 this afternoon."

In the afternoon session, Emma Culpepper serves as the main witness for the defense. Her assignment, carefully spelled out by Mr. Harris, is to undermine her husband's testimony by providing evidence that he is jealous of the relationship between his wife and son.

Before calling on his witness, Mr. Harris offers a brief introduction. "This morning we heard something very unusual…we heard a father testifying against his own son. This is so unusual as to make one wonder if something extraordinary is going on behind the scenes. To help answer that question, I call Emma Culpepper to the stand."

Amidst gasps from the audience, Emma strides to the witness box, sits quickly and folds her hands. Harris wastes no time getting to the point. "Now Mrs. Culpepper, how would you describe your relationship with your husband?"

Oswald rises to object. "Your honor, this has nothing to do with the question of the defendant's guilt or innocence. Counsel is just fishing for some way to impugn the Sheriff's testimony."

"I disagree, Mr. Oswald. I think it is quite pertinent. Please continue Mr. Harris."

Harris nods, then returns to his witness. "Please describe your relationship with your husband. It is important that you be completely honest, even if it means divulging matters you might prefer to keep private."

Emma's nervousness is obvious from the way she wrings her hands. Speaking in a whisper, she says, "Well, we don't really talk anymore. He's pretty angry at me and doesn't want to be close."

"Could you speak a little louder Ma'am?"

"Oh, sorry."

"So, how long has it been like this, Mrs. Culpepper?"

She raises her voice slightly. "It's gotten real bad lately because of Eric… but it hasn't been very good for years…really, ever since the boy was born."

"Because…"

As she looks at the Sheriff, she continues to wring her hands, contradicting the lack of emotion in her voice. "Earl couldn't stand seeing how close I was to the baby. I thought I was just being a good mother but Earl got jealous every time I held him or kissed him…even when I breast-fed him. He didn't say anything about it, but I could tell he was upset. A few months after Eric was born, Earl and I stopped being intimate in bed. Later that year I moved into the guest room where I've been for the last 18 years."

"And have things changed recently?"

"Well, yes…they've gotten worse…especially between Earl and Eric. My husband was never was much of a father but as soon as he met Asanté and began going to his soccer games, he completely ignored Eric."

"And how would you say your husband feels toward his son now?"

Emma pauses, then looks out at Eric. "He despises him …(*crying*)…Yes, he despises his own son."

Mr. Harris waits for Emma to blow her nose. "You heard the Sheriff's testimony this morning, Mrs. Culpepper. Do you think your husband's feelings toward Eric affected his testimony?"

Oswald leaps to his feet. "Objection. Counsel is just fishing, your honor."

"Objection sustained," says the Judge. "Unless you can be more specific, counsel, this is not an appropriate line of questioning."

"O.K. Let me get more specific…(*turning back to Mrs. Culpepper*)…Your husband claims that Eric knew the Aguilera boy before the collision. This is extremely important. He bases the claim of prior knowledge on the fact that Eric admitted following him to the soccer game where he saw Santé in the flesh. He saw the Mexican boy again when he and your husband came out of the restaurant…and then a third time when he went back to the Repair shop to pick up his backpack. Without this claim of prior knowledge, the charge of premeditated murder is laughable. Why would Eric want to kill someone he doesn't even know? …(*pause*)…So, here's my question. Remember now that we don't have Eric's testimony. All we have is what your husband said. In your opinion, is it possible that the Sheriff, feeling jealous of your relationship with your son, made it appear that Eric had recognized Asanté when in fact he never got close enough to identify the boy?"

"That's exactly what I think happened. Eric followed his father because he thought he was having an affair with a woman. He hung around after the game, still looking for such a person. When he didn't see any, he concluded that there wasn't any affair after all and that his father just enjoyed soccer…or perhaps wanted to get out of the house…you know, to get away from me."

"But Eric did see another boy with your husband, didn't he…going into and coming out of the restaurant?"

"Yes he did, but it was probably a different member of the team every week…perhaps a reward that Earl promised them for winning the game."

"So, in your opinion, Eric did not know the Aguilera boy at the time of the collision up on Bristlecone Drive. He never saw him before."

"That's right."

Judge Foster leans toward the witness. "Thank you Mrs. Culpepper; you may step down now unless Mr. Oswald wants to cross-examine. Mr. Oswald?"

Oswald shakes his head.

In the following days, a number of character witnesses are called to testify in Eric's behalf. The defense also calls its own automotive expert who claims there are newer 18-wheel truck models capable of driving up steep inclines even with a heavy load. The prosecution counters with the Attorney General's secretary who says she called every truck company within 50 miles of Phoenix and they all denied that one of their fleet was in the vicinity of Bristlecone Drive on the night of August 16th. In addition, the assistant manager of the Hennessey Transportation Co. testifies that "no trucker in his right mind" would take that route when other, much easier and less dangerous roads were available. As its last witness, the prosecution calls Anna Erickson who confirms that Santé was at her house on the night of August 16th…and left at approximately 6:30. Upon further questioning, she says that Santé was in the habit of coming to see her in the late afternoon, right after he finished work. When cross-examined by the defense, she admits that she didn't notice anyone following him as he drove away.

When all witnesses have had a chance to testify, the Judge asks for summations. "Mr. Oswald, are you ready?"

"Yes your honor." Not surprisingly the attorney has spent hours rehearsing his speech…his last chance to sway the jury in a case that could easily go either way. To be sure of his delivery, he has even practiced it out loud to his colleagues over tequila and lobster at Romo's Tavern.

He begins by clearing his throat. "Ladies and gentlemen of the jury, to convict the defendant on the charge of first-degree murder, you must be convinced that the collision on the night of August 16th was not accidental but premeditated and intentional. So, how convincing is the evidence presented thus far? To answer that question, let us consider what has been said about the relationship between Eric Culpepper and Asanté Aguilera. Did they know each other or not? This is critical. When Eric followed his father to the soccer field and watched from his truck while the game was played, did he notice who his father was looking at? It's hard to be sure. How about when his father and Asanté entered the restaurant together? Is it possible that he saw the other boy's face then; if not, how about when he observed them coming out of the restaurant? Think about it. He had three separate chances to identify Asanté Aguilera as the boy his father had befriended. What can we conclude from this? I think it reasonable to conclude that Eric knew who was in that white pickup when their trucks collided on Bristlecone Drive. He knew that it was the same boy whom his father went to see every Saturday, the same boy who took his job at the TV & Radio repair shop.

"Although we have no direct knowledge of the defendant's plans, circumstantial evidence suggests that he followed Mr. Aguilera to his girlfriend's house that night with the intention of doing him harm. Why else would he bother to go up to Bristlecone Drive at that time of day…

the very time of day that Asanté was in the habit of leaving his girlfriend's house? To watch the sunset?…hardly. He waited until his rival came out of the house, then followed him down Bristlecone Drive. When they reached the steepest part of the road, he pulled up beside the Mexican boy's pickup, rammed into him and forced him over the cliff. Then he went home and spray-painted his fender.

"That's the big picture. To understand better how events actually unfolded, let's look at the scene again from the defendant's perspective. Put yourself in Eric's position on the night of August 16th. You're coming down Bristlecone Drive, preparing to pass a white pickup on your right. You've been following the pickup ever since the driver left his girlfriend's house. You honk your horn and look over at him. There's no question about it. He's the boy you followed to his girlfriend's house, the boy you saw with your father at the soccer game and again outside the restaurant…the same boy who stole your job at the repair shop. O.K. so far? Now plug in what we know about your jealousy toward the Mexican, a jealousy springing from years of neglect on your father's part. Isn't this the perfect time to do your rival in…to get rid of him once and for all? Nobody is around to see you…no one behind you, no imaginary 18-wheeler coming up the hill toward you…(*pause*)…So, what do you do? It's pretty obvious. You start to pass, then pull your steering wheel hard to the right and drive your rival into the canyon…(*pause*)…Ladies and gentlemen, there is no other way to interpret the evidence; this is murder in the first degree….murder with the intent to kill."

Before continuing, he waits for the jury to digest his summary. "One other thing you might keep in mind as you make your decision. Think of the courage it has taken for Sheriff Culpepper to testify against his own son…especially when a guilty verdict could condemn the boy to years behind bars. The fact that he did so…despite his fatherly feelings… adds to the credibility of what he told us. Yes, he may have been jealous of the affection his wife bestowed on their son, but that's hardly enough to make him set Eric up for a lifetime in prison. You heard him say that he may have lost respect for his son but that he still loves him. So why did he testify for the prosecution? He felt he had to testify because he believes in telling the truth. Most of us know that about him; that's why we made him our Sheriff.

"One final note. It's important that we not send the wrong kind of message to the Latino community. Given the preponderance of evidence against the defendant, that's exactly what we would be doing if we were to let Mr. Aguilera's death go unpunished. Eric Culpepper ended a brave young boy's dreams because he was jealous. He deserves to go to prison."

As visitors start whispering among themselves, the Judge bangs his gavel, then turns to the defense. "Mr. Harris…your turn."

Mr. Lloyd Harris brushes back his curly hair and moves to the front of the jury. "Ladies and gentlemen of the jury, what we have here is a regrettable accident, but hardly a murder. Let's look carefully at the facts and what it is reasonable to infer from those facts. We don't challenge the prosecution's claim that the defendant tried to cover up the damage to his pickup. But let's be clear what that means. The fact that Eric painted his right front fender to cover up some dents may be consistent with his having been up on Bristlecone Drive the night of August 16th. It may even be consistent with a collision between his pickup and that driven by the victim. But under no circumstances can it be taken to mean that the defendant deliberately caused the other boy's death. There is absolutely no evidence here of malicious intent…thus no reason to believe that the contact was anything more than a regrettable accident.

He pauses to let his remarks sink in. "I think we can accept that Eric was delinquent in not reporting the accident.…but let's remember that he had no way of knowing initially that the driver of the white truck went over the cliff to his death. When he found out the next day through the media, he should have reported his involvement. Why didn't he? Understandably, he was afraid he might be considered culpable of more than non-reporting. At worst he might be accused of a hit and run offense. So he painted his fender and kept quiet…until his father, the Sheriff of Maricopa County… confronted him. From that point on, we know from his wife's testimony that the Sheriff, having developed strong feelings for the Mexican boy, proceeded to distort the facts in such a way as to suggest his son committed murder out of jealousy. Much of what we have heard from the Sheriff in this trial is opinion disguised as fact. He says he loved his son but his behavior suggests that he had much stronger feelings for the Aguilera boy. His wife confirms the fact that he actually despised his son. So, of course, the defendant was jealous. Wouldn't you be jealous if you knew your father was befriending another boy…a boy your own age at that…instead of doing things with you? But wait…just because you're jealous, does it follow that you want to murder your rival? That's what the prosecution would have you believe; it's simple mathematics they say: jealousy equals murder."

Mr. Harris pauses to enjoy the laughter rippling through the audience. He continues: "Even if we grant, which we don't, that Eric recognized the Aguilera boy just before the collision, it doesn't follow that he was out to murder him. The prosecution would have you believe that the recognition equals intention to kill…that the mere fact of recognizing someone means you want to kill them. This is more twisted mathematics. Let's be clear. With or without the assumption of recognition, the contact between Mr. Culpepper's pickup and that of Mr. Aguilera remains an accident. The prosecution has tried to make a first-degree murder case out of an accident. You the jury have the responsibility now to correct their mistake. There is more than enough 'reasonable doubt' to justify a verdict of not guilty. You must vote to acquit."

The jury comes to a decision within hours of leaving the courtroom. Before the verdict is read, Earl looks over at his son who is staring at the jury foreman. What he sees is unnerving. It's the same irritating smirk that Eric sports when he wants to put someone down without appearing to do so. "He thinks he's going to get away with it," the Sheriff muses. "It's gonna come as a shock if they find him guilty."

The Sheriff turns out to be only half right. The jury agrees that the defendant is guilty of vehicular manslaughter but not of murder. Later, in a post-trial interview, one juror reports that "the grounds for first-degree murder were not there. We all agreed that the defendant was criminally negligent in his driving but we were never convinced that he actually intended to kill the Aguilera boy."

As Eric is led out of the courtroom, he turns to look at his father. Earl lifts his hand to wave, then changes his mind. Something is different in his son's expression, something unexpected. The Sheriff looks again. Wiping the tears from his own cheek, he smiles. It's true; the boy's smirk is gone.

At the sentencing session a week later, Eric is given a prison term of five years. With good behavior, he is told, he can be out in three.

Two days after Eric is sentenced, Emma files for divorce.

35

The Raid

Two weeks later, Earl is sitting alone in his new apartment in an upscale section of West Phoenix. The TV is on but is not being watched. He has been to visit Eric in prison twice…and been informed on both occasions that he is not welcome. As he pours himself another Scotch, he struggles with disparate feelings…guilt for putting his son behind bars and sadness that Santé is no longer alive.

Early in the evening he gets a call from Herb at the Phoenix Police Station telling him of a plan to round up a bunch of Latinos at the Senden Meat Packing Co. just outside of town. An unknown insider at Senden's has leaked information to the FBI indicating a widespread practice there of hiring illegals. The FBI has decided to organize a raid and wants the Phoenix Police, Arizona State Police and Maricopa County Sheriff's office to get involved. Given the large number of workers thought to be undocumented, the case is considered high priority.

Earl responds by asking a series of questions about the reliability of the source, jurisdictional boundaries and the urgency of the problem. Herb is not pleased with what he is hearing. "You with us on this one or not, Earl?" he says, not bothering to conceal his impatience. "The FBI wants you in… that's why I'm callin'…but you don't sound too enthusiastic." Hoping to make the raid more interesting, he adds, "There should be some good publicity in this for all of us…assuming we catch lots of them. But like lemmings., they're goin' to run and hide…makin' it hard to haul 'em in. That's where you come in, Earl."

"So…what do you want me to do?"

"My men are goin' in at the front door; when the aliens catch on that we're there to grab 'em, they're goin' to scatter. So we need you and a couple of your guys to wait down below at the west entrance and catch anybody who comes down the stairs headin' for the door. All you gotta do is nab 'em and bring 'em to me upstairs."

Silence.

"Earl, you there? Did I lose you or somethin'?"

"No, I'm here. Had a little problem with my phone…sorry. Yeah, count me in. What day and time?"

"Next Friday…(*chuckling*)…they'll all be there to pick up their checks. Mid-morning is best…say 10:00. We'll rendezvous first across the street… then move in. Like I said, you and your guys take the west entrance. We'll cover the others. O.K?"

(*Barely audible*) "Yeah. O.K. We'll be there."

On Friday Earl is at the side door when two young Latinos come racing down the stairs, heading for the exit. Earl steps in front of the door to stop them. Both are teenagers, around Santé's age. The taller one sports the beginnings of a mustache, the other a tiny goatee. Both are wearing t-shirts with the name SENDEN on the chest; one has a sweat band around his forehead, the other a large silver buckle. Both are wearing blue jeans and rubber boots.

Earl asks where they are from…in English. When he fails to get a response, he tries the few Spanish words he knows: "De donde sois? The taller boy hesitates, then says "Chicago"; the other nods his head. Earl smiles, "Hmm yeah, I'll bet." While his words go untranslated, his smile conveys the message that he means no harm. Gradually the boys relax and return the Sheriff's smile with smiles of their own. For the next few minutes the three stand there at the door, doing nothing while Earl figures out what to do next. It is not an easy decision. His career as an officer of the law hangs in the balance. He's already lost his family; does he want to lose his job as well? Breaking eye contact with the boys, he stares out the window. When the awkwardness becomes unbearable, he turns back, glances up the stairwell to make sure he can't be seen…then tells the boys to wait at the door while he gets some forms from his cruiser.

When he reaches the cruiser, he stops and turns around to see what's happening. What he sees brings a smile to his face…two boys dashing from the building and heading up the street. He waits until they are completely gone before returning to the west door.

A few minutes later Herb yells down from upstairs. "You catch anybody, Earl? We got a whole bunch up here."

Without looking up, Earl answers, "Nope. Nobody's come this way…at least not while I've been here."

"Really? Well then, I guess we got 'em all. You might as well go back to your office. Thanks for comin', Earl."

"Sure. No problem."

Back in his cruiser, the Sheriff of Maricopa County sits quietly, staring out the window. Musings about the law, duty and family alternate with thoughts of another night alone in his apartment. Once he sorts things out, he reaches into the glove compartment and withdraws a photo of Santé, the one where he's wearing an orange jacket with lettering on the back. His hand begins to shake; he forces a smile then bites his lip. Gradually words stir in the depths of his psyche, rise to his lips, then spill into sound. Nodding to the boy in the picture, he whispers, "That's one for you, kid."